CORVITIC⌐ᴜ UNIVERSITY

J.E. CLUNEY

GLOSSARY

Arvo - afternoon

Bogan - is Australian and New Zealand slang for a person whose speech, clothing, attitude and behaviour are considered unrefined or unsophisticated.

Bottle-o - Liquor store

Chippy - Carpenter

IGA - Grocery store

Fortnight - two weeks

Gumtree - either a tree or the Australian Craigslist

Kiwi - New Zealand origin person

Op Shop - Second-hand store that donates money raised to causes

Singlets - tank tops

Skippy - Australian Kangaroo show (popular and known)

Stubbies - bottles of beer

Thongs - flip-flops

Trackies - Tracksuit pants

Verandah - Porch

Woolies/Woolworths - Grocery store

1

Sometimes change is what you need. Making one big choice to better your life, leaving behind all you know to start a brand new chapter in your life.

Little did I know that this choice would lead to a life I could never even dream of.

The ugly orange taxi rumbled off into the darkness, spurting soft clouds of grey smoke as it struggled along the quiet street. I watched it leave, my chest tight as I stood on the sidewalk with my measly navy suitcase and green gym bag. It carried all my belongings from my life, everything that had any meaning to me. And my clothes and toiletries, of course.

I bit my lip as the taxi turned the street corner and disappeared from view, taking any chance of returning to my old life with it.

This was it. This was where the next step in my life began.

I sighed as I turned back to take in the building before me.

The large two-story house was quite the sight. Lucas had

informed me through emails that it was an old Victorian Georgian-style Villa built by his great grandfather. Apparently, it was inspired by the 'Baddow House' in Maryborough after his great grandfather glimpsed the home in the early 1900s.

Both levels had beautiful wrap-around verandahs, with a staircase joining the top and bottom on either side of the home.

The bottom half had a wicker table set off to the side of the front door before a large window with the drapes drawn. It was painted white like the majority of homes these days, with a heavy looking wooden door, set with a stained glass window. From my position, I could just make out the dragon presented in the stained glass with red pieces, the surrounding glass a deep purple and blue.

I spied the ginger and white cat in the window watching me curiously, and I waved as I smiled at it. The housemate ad hadn't said anything about a cat. Not that I minded, I preferred the company of animals over people. People were nasty pieces of work, I'd learned that with my Aunt and her boyfriend while I'd lived with them. I'd stayed with them until I was a teen before I ran away.

I pursed my lips as I rearranged my bag on my shoulder and started up the path. My suitcase bumped along the uneven pavement behind me, the one broken wheel scraping and making me cringe.

I left it at the base of the steps leading up to the verandah, jumping up them and smiling at the cat as it watched me inquisitively. Someone had left the light on, a small lantern fixed on the wall beside the front door.

I drew in a shaky breath as I calmed my nerves. I was eager to meet Lucas and take my first step into this new life I'd started, but I was still nervous as all hell.

I barely had the chance to raise my hand to knock before it swung open.

My breath caught at the utterly drop dead gorgeous man that stood before me. His jet black hair was spiked up at the front, cut in a crew cut style, his high cheekbones defined under the outside light. He had a neatly trimmed, short, boxed beard that only made him look more dazzling. His skin was pale, and that nose was sculpted to perfection, perfectly straight, while those frosty blue eyes took me in with a look of instant distrust. Those eyes were both piercing and bored, all at once. And he pulled the expression off perfectly.

My knees went weak before this stunning male model, my heart skipping a beat as he scrutinized me. He was perfection squeezed into one man, in a tight black shirt that showed off his muscular frame, and baggy trackies. I could only picture what was hidden beneath them.

He'd look so much better in jeans.

"You're Allison?" he asked, raising one perfect eyebrow as he scanned me. The once over wasn't unsettling like he was undressing me, it was more like he was looking down his nose at me as his lip curled upwards. Not that I would've minded if it was an undressing one.

I wished I'd worn a dress or something nice rather than my old ratty jeans and red and white long-sleeved flannelette shirt over a white singlet.

I was suddenly very aware of how I looked, probably something he threw in with trailer trash or country bogans.

I ran my hand over my pocket, comforted by the lump of my scratched up iPod I had tucked there.

"Yes." I managed to not squeak under his stony gaze, that slight smirk pissing me off. He may look like a God, but he certainly didn't act like one.

He'd just dropped a few levels in my books with that

smug, uppity expression. Like he was above me. Maybe he was, but it still didn't make me feel any better.

He was supposedly my housemate. Unless he was just a guest, which a part of me hoped not. I could ogle this sexy slab of divine beauty any day. Even if he seemed like he was going to turn out to be a jerk. No, I already sensed he was one. With that look he gave me, one of disapproval and annoyance.

"Right, I guess I'll have to show you around since Lucas isn't home." He sighed, as if the idea was too much work for him. He ran a slim hand through his hair, one that looked like it would be soft and smooth to touch.

Lucas had been the one I'd exchanged messages with. He'd wanted me to meet everyone and see the place before deciding if it was where I wanted to live, but I didn't have the cash to make two trips if I did like it. Not to mention classes started next week, and I was running out of time to find a place, this being one of the only places left.

There'd been plenty of wonderful photos and the price was quite reasonable, and the fact I'd be sharing with four men didn't bother me as much as I thought it would. I'd lived with my cousin, a girl a year younger than me, and that had been a nightmare. Men were easier, they weren't bitchy, just straight to the point most of the time. They didn't care much about the same things girls did. No squabbling over the hair curler or losing their shit over misplaced eyeliner, which she'd lost herself.

So I'd applied and gotten the room. I'd already landed myself a position in a local cafe as a barista and waitress, so I was set. I was excited to finally be able to save and buy myself new clothes. I'd worked previously while I lived with my Aunt, but she took most of my pay, and then when I ran away, I barely scraped by with my bills and rent.

"Name's Marcus," the devilishly handsome man said as he stepped aside to let me in.

I glanced back at my suitcase wistfully, wondering if I should try to lug it up and risk scratching the paint on the verandah and the beautiful wooden flooring inside the house.

"I got it." Marcus sighed, noting my despairing look. He brushed past me, and I caught the softest scent of vanilla wafting from him. My favorite.

He picked my suitcase up with ease and carried it under one arm as he led me straight up the stairs, brushing past me again in a delicious wave of sweet vanilla. Not too strong either, just enough to catch my nose.

"Rooms are upstairs with a bathroom, Lucas' room is downstairs with his own bathroom. You'll be sharing a bathroom with me, Red and Kit," he said as he glided upstairs silently, carrying my suitcase with no effort, like it was as light as a feather.

"Got it." I nodded as I tromped up the stairs after him with not even the slightest hint of perfect grace like him.

So Red and Kit were the other two. Well, I assumed that wasn't their real names, Lucas had emailed me with their names but I hadn't memorized them. And without access to my email, since I had no laptop or smartphone, I couldn't check the names Lucas had sent me.

My room was at the end of the hall right next to the bathroom as Marcus had pointed out. It was an elegant hall with a deep royal red hall runner to save anyone slipping on the beautiful wooden flooring. No need for someone to take a daring fall down the staircase.

Marcus led me to my room, moving sleekly like a cat. So fluid and silent that it unnerved me a little.

I smiled brightly as we entered my room. The single bed was ready for me, I'd paid a little extra for Lucas to get some bed sheets and a blanket for me, which he informed me would then be mine to own. The bed was positioned right before the door, so we stood at the foot of the bed upon entry. An arched window had navy blue drapes pulled over the head of the bed.

There was a desk set up under the large back window looking down onto the backyard, an old wattle tree standing strong in the back corner, barely visible in the night shadows. My room was set in the back corner of the top story, and I wondered which way the sun rose. I'd love the early morning sun flooding in.

The built-in wardrobe had one mirrored sliding door which I'd loved the thought of, and there was a small set of teak wooden drawers to the left of the doorway.

"Kitchen and living room are downstairs, same as the laundry. There's a library room, too, and a games room. Most things in the fridge are shared, if you don't want to share, you put your name on it. Doesn't always mean it won't get touched, though." Marcus shrugged as he set my suitcase down at the foot of my bed. The movement made his muscular arms bulge against his sleeves, and I bit my lip at the sight. Damn, he sure was fine.

The orange and white long-haired cat scurried into the room, peering up at me with keen interest, its bright amber eyes stunning. It sat down on the floor at the foot of the bed, glancing between Marcus and I curiously before letting out a soft meow.

"He lives here, too." Marcus scowled at the cat. "You'll get used to his tendencies."

"Got it." I nodded. I wanted to ask about the tendencies, but let it slide.

"Well, here you go," Marcus said as he glanced around

my room once before striding out. He didn't even say another word, just ditched me.

"He sure is interesting, huh," I murmured to the cat once I was sure he was out of earshot. "He didn't even tell me your name, handsome." I smiled as the cat leaped up onto my bed.

I sat next to him, loving the bed set Lucas had picked out. A deep ocean blue blanket that was soft and plush, and the sheets and pillows were sky blue. It was made of pure cotton from the feel, and I inhaled the fresh scent of washed sheets, a hint of lavender wafting from it.

He'd asked what my favorite color was, and I'd said blue. Blue was a calm, natural color that soothed me.

I stroked the cat's soft fur, bummed that he had no collar for me to check his name. I'd wait until Lucas or one of my other housemates was home. Marcus was not someone I wanted to bother, I could already picture him groaning and rolling his eyes.

The first thing I intended to buy with my new job would be a mobile phone, since my last iPhone had died after an unfortunate fall off a counter.

Thankfully, Lucas had given me the landline number to give my new place of work.

I had a feeling I was going to like Lucas, he'd sounded quite friendly and sweet on the phone when we'd discussed the place.

"Well, I guess I'd better unpack, you going to keep me company?" I asked the cat. He just meowed and watched me carefully as I stood back up.

My stomach growled, and I wondered if there was anything open still that I could grab a bite from. There were a few small shops nice and close, within walking distance, same with the campus.

I'd moved to this tiny town of Maple Grove to attend the

Corviticus University here. It catered to others like me. Other unique people.

It made me wonder how my housemates were peculiar. Lucas hadn't said anything, but the entire town of Maple Grove was special. The University only allowed entry to those like me.

From what Lucas had said, it was probably the only thing of any worth in this tiny country town. He told me it was better to head into the township of Maleny or head back down to the coast to where I'd grown up if I wanted to do shopping or anything of the sort.

I knelt down and unzipped my suitcase, the cat peering off the end of the bed as he watched me quietly.

I put away my few clothes in the wardrobe, leaving it looking still sparse and empty. I had a few pairs of jeans, one set of denim shorts, one pajama set and a few shirts. I hung up the two dresses, a striking bright red one that I loved to wear, and a more inconspicuous sky blue one.

I sighed as I shoved my underwear and bras into the drawers beside the door, contemplating whether I should move my pathetic wardrobe of clothes into the drawers instead.

No, I could save them for something else.

I flicked on the bedside lamp, pulling out the drawer to my bedside table to inspect it. I dug my iPod out of my pocket and set it inside, before searching through my gym bag for my charger to toss in alongside it.

I rose and strode over to flick off the main light before sprawling on the bed beside the curious cat.

This was it. My new home. And it would remain my home until I completed uni, at least, that's what Lucas and I had agreed on. Technically, I was only locked into a yearly lease, but I intended to stay the whole time. It was a beautiful house, a huge step up from my last rental, that had cost nearly twice as much even though I'd rented it with a housemate.

"Pretty big place Lucas has here, I wish my family had left me a house like this," I mused as I stroked the soft, fluffy cat. He purred and nuzzled my hand as I rolled onto my stomach, his whiskers tickling my palm.

"Lucas said I can use his laptop till I buy my own, you know, for research and assignments. I'll have to get one asap, I don't want to put him out," I murmured to the cat. Animals had always been important to me. They never got angry with you or shouted at you, they were just there, willing to love you if you showed them even a smidgen of affection.

My stomach growled again, and the cat cocked his head at me, those amber eyes staring at me in amusement. Strange, how he actually looked amused.

"I haven't eaten since lunchtime," I defended myself as the cat just blinked. I grinned as his tongue slowly slid out, and he just looked at me with that tiny pink tongue peeking out.

"You're a cutie." I chuckled as I scratched behind his ears and his eyes half closed.

Lucas had said we were to buy our own food if possible, but there were basics for us to share.

Even just some pasta and shredded cheese sounded good. But first, I wanted a shower and to see if there was a set place in the bathroom that I could store my toiletries.

I rolled off the bed and collected my old, faded set of pajamas. A grey short-sleeved shirt with a long since faded red heart on the front. The vinyl heart had cracked and many pieces of it had come away. There wasn't much left of the heart to be honest, but at least the grey pants with small red hearts had fared well.

I shuffled through my gym bag and pulled out my small bag of toiletries before heading out into the hall.

The bathroom was decently sized, and the door to the right of it just before the stairs was the toilet. I had to assume all the other closed doors were the rooms of my housemates.

Past the stairs was a door to the verandah, along with a window that allowed the moonlight to seep down onto the staircase. It gave the area an eerie, whimsical look. I headed straight into the lavish bathroom, loving the large, luxurious room with a separate bathtub and shower. It had been a major pull for me to apply as well. Who didn't love to shower in comfort?

There was a wooden cupboard behind the bathroom door, and I opened it to find all the fresh towels, the stash of toilet paper, soaps, and shampoos.

I moved on to the vanity sink and cabinet underneath, which housed some shaving equipment labeled with names. Skip and Oliver had their electric razors there, and I wondered if Marcus kept his in his room. So these were my housemates' real names.

I looked forward to meeting them, a flutter in my gut making me roll my eyes. Yeah, being single made the prospect of living with a bunch of guys even more thrilling, if not terrifying.

Damn, I seriously needed to get a vibrator. Especially with how Marcus' looks melted me. Too bad his personality worked against him.

No. Housemates were off limits. I'd already told myself that when applying. No need to make things awkward.

The mirrored cabinet over the sink had toothbrushes, and I set mine on the bottom shelf near the painkillers. It also housed an assortment of other things to be expected, burn and bite creams, earbuds, cotton balls, antiseptic creams, the works.

I slipped my toiletries bag with my other few items under the sink and out of the way.

I turned back to find the cat sitting beside the bath, watching me as I explored the bathroom. The bathtub was a clawfoot porcelain tub, and it wasn't a pathetically tiny thing like the one I'd grown up with. I could actually soak properly in it. The shower was quite fancy and gorgeous as well. I wondered how good the pressure was too? If it was halfway decent, then I'd be in heaven.

I strode over and closed the door, clicking the lock before tugging my shirt off.

I tossed it on the floor, making a mental note to buy myself a hamper or washing basket. I didn't need my house-mates finding a pile of clothes on the floor in here. I'd just keep them in my room for now.

My eyes dropped to the cat, who was staring at me wide-eyed. Weird little fur ball.

I shifted awkwardly under its gaze and even wrapped my arms around myself. It looked genuinely stunned, and it was weirding me out.

"Look away, weirdo," I muttered as I collected a cream towel from the cupboard. Surprisingly, the cat averted his eyes, and I couldn't help but smile at it. Guess he was a smart little guy, or maybe he'd spotted something I couldn't see.

I stripped down and climbed into the shower, pulling the cream curtain across.

I took my time showering, lathering up my body and enjoying the fragrance of the vanilla soap. I guess that was where Marcus got his sweet scent from.

I didn't bother with my hair, instead having tied it up with the flimsy hair tie from around my wrist.

When I finished, I stuck my head out from behind the curtain and scolded myself. I'd forgotten to flick the overhead fan on. Damn.

I spied the cat lying bread loaf style with his legs folded under him over by the door.

He opened his eyes to peer at me, and I chided him as I climbed out of the shower. It was rather adorable how he actually looked away, turning his whole head as I reached for my towel on the edge of the sink and began drying myself.

I hummed as I dried off, looking forward to having something to eat and settling down for the night. I did wonder if the other boys would be back tonight, as I would've liked to make their acquaintance.

I pulled on my pajamas, wishing I had some pajama shorts considering how warm it was tonight. At least my room had an overhead fan.

It was mid-February, and summer was a hot bitch.

I flicked on the overhead fan before gathering up my dirty clothes and heading out into the hall. I made a mental note to switch it off on the way back up after dinner.

Marcus was just exiting his room when he turned to spy me.

His icy gaze dropped to the cat as it slinked out after me. Marcus' face took on an amused expression.

"Did he go in the bathroom with you?" he queried with a half-smile playing at his lips.

"Yes, why?" I asked as I arched an eyebrow at him.

"No reason." He shrugged, his eyes glittering in amusement as he continued towards me.

"But, just some advice, I wouldn't do that again." He smirked as he moved past me, forcing me to lean into the wall to allow him to pass.

I scowled after him as he tromped down the stairs and

shook my head. I turned and headed back to my room, wondering why the cat bothered him so much.

Weird guy.

Too bad he had the face of a bloody God. Hell, I bet his body was just as divine.

And mine was more than willing to remind me of just how it made me feel if I thought about it too much.

I tossed my dirty clothes into the corner, covering them with my gym bag before heading downstairs.

The muggy heat was beyond ridiculous, and I wiped at the sweat forming on the back of my neck already. The shower was almost pointless. Tonight was a hot one, and I couldn't wait for it to cool down. Although, being on the mountain range now, I doubted I was going to like autumn and winter any better. Spring was pretty much the only season I liked.

Australian humidity was a joke sometimes. But with this rising heat, I suspected we had a storm due in the next day or so.

I descended the staircase as my mind wandered to food and what the small town may offer. Surely it had a grocery store or something, right?

The University was only a stone's throw away from the house, a five-minute walk down the street and onto the campus at the far end.

This home was nestled on half an acre, apparently it was once part of a larger area of land and used for farming, but Lucas' father had sold off the surrounding lands years ago when developers wanted to put in some estates to provide additional accommodation for the students attending Corviticus. Many were owned by families in the area or by the University itself, and they rented them out as share houses.

Lucas was very forthcoming and open in his emails, nothing like the brooding male who had welcomed me.

I found my way to the kitchen, passing through the living area where Marcus sat on the red lounge with his laptop propped on his lap and headphones on. He glanced at me as I passed in front of him, but he didn't say a word as he focused on his screen.

What a tool.

Fingers crossed that the other guys were friendlier.

I checked the fridge out, there were a few things in there, including a few tins of cat food and some old pizza with 'Skip' sprawled on the box. Fruits, veggies, leftovers—the standard things expected.

I found the shredded cheese, making sure it was there before hunting down some pasta in the kitchen cupboards. The kitchen was quite spacious with white marble-topped benches and had an adjoining dining area. There was a center island that I navigated around as I searched the kitchen. It didn't take me long to find the bow tie pasta and pots. During my search, I made mental notes of where the plates, bowls, mugs, and glasses were located.

I'd considered asking Marcus for guidance, but I'd rather go in blind than see his displeased scowl again.

I got to work boiling my pasta as I wondered about my classes and housemates, and how I would need to buy some food tomorrow. I'd used nearly all of my savings for the bond and first two weeks of rent, and what I did have left was for groceries and to save for a laptop.

I jumped as something brushed my calf, and I smiled down at the cat weaving through my legs.

He was probably hungry.

"Do you want me to feed the cat?" I called out.

"He's been fed!" Marcus called back, his smooth voice laced with mild annoyance.

Seriously? Way to welcome a new housemate. I guess he was part of the reason the room hadn't been snatched up already.

"Sorry little guy," I murmured as I leaned down and scratched the cat's chin. He purred before walking off, his little fluffy tail flicking in the air.

I got back to my pasta, watching it boil as I drummed my fingers on the bench.

A glance at the clock on the microwave informed me it was already 8pm. God, you wouldn't have thought so considering the sun had only set just over an hour ago.

That was long summer days for you. It still caught me off-guard sometimes, as I'd grown up having dinner almost exactly at 6.30pm every day.

I had a few days to settle in before I started at uni. From what Lucas had said, everyone in this house was either currently studying or about to start.

I wanted to ask Marcus some questions, to find out more about the others, what they were studying, that kind of thing.

If I was going to be living with them, I wanted to get to know them. It would make life easier all around. Not to mention I was secretly hoping they were all divine Gods like Marcus. Preferably with friendlier attitudes.

I was going to study veterinary science in hopes of becoming a vet. It was a long degree, but worth it. And thanks to what I was, I had abilities that could help.

I zoned back in as the water boiled, and I stirred the pasta as I wondered about Marcus. What was he? And why was he such an arrogant prick?

I finished up with my pasta, finding a strainer easily

enough, and with a sprinkling of shredded cheese, I was on my way.

I contemplated going to investigate the library, but decided against it.

I'd just bite the bullet and sit in the living area. I really did want to ask Marcus a few things. Like how far away was the town, was it an easy walk, what did the town have to offer?

Marcus would just have to get used to me, I was paying to live here, too.

I marched out and sat on the duplicate red lounge across from him, shoveling the cheesy goodness into my mouth.

He barely even glanced up from his laptop to acknowledge my presence.

What was up his butt? Was I really such an irritation to him? He didn't even know me. Hell, he made it quite clear he had no interest in getting to know me.

God, what I wouldn't do...

Marcus' eyes widened as he glanced at me, his eyes falling to my bowl of pasta.

"What the fuck is that?"

"Pasta and cheese?" I frowned as I looked down at my bowl.

Well, it was a few seconds ago.

Now it was a wriggling mass of pasta, the little bow ties fluttering, ensnared in the cheese.

Goddamn fudgsicle.

A piece of pasta broke loose, fluttering up into the air as it beat its little wings like a butterfly.

More and more began to free themselves from the sticky cheese, fluttering into the air as Marcus just stared, dumbfounded.

"Well, don't just sit there, help me!" I snapped as I stood up, slapping down the flying bow ties like a madwoman.

"Why the fuck is the pasta flying?" Marcus gaped as he stood.

He knocked a pasta piece away as it fluttered too close, a look of sheer confusion etched across his godly face.

Get it together, Ally, now's not the time to check him out.

The cat had wandered in at some point, and was batting at them from his position on the floor. His little tail was twitching like mad as he watched the pasta glide through the air.

I reached for a piece of pasta as it fluttered past, struggling as a string of cheese hung from it, weighing it down.

I snatched it up and tossed it into my mouth, crushing the little thing and swallowing. Marcus was just giving me a very odd look as I began eating the flying pasta.

It was the only way.

Each time I slapped one down, it would glide back up before hitting the floor.

Time to get serious.

I jumped and danced around, catching the pasta butterflies and consuming them as I went. All the while Marcus watched, a mix of both confusion and amusement dancing behind his frosty eyes.

"Are there any more?" I mumbled as I shoved what looked to be the final one into my mouth.

Marcus took a moment to answer as he just stared at me.

"I don't think so."

"Good," I breathed as I sat down and stabbed the remaining few pieces in my bowl. They were trapped under too much cheese, but I wasn't taking any chances as I wolfed them down.

"You going to tell me what the hell just happened?"

Marcus asked as he crossed his arms. The movements made his biceps bulge against his tight shirt, and I wondered just how toned the rest of him was. If he'd just take that shirt off, that would be lovely.

No. Marcus was a jerk. I'd established that, so no more drooling!

"Um, well, I'm part pixie." I sighed, my stomach grumbling unhappily at the way I'd wolfed down my food.

"Right." Marcus rolled his eyes. "Mischief magic then. Didn't you get taught how to control it?" He frowned, the expression only making his icy eyes more prominent. Damn, that face was carved from marble.

"No, my parents died when I was young," I said as I set my bowl down on the coffee table between us. I averted my eyes from the probing man, taking in the cream walls and the flat-screen TV over on a cabinet before you walked into the kitchen. Not the greatest setup with the lounges in my opinion, it'd make watching TV hard unless you laid out on them.

"Well, best learn how to get it under control, we don't need mischief magic in this house," he muttered as he ran a hand through his dark hair. I wondered just how soft that raven hair was.

Wait. My eyebrows knitted together at his disregard for what I'd just told him.

He just looked rather displeased at this new knowledge as he sat back down and reached for his laptop. No 'sorry for your loss' or whatever like I was accustomed to when I told people of my dead parents.

"Not too friendly, are you," I said, not caring about keeping my words to myself or upsetting him. He was quite an arse to be honest.

"Nope," was his instant reply as he put his headphones back on.

Guess I couldn't ask him anything anyway.

I huffed as I stood, snatched my bowl up, and stormed into the kitchen. The cat watched me leave, his little legs working hard to follow after me.

I hoped to dear God that the other boys had some friendliness. Because I wasn't sure if I could live with such a rude little shit like Marcus.

I rinsed my bowl before tossing it in the empty dishwasher and tromping up the stairs. I would gladly hide out in my room until someone else showed up that I could talk to properly.

I made sure to flick the bathroom fan off on my way past before heading into my room. I'd finish unpacking my bag and suitcase.

Stupid, sexy man.

2

MARCUS

"Excuse me, what's this?"

I turned to spy the dark-haired beauty inspecting one of the paintings closely.

"It's darkness," I shrugged. I doubted she'd understand my art. Few people ever did.

Those bright red lips parted, a stark contrast to her porcelain skin and almost black hair.

"It's beautiful." She smiled, focusing her attention back on the painting. "You can see the break of darkness, the emotion in these flourishes. In darkness and silence there is true beauty."

"Thank you." I frowned. She was seeing more in my piece than I had. I was just flustered one night and had hurled all my annoyance at the canvas in a splash of blacks and grays. To be honest, I wasn't sure why it had captured her attention. I had many other pieces with far more detail, like the woman standing in the lake or the galaxy piece. Even the mountainous landscape was drawing more eyes.

"Tell me, what's your name?" She smiled as she pulled back, those jade eyes capturing my own.

. . .

Allison was an intriguing girl, and I knew she was going to be an interesting housemate from the moment I opened up the door.

Her scent carried with it the sweet goodness of fae, something us vampires were drawn to.

But there was something else that lingered in that blood, something darker. And I swore I could smell canine.

What was she?

When she gazed at me, her cheeks flushing softly as she took me in, I slammed up my defenses.

I did not need any more dramas in my life. Living with the other three guys was enough, and this vampire bait was not something I wanted to get involved with. She'd be a magnet for vamps, and I hated mingling with others of my kind. Hell, I hated mingling in general.

I begrudgingly helped her bring her suitcase inside, giving her a quick rundown of where everything was located. I even introduced her to Kit, who was currently stuck in cat form. Again. She'd smell what he was. Or at least, I assumed she would, considering there was something canine in her blood.

Werewolf, perhaps?

Not dingo or dog. Something more primal. I was more than happy to leave her to her own devices once I showed her to her room, and I returned to my laptop in the living area to continue playing Grand Theft Auto.

The night turned to a surprisingly interesting one when I discovered she'd taken Kit into the bathroom. That little shit. She obviously hadn't sensed what he was, but there was no way in hell I was going to tell her now. I'd just enjoy the amusement it gave me.

I discovered just what kind of fae she was to my annoyance in the living room, when her mischief magic ran havoc.

Those flying little pasta pieces had been rather infuriating, although entertaining a little.

A pixie. Just what we needed.

What was Lucas thinking? We didn't even need another housemate. It wasn't like he needed the extra rent, the rent he got from us was practically his wages. His grandfather had left the house to him, so there was no mortgage, just standard bills to pay, and his grandfather had left him a sizable inheritance, too. He was easily set for life.

Unlike the rest of us.

Allison opened up about her parents' death, and for a moment, I shared her pain. She'd had no one to teach her about her powers. At least I'd had mine until I was a teen.

I wanted to say something comforting as she averted her gaze, but then I remembered just what she was. I was not going to get close to a fae. That would end in disaster.

I instead told her to get control of her magic, knowing it was brutal and would make her hate me.

Good.

I didn't need the dramas of a fae girl.

Even if she drew me like a moth to a flame.

3

"Tell me, little one, how does it feel, how does it feel for your flesh to burn?"

I awoke from the nightmares tinged with darkness, fighting to pull me under.

I groaned at the weight on the end of my bed, my mind flitting back to the small orange and white cat that I'd met last night. Such a sweet, soft little guy. He'd stayed with me as I'd listened to some music on my iPod before calling it a night.

I certainly didn't remember him weighing so much when he'd curled up last night.

I shuffled my legs, trying to shift the cat off my foot, but finding the weight too much.

A groan welcomed me, and it took me a moment to register it.

Wait, a groan?

I sat up, my mouth falling open at the stark naked young man curled up on the end of my bed.

"Hey!" Was all I could come up with at this strange situation. Really could've done better there.

The young man's eyes shot open as he struggled to sit up at the fright.

My eyes dropped to his sizable member, nice and stiff first thing in the morning. And... covered in tiny barbs? What the fuck?

My cheeks flushed as I dragged my eyes back to his, those confused and sleepy amber orbs flicking around the room as he got his bearings, his short brown hair a ruffled mess.

Wait a minute...

"Oh my God," I gaped, everything clicking into place as he realized his nakedness and hastily covered himself.

"I'm so sorry!" he blurted as he scrambled off the bed.

I just stared in utter shock as that firm little arse rocketed out of the room.

That little fucking cat.

I groaned as I realized something else.

I was going to kill Marcus.

I threw my sheets back, cursing as I stormed over and slammed my bedroom door and turned to the wardrobe. I picked out one of my two dresses, the faded sky-blue one with a heart neckline that ended just above the knees. Just a nice little day dress, not too revealing. Nothing like my glaringly obvious red one. That was saved for tinder dates and other special occasions.

I gave my hair a quick brush with my fingers and tied it up into a ponytail. I shivered, glancing out my bedroom window where rain pattered against the panes softly.

I'd been right about a storm coming yesterday. And it had cooled right down now, enough that I reached into the wardrobe for an old gray jacket to throw on.

Now, I needed to go have a not so nice chat with Marcus, that arsehole. He knew about the cat-boy. And he didn't tell me, even though…

I scowled as I stormed out of my room, eyeing the bathroom door with a flush of embarrassment. I was going to rip into the cat shifter too. That little shit.

Which one of my housemates was he, anyway?

I padded down the stairs in my bare feet, marching into the kitchen, expecting to find Marcus at the dining table.

Nothing.

The kitchen and adjoining dining area were empty.

I sighed as I accepted this would have to wait. I was not about to barge into anyone's room.

I found the cereal in the pantry, going with some weet-bix for breakfast. I flicked the kettle on as I leaned against the island, mulling over the cat-shifter. I'd gotten a good look at him today. Too good of a look. My cheeks warmed as that erect penis sprang to mind, and I shoved the image away, despite how my body reacted.

"Spider-man," I muttered. That's who he'd looked like. Not Andrew Garfield or Tobey Maguire, the new one. I'd caught the latest Avengers movies with him in it.

I frowned as I mulled over his name, tapping my fingers on the counter as the kettle whistled.

I poured the hot water over my weet-bix and then sprinkled some sugar on top before adding the milk.

"Tom Holland!" I grinned, grateful that my memory had come through.

"Who are you talking to?"

I nearly dropped my bowl on the floor as I spun around, ready to rip into the cat-boy or Marcus.

I caught myself as I took in this new, stunningly hot man standing in the kitchen.

And he'd lost his shirt, apparently.

His dirty blond hair was crew cut, and those bright blue eyes were amused and trailing over me in a much more pleasant fashion than Marcus.

And that chest, holy hell. Almost completely hairless save for a sprinkling around his nipples and tanned to a beautiful golden like the rest of him. He had a tribal tattoo that adorned his left arm and swirled down over his left pec. He was ripped to perfection, and those abs looked like they'd been manufactured in the men's hottest weekly workshop.

Someone certainly ate his weeties.

"Allison, right?" He smiled, forcing me to drag my eyes back up to his. I flushed, my body heating up at the sight of this handsome muscle mass.

"Um, yeah," I managed to say, struggling to not drool over that sexy body. He never missed leg day either. He was a little taller than Marcus, and much broader and toned. Not that I'd seen Marcus shirtless.

I bet he's just as big down there…

Nope. Let's not do that.

"So, who were you talking to?" he asked as he continued to the fridge to pull out some orange juice.

"No one," I mumbled, embarrassed that he'd caught me talking to myself.

"Okay then." He chuckled. "I'm Skip, but some of the guys call me Red. You probably met Marcus last night, he never leaves really except for classes. Then there's Oliver, and Lucas," Skip said as he poured himself some juice.

"Yeah, Marcus is… interesting." I shrugged as I took a mouthful of my breakfast.

"Well, he's a vampire," Skip stated.

Right, that explained the pale skin, and vampires weren't exactly known for their cheery personalities.

"So, who's Kit?" I questioned once I swallowed.

Skip let out a deep chuckle, his stomach heaving with it and drawing my eyes to his defined abs once more.

"Oliver, Marcus calls him Kit, short for kitten." He grinned as he sipped his juice and leaned against the counter.

Right, the cat shifter.

"Speaking of, I need to have a chat with him," I scowled.

"Uh-oh, what'd he do?" Skip cocked his head with a smile playing at his lips.

"Well, Marcus failed to mention the cat was actually a shifter," I muttered.

Skip just narrowed his eyes at me before he grinned widely.

"Did you get changed in front of him?" he instantly asked.

My cheeks must have flushed badly because his throaty laughter rung out as he clapped his hands.

"Damn, Ollie!" Skip slapped the counter in amusement. "Lucky bugger."

I groaned inwardly as he grinned at me. I tried to ignore his quip about being lucky. That naughty side of me wanted to say how he could get lucky too if he played his cards right.

Hot hell, what was going on here? Why was I reacting so much to these men all of a sudden? I mean, it didn't help that all of them looked sexy as hell, even Oliver, the lean, yet muscular young man from my room. I forced away the image that dared to slip into my mind of his nakedness.

"So, you've met those two, which means Lucas is the only one you haven't met yet," Skip mused as he finished his juice. He seemed oblivious to the effect his naked torso had on me.

"Yes, so Marcus is a vampire, Oliver is a cat-shifter, and

you are?" I asked, wanting to learn just who I was going to be living with.

Besides, I was loving Skip's easygoing attitude, and the sight of him only added to it.

"Red kangaroo," he said proudly. Well, now I could see why he was so ripped, it was in his DNA. "And Ollie isn't a cat-shifter, he's a true shifter," Skip corrected me.

"Really?" I breathed. True shifters were rare, practically royalty. They possessed the ability to shift into any animal, unlike most shifters these days who were stuck to only one animal.

"Yeah, cat's his go to though," Skip said quickly, but I sensed he was hiding something from me from the way his mouth set. "Lucas is a witch, he's… interesting, to say the least. He'll be back today sometime, he spent the night out last night, I got home quite late, local party," he admitted.

An instant tug of curiosity and jealousy made me do a double take. What the hell was that about? Was I seriously jealous about a guy I'd just met being out at a party? With girls most likely?

I shoveled some more weet-bix into my mouth to squash the feeling as Skip began getting himself some breakfast.

I watched the muscles ripple in his back as he served himself some weet-bix. Twice as much as me.

"What are you going to study?" I asked through a mouthful of food.

"I'm in my second year studying a Bachelor of Environmental Science," he informed me. "You?"

"Veterinary science," I said.

"Oh cool, so you want to be a vet?" He grinned as he added sliced banana onto his weet-bix.

"Yeah, I think it'll be good." I nodded.

"Why?" he asked as he began eating.

"Um, well, I love animals, they're much nicer than people, and I seem to know when there's something wrong with them already, I can... well, sense it, I guess," I said between mouthfuls.

"Right," he breathed, cocking his head at me. "So, what are you? You know what we are. You smell a bit canine, but not a dingo or dog shifter, I know enough of them to know what one smells like. Something else, too."

"Um, well, I'm part pixie, and my father was a werewolf, so I'm part werewolf, my mom was fae with mostly pixie lines," I said. So he'd sniffed me out, that was a little weird, although natural for shifters, I guess.

"Damn, a pixie." He chuckled. "No wonder Marcus is avoiding you, fae are pretty much vamp bait."

That wasn't new news to me, but now I was intrigued. Was that why Marcus was such a jerk towards me? I hadn't known he was a vampire. And fae blood was very appealing to vampires. Normally, they didn't treat us like something to be avoided, they'd rather take what they wanted, which made Marcus' treatment of me even stranger.

"If you're part werewolf, no offense, why couldn't you scent us? Tell what we were?" he asked.

I scowled as I finished my last bite.

"My nose doesn't work," I mumbled.

"What?" He just frowned.

"My nose, it has no special werewolf qualities. I can't smell shit," I groaned as I moved to the sink to rinse my bowl out before placing it in the dishwasher.

"Seriously? Huh, that's weird, most half-breeds still retain a decent amount of their abilities from each side," he said as he pondered it.

"Yeah, well, my nose is broken, works just as well as a normal pixie's, which is the equivalent of a human's," I huffed. I was not too happy with this piece about myself, but it was something I'd accepted a long time ago.

"Can you shift into a wolf then?" he questioned.

"Yes, surprisingly," I said with a sigh. At least I had that part.

"Huh, strange. There aren't many werewolves around Australia, you know, not their normal environment," he mused.

"Yeah, my father moved here from the States as a kid. Apparently they're quite strict on predator shifters coming in from overseas. They prefer to have only those native to the country. There were rules where we couldn't shift unless we were in a safe area. Like here, Maple Grove," I said.

Maple Grove was for all kinds of supernatural creatures, and had a protective warding around it. You could actually feel it when you passed through, and it was a welcome relief.

Powerful warlocks and witches had cast warding spells around a number of towns and even the odd city so that we could shift freely without being seen. At least, those of us who didn't belong. Apparently, if I shifted and got seen in a warded area, I'd look like a wild dingo instead of a wolf. The big cats just looked like large feral cats or even dogs. Although, there were a few real sightings outside of warded areas. There'd been a handful of panther sightings and big cats over the years, although thankfully none of them were confirmed. The Supernatural Council would cover it as best they could and deal with those responsible.

"So, do you think Oliver will make an appearance for breakfast?" Skip asked with a mischievous grin.

"I hope so," I mumbled. He was in trouble for the stunt he'd pulled.

I leaned back against the counter, contemplating whether or not to make a tea as well.

"So, have you been to the uni yet to get your temporary schedule and textbooks?" he asked.

God, I was struggling to keep my eyes off him. He seriously needed to pop a shirt on.

"No, I was planning on doing that today, and maybe checking out the town," I said as I decided to flick the kettle on again to reheat it.

"I can walk you there? Show you around town too if you want, although it's pretty pathetic. We've only got a corner shop and a fuel station. Everything else is over in Maleny, it's only ten minutes from here, has the post office, IGA, Woolworths, butcher, cafes, you name it. Although if you're wanting to do some proper shopping, you'll have to go down to the coast, to Caloundra or Maroochydore," he stated as he finished his breakfast.

I just watched happily as he bent over to load up the dishwasher, his blue board shorts falling down a little to show me a little of his lighter colored arse. Guess someone didn't believe in nude tanning.

"Apologize!" He shot up straight, startling me, and then I realized his eyes had moved past me to the doorway leading to the living room.

I followed his gaze and my stomach flip-flopped at the sight of Oliver standing there hesitantly, his face going bright red.

"I'm sorry," he mumbled as he shoved his hands into his jacket pockets. The flimsy black jacket looked like it wouldn't even be remotely warm. The rain was only a distant spatter now, having died down by the time I got to the kitchen. I wasn't sure I wanted to walk to the uni with such unpredictable weather.

"I didn't realize she was going to lock me in the bathroom

with her!" Oliver defended himself, pouting as Skip's eyes widened.

"Wait, you watched her shower?" he asked quietly.

"No, I looked away," Oliver shot back, unable to even look at me.

"No, you watched me undress," I retorted.

"Damn." Skip clucked his tongue, but a grin was forming.

"Why'd you pretend to be a cat?" I demanded answers. "Why?"

"I wasn't pretending," Oliver crossed his arms. A flash of his naked body, smooth and toned, and that nice erection…

"You can turn at will," I shot back, stomping down the images. Damn, I was going to have his dick in my head for a while. He was a nice size, I'd give him that.

Oliver pouted, grumbling as he averted his eyes.

"Actually, he can't," Skip corrected me.

"What?" I turned on him.

"He can't control it." He just shrugged.

I moved my eyes back to Oliver, who was giving me a sheepish look as he rubbed his arms.

"Why not? Don't shifters learn how to shift at puberty?" I asked.

"Yes," Oliver stated with an eye roll.

"So…?" I raised an eyebrow.

"He pissed off a witch and got cursed, so now he can only turn into a cat. And it happens randomly, normally with emotions. He's been stuck like that for the last two days actually," Skip informed me. "Speaking of, Lucas will give you a bracelet to wear, we all have one, to allow us to communicate with him when he gets stuck," Skip said as he raised his arm up to show off the leather bracelet. Now that I thought about it, Marcus had had one, too.

"It's bloody embarrassing," Oliver groaned. "And I'm

sorry, Allison, I didn't mean to see you naked. I was just curious about you, and then you locked me in the bathroom with you, it all happened so fast. And seeing your mischief magic last night, that was interesting. Sorry about this morning…" He gave me a boyish grin as he tried to apologize.

Yep, he could pass as Tom Holland on the right angles.

"What happened this morning? And mischief magic? Why'd you use your magic?" Skip was thoroughly intrigued now.

"Um, well, I woke up to someone naked on my bed," I shot Oliver a look, and he bit his lip as he looked away. Someone with nice morning wood, but still.

"Wow, now I'm curious." Skip laughed, a full-on belly rumbling laugh. It made all the muscles in his abdomen tense and release, and I struggled to not stare at that gorgeous body.

"I fell asleep there by accident last night, nothing happened," Oliver said instantly.

"Sure, sure." Skip grinned, his amused blue eyes moving to me.

Was he suggesting…?

"You guys are nuts," I mumbled as I ran a hand down my face.

"So, mischief magic, why?" Skip moved on, although he kept a playful smile.

"Her parents died," Oliver jumped in. "So no one taught her how to wield it."

"Oh, I'm sorry to hear that." Skip's light-hearted attitude dropped, as did his smile.

"Don't be, it happened when I was little." I shrugged. I ignored the pang in my chest at the reminder. I'd been left alone in this world, tossed into a shitty household to survive in.

"Didn't family take you in?" Skip asked.

"Yeah, but they weren't interested in helping me understand my abilities. My Aunt had a witch craft a pendant that was spelled so I couldn't remove it. It stopped my powers." I gritted my teeth as I shared that part of my history.

"Shit, that's messed up. Mischief magic isn't normally dangerous, but you need to learn how to use it, that's just what happens with us supes. Us shifters don't shift until puberty, but magic in other creatures, like the fae, can manifest while they're children. They need to be taught about it and learn how to use it and control it," Skip growled, annoyed on my behalf. It warmed me, seeing him ruffled like on my behalf.

He barely knew me.

"Well, I think I'd best head over and pick up my temp schedule. I wouldn't mind popping into Maleny for some shopping later, are there any buses?" I asked, wanting to move away from the topic of my family and magic. I'd rather not share too much with them. I'd only just met the pair.

"I'll take you, the rain's getting heavier, so I'll drive you to the University, then we can go to Maleny. Lucas will be home by the time we're back I imagine," Skip said instantly, leaping at the chance to drive me.

"Can I come?" Oliver piped up.

"Sure, if it's okay with Allison." Skip grinned.

I rolled my eyes as I focused back on Oliver.

"He can come."

I collected my schedule from the office while the two boys waited in the car. The drive over had revealed that Oliver was indeed the youngest of us at just over eighteen years old. Apparently his birthday fell just after Christmas on the 27th.

I was nineteen, along with Marcus, although technically

he was twenty-one, he'd been turned into a vampire at nineteen. I didn't ask how or why as it seemed a touchy subject for the pair. Lucas was twenty-one as well, while Skip was twenty, his birthday having just passed us by on the 23rd of January.

I told them I was the 20th of April, which they were excited to hear. I was next in line for a party apparently, and it fell around Easter.

Lucas' birthday was the 20th of June, while Marcus was the 5th of August. Although there was a debate as to whether that was his birthday or if his turned day should be his birthday, which had been early October, although neither of them knew the exact day.

I pulled my hoodie up as I sprinted back to Skip's big sixty series Landcruiser, a model normally known to become rust buckets, but his had fared well. He'd even had it repainted forest green recently, which he was proud to inform me of. It was obvious he loved his car, which I'd never understand. I had my license, but I'd sold my last car to cover bills and add to my savings in order to move here to study.

Skip flung the door open just as I reached it, and I leaped into the passenger seat and tugged the door shut.

The rain was really coming down now in sheets.

"Still want to do some shopping?" Skip asked with a chuckle as I rubbed my arms. God, this weather was ridiculous.

"I know there's shared food in the house, but I need to buy my own stuff," I groaned as I dumped the bag of textbooks and papers on the floor. I was extra grateful that Skip had had a reusable bag handy for me to use.

"Okay, well, Woolworths has undercover parking, we should go there," Oliver chimed.

"Sounds good," I mumbled as I rubbed my hands

together. The rain really did cool everything down, too much for my liking. And Skip's heater in the Landcruiser was abysmal.

The old beast of a vehicle rumbled to life, and we pulled out of the University parking area to head into the neighboring town. I was pleasantly surprised that the uni didn't charge for its parking. That was a bonus, if I did get a car eventually. Although walking was easy enough, it wasn't far.

"So, you never did say what happened with the mischief magic last night?" Skip mused as he focused on the road, his wiper blades working overtime in this rain.

"Well, my magic likes to affect food mostly. I'd cooked myself some pasta, and I was getting agitated with how much of a dick Marcus was being," I muttered. "It just flared up and the pasta came to life."

"Damn, that must be interesting. I hear mischief magic can take on many forms." Skip gave me a lopsided grin. "What's yours like?"

"Flying pasta butterflies!" Oliver declared, causing Skip to laugh, that throaty sound making me grin.

"Seriously?" Skip snorted.

I loved how his naked chest moved when he laughed; it was hard to keep my eyes off of him. Why he'd not bothered to grab a shirt was beyond me, and he'd thrown on a pair of black thongs to finish his outfit, or lack thereof.

"I can't help it! It just happens, normally when I'm annoyed, but other emotions can trigger it." I managed a smile as the pair chuckled.

Oliver was leaning forward to chat with us, straining against his seatbelt as he rested his arms on the back of the front seat. Skip's cruiser's front seat was one of those full length ones, where technically we could've all squished into the front, but I was glad Oliver had taken the backseat.

Then again, that lean body would've been nice and warm, and quite welcome all pressed up against me…

I pursed my lips as I forced my naughty thoughts away. God, I was terrible.

"So, how'd you deal with that? You said your Aunt gave you a pendant, but you're not wearing it now?" Skip said as his eyes dropped to my neck. I couldn't help but notice how his eyes dipped down to the slight cleavage I showed.

"I got a witch to unbind the spell once I left home at sixteen, but I kept the pendant with me. I wore it almost all the time afterwards anyway when I was away from home, as I accidentally made… something come to life once. I realized what could go wrong if a mortal saw it, my Aunt at least taught me that our abilities and powers were to be hidden from non-supes. It's strange, here, inside the wardings, I can't feel when my magic is coming over me. When I'm outside of it, I can sense the mischief magic coming to the surface, that's why I still wore it, because it was unpredictable. I tried to teach myself how to wield it when I was alone, but it's not easy. It's a strange magic to have, not overly helpful," I said with a sigh. I reached for my black handbag, a crappy little thing I'd picked up from an op shop for a few dollars over a year ago. The strap was falling apart, and I had a safety pin holding the strap onto the handbag on one end. It held my trusty iPod and pendant, within easy reach if needed.

"Yeah, I've heard about mischief magic. Usually you have more fae bloodlines that carry other magic too, though, you don't have any other magic?" Skip asked.

"No, not that I'm aware of."

"Strange, but you can shift into a wolf," Skip murmured. "You're an interesting little mix, aren't you?"

"Apparently," I said. "Hey, you said Oliver was cursed, can't that be fixed?" I asked as I turned to look at Oliver, finding his face a little too close when I turned. Those amber eyes were bright and flecked with the tiniest hints of gold. He also had the slightest dusting of freckles over his nose.

"Nope, she was a strong witch, it will apparently lift when I turn twenty." Oliver sighed as he picked at a small hole in the top of the seat.

"Don't make it worse," Skip scolded him as he slapped the seat while staying focused on the road.

"That sucks," I said as I pursed my lips.

"I deserved it." Oliver shrugged.

"I highly doubt that," I shook my head. "What'd you do?"

"My cousins, brother, and I were harassing her, she got pissed, and I ended up getting the curse, the others didn't," he frowned as he pulled back to look out the window.

His sudden change from bubbly and sweet made my brow furrow, and I glanced at Skip who just gave me a thin smile. I wouldn't pry, I knew what it was like to have a history you'd rather keep hidden.

"So, where's Marcus today?" I asked as I looked out the window. The drive into Maleny was beautiful, so green and lush up here on the mountain, the farmland dipping into valleys and the hills rising and morphing into heavily treed areas. Dairy country mostly, with the black and white cows scattered throughout the paddocks.

"He'll be hiding out in his room. Waiting out the daylight hours, y'know," Skip said.

"Why? The myths that vampires burst into flames isn't true," I scoffed. "They just burn easier than others, even I know that."

Vampires didn't burst into flames or disintegrate as soon as the sun touched their skin like the movies portrayed, they just burned easier if in the sun for too long, like a bad sunburn that manifested in minutes rather than hours. If they stuck to shaded areas or the indoors, they were safe.

"Yeah, but he'd rather completely dodge getting any kinds of burns," Skip said. "And what do you mean even you know that?"

"Oh, well, my Aunt, she couldn't send me to a supe school, but I learned a little from my cousin about supes. She went to a supe school," I mumbled, regretting saying anything.

"Wow, your Aunt was a real tight-ass, wasn't she?" Skip said. "I'm pretty sure it's actually mandatory for a supe to only attend supe school."

"Yeah, I guess so," I murmured. "I didn't know it was mandatory." Supe schools weren't too common, they were spread out and set in the warded areas. Sadly, the area we lived in, Maroochydore, only had one supe school within a fifteen-minute walk, and it was one of the higher end private ones, where you had to pay to attend. So my fae cousin went there.

While I got sent to the public schools, despite there being a public supe school in Caloundra that I could've caught a bus to. Nope, I got shoved into a mainstream, normal school. It was easier for my aunt, less costly. Besides, technically I didn't have any powers with my pendant on. Guess that was how she evaded the mandatory thing.

"I hear Maleny is full of hippies, that true?" I asked, wanting to move away from my family. I hated talking about them. They were a memory, a past I wanted forgotten.

Skip seemed to register this, but allowed my subject change as his mouth set for a moment before he grinned.

"Yeah mate, we got a few of 'em, they're harmless, just potheads and at one with nature, y'know?" He chuckled.

I smiled at his choice of words for the hippie locals. I'd

heard a bit about the people up here on the range, but I doubted it was anything bad. Hell, down on the coast was pretty wild at times.

"So, you got any magic classes on your schedule?" Skip asked, glancing at his rearview mirror.

I hated how silent Oliver had become; I was already growing fond of his cheery personality, and I couldn't stop remembering his morning glory from earlier either. I hoped I hadn't upset him too much by asking about his curse.

"I don't know, I asked to take some, I chose fae," I answered honestly. Being a supe university, we were given some elective magical classes, depending on our bloodline. There were ones for shifters, vampires, witches, fae, and more. I'd asked to be put into the fae classes, although due to my mixed blood, I was allowed to also attend shifter classes if I chose to.

"Huh, cool, I'm sure they've scheduled you in, I wonder what days you'll have them?" Skip mused.

"It'd be good to finally learn how to wield these powers," I said. "I hate how they can just take over so randomly. I need to learn control."

"That's definitely true," Skip agreed. "Mischief magic can become a pain in the arse if you don't get a handle on it."

"What experience do you have with mischief magic?" I asked, intrigued. He seemed to know more than I'd expect from a shifter.

"My sister dated a pixie, he was a wanker. Always causing trouble around the house. His magic affected fixtures and anything that had electricity. Even cars. Fucked with this baby a few times, too," Skip growled as he patted the dash of his cruiser.

"Wow," I arched my eyebrows. "Is your sister here too?"

"Oh hell no." He gave a sharp laugh. "That slut is back

home running the place like usual. You know what it's like, baby of the family, got mummy and daddy wrapped around her little finger," he growled.

Wow, I had not expected such words from him. Someone certainly wasn't close to his sister.

"So, you said you made something come to life?" Skip asked.

"Huh?" I frowned.

"Earlier, you said you brought something to life that made you always wear your pendant when out and about, what was it?"

"A muffin," I answered quickly as my mind jumped back to it. Let's just say, pixie orgasms contained mischief magic. And a flying, honking vibrator was not what I wanted to share right now.

"Oh, cool," he shrugged.

I fell silent as we passed through the warding as we exited Maple Grove, and I relaxed into the seat with my arms wrapped around myself. The rain had grown heavier, hammering down on us, and Skip flicked on his headlights to make it easier to navigate.

"I think we should head straight back after woolies, we don't want to stay out in this," Oliver finally spoke up from the back.

I glanced back at him, hating the forlorn look on his face.

What was he not wanting to share? What was so secret about his curse?

4

I laughed as Skip turned up the radio, clapping my hands along to the AC/DC song playing over the speakers. God, how I loved them.

My bags of groceries lay nestled at my feet, and I was beyond grateful that I'd somehow managed to afford them. I was running low on cash, and I was looking forward to starting my new job next weekend to start saving again. I'd also work short day shifts around my uni schedule, which my new employer had been more than flexible with. I even told Skip about my new place of work, and he laughed, saying it was the only little cafe in Maple Grove, recently opened too. He was surprised they'd dared to open up shop there as many of those local to the area just went straight into Maleny for everything.

I'd applied at the right time, right when they were just starting to hire.

"I guess I'll have to drop in sometime and see you there, aye?" Skip chuckled as we headed home.

Home, still an interesting concept to me. My new home was living with four men. A unique new change.

"I know the couple who are running it, they just want Maple Grove to start growing more, supporting the locals, that kind of thing," Oliver piped up. They'd both joined me in woolies, and Oliver had slowly returned to his cheery self.

Apparently, he had a thing for caramello koalas. I was a freddo frog girl myself, and Skip loved his salt and vinegar chips and coke.

I'd chosen more nutritional food than my two counter-parts, and I'd had to pay extra for my green bags since I'd left mine in my car when I'd sold it.

"We'll see how it goes, for your sake, I hope they last," Skip said with a sideways glance at me.

"I'm sure they'll do fine," Oliver assured me.

"Hey, want anything from the bottle-o before we head back?" Skip asked as he indicated left instead of right to go home.

"Nah thanks, I'm good," I shook my head. I didn't drink. Ever. That was just a rule for me. I'd seen what it did to people.

"Well, I'm going to grab some stubbies for the weekend, Lucas has invited Richo and Issac over, so I'd best make sure we're stocked up."

"Grab me some Midori?" Oliver asked as he pulled out his wallet.

"You with your fancy drinks," Skip sniggered.

"Beer tastes like piss." Oliver scrunched his nose up, and I cracked a grin as I glanced between the pair as Skip pulled in before the bottle shop.

"It's the stuff men are made of," Skip declared. "A real man's drink."

"If they like piss," Oliver muttered.

I just giggled, agreeing with him. It did taste like piss from memory of the time I'd sipped one out of curiosity.

"Well, give me the money if you want your green shit," Skip said as he shut the engine off and offered his hand over his shoulder.

Oliver slapped the fifty dollar note into his hand, and I just rolled my eyes.

Alcohol cost too much, just another reason I hated it.

Skip braved the rain, leaving us in the rather cool interior of his cruiser. His heater was useless. Although, what did I expect from such a fossil of a car?

"Who's Richo and Issac?" I asked.

"Richard Cooper, and Issac Ellison. Just some of Lucas' friends." Oliver shrugged. "They like to play pool some nights, bet money, drink, you know, usual."

"Huh, okay, I didn't realize we could have friends over," I said.

"Well, it is his house," Oliver reminded me. "But we can have friends over too, as long as they're respectful of the place."

"Of course." I grinned. As if I even had friends. I had work colleagues, and that was it. No one that I really considered a friend, I'd been working too much to even consider a social life just to afford my rental down on the coast. I'd worked thirty-eight hours a week for a fair while as a retail clerk, then moved into a barista position when the small clothing store got shut down in the plaza. We just couldn't make a decent enough profit with the rising rent costs of the plaza storefront.

And despite sharing a rental with another lady, it was eating up half my pay-slip easily, then I'd had my phone plan on top of that, my car expenses, and groceries. I'd struggled to save, and I was still surprised I had. At least this new housemate situation cost just under a third of my last rent. I could work, study, and save a bit, as long as I didn't party.

The thought made me roll my eyes.

I was certainly no party girl.

"So, Ally, Lucas told me you were studying Veterinary Science, so I guess we'll be sharing some classes." Oliver grinned as he bit into his caramel koala.

"You're studying it too?" I relaxed. At least I'd know one person. Well, I guess I knew him, I'd seen his dick already, surely that made us friends.

"Yeah, being a true shifter, I can sense things with animals and all sorts. It's just a special knack I've got, what about you?" he asked, cocking his head curiously at me.

"I can tell if they've got something seriously wrong with them. I found out back at my first job, my colleague, Sue, asked me to pet sit for her while she was away one weekend as her pet sitter canceled last minute. She even paid me, but I was patting her Labrador when I just, well, knew something was wrong. I told her to take him to the vet, and she did, turns out he had a tumor. If she hadn't caught it so soon, they said it would've killed him," I explained, remembering the scene so clearly.

I was on the beige lounge, watching some Law and Order, when Crow, her black lab, jumped up to join me. I began patting him, and the alarming sensation coiled inside me. I could almost pinpoint where the issue was in his chest, it was that clear.

"Wow, that's pretty wicked. Does it work with other animals? Maybe it's some sort of combo werewolf/fae ability," Oliver contemplated.

"I used it on a cat too at my last rental, this big grey tabby cat would visit me sometimes, I patted him once and sensed something was wrong, but I didn't know who owned him. He died a few days later I found out, some kind of cancer," I said sadly. I'd hated that. I'd grown fond of the fat cat that would greet me when I got home from work, sprawling on the driveway and demanding attention. I never even learned his name, although I'd ended up just referring to him as 'handsome' most of the time.

My housemate had informed me that he'd died, she'd seen a girl crying out on her lawn one day and asked, learning that 'Billy' had passed away from sudden cancer.

"Hey, wanna know a secret?" Oliver leaned forward, resting his arms on the back of the seat.

I quivered at his sudden closeness, of that boyish grin as he moved his face closer.

"What?" I breathed.

"Skip's name, he hates it. His parents are dicks, they thought it was funny," Oliver murmured.

"Skip?" I raised an eyebrow.

It wasn't that bad of a name, although rare. More known in the States. "No." Oliver chuckled as he leaned forward to whisper into my ear.

My cheeks flushed as his hot breath washed over my ear, but then my chuckles rose up, turning into giggles as I registered the name.

Skip returned, diving into the cruiser to try to flee the rain. Too bad he brought most of it in with him. He was dripping wet, but damn, that slick, chiseled chest was a sight for sore eyes. I could look at it all day.

He handed me the carton of stubbies and thrust the bottle of Midori at Oliver.

"Skip, I'm so sorry," I murmured, unable to stifle the soft giggles that escaped.

"For what?" He frowned, and Oliver snickered, causing him to glance between us, confused.

"I really did love little Skippy," I said, bursting into chuckles as Skip's face dropped and he rounded on Oliver.

"You cunt, you told her?" he groaned. "Not cool, man."

"Hey, if she's going to be living with us, we shouldn't have secrets." Oliver grinned as he moved back into his seat to pull his seatbelt back on.

"Seriously though, that's a little cruel," I said once I reined my chuckles in.

"Yeah, well, they're not exactly the world's best parents." Skip rolled his eyes. "Could be worse, though."

"What's worse than a kangaroo shifter called Skippy?" Oliver snorted.

"The dairy kids," Skip shot back. "That was a marketing stunt right there, everyone knows it."

"What dairy kids?" I asked, feeling like I was missing some common knowledge.

"Locals here know all about them, one of them's called Cheeky." Skip grinned. "Don't even get me started on the others."

The cruiser started up, and I managed to get the pair to tell me more about these kids of the local dairy farmers, and I couldn't contain my groans on the behalf of the children.

"Do you know what bothers me? How Christmas is barely over, and yet Easter stuff is all over the shelves," Oliver stated as we headed back.

"I know, right?" I groaned. "As if I need the extra temptation."

"Right, you're a fae, and a pixie at that, your sweet tooth must love it." Skip smirked.

"Yes, and I'm a sucker for chocolate bunnies and eggs." I sighed in defeat. "I actually gave in just last week and got myself a big bunny. I ate it all in one go, I'm a pig." I pouted.

"Wow, no willpower at all." Skip laughed.

"You're not a pig," Oliver snorted. "Don't call yourself that."

"Oh, but I am, what little money I have leftover from work after paying my bills and rent, usually goes on food. And normally it's something yummy. Like bee stings! God, the bakery down in Landsborough makes some of the best ones," I moaned. I'd caught a bus into the station there before catching another to Maleny to then get my taxi.

While I waited for my bus to arrive, I'd popped across the street to the renowned bakery and selected a small bee sting. Small meaning it could maybe be shared between two people.

Nope, I annihilated it in one go.

"The bakery in Maleny sells bee sting slice, it's amazing." Oliver grinned.

"Don't egg me on," I chided him.

"Bee sting. I like it," Skip stated.

"Who doesn't," Oliver said.

I felt completely at ease with my two companions. Like I'd known them for years.

I loved it.

I smiled as we pulled up before the gorgeous house, Skip parking out the front of the small two bay garage to the left of it. I'd noticed it yesterday when I'd arrived, but I hadn't seen this big beast of a car. I wondered why he didn't park inside the shed.

"Lucas has his inherited old Ford Falcon in there. Got it from his grandfather I believe," Skip explained when I asked. "Fancy little beast."

"Cool," was all I could say to this, and Skip just raised an eyebrow at me.

"You're really not a car gal, are ya?" he questioned.

"Nah." I gave him a half smile. I certainly was no car

fanatic. If it ran and got me from point A to point B, then that was good enough for me.

"Ready for a mad dash to the house?" Oliver said, the rain beating down on the windows.

What I wouldn't do to curl up on the lounge with a hot chocolate in hand.

"Guess so," I said, glancing down at my two bags of groceries and my bag with my textbooks and schedules.

"Here, I'll take your groceries," Skip offered, leaning over to grab them.

My breath caught as his warm arms brushed my bare legs, and I got a closer look at his chest and that tribal tattoo.

He seemed to sense my change, and he gave me a sly smile as he pulled my bags up.

"C'mon, don't want those textbooks getting wet." He grinned. My heart jumped as I tried to focus only on his glittering blue eyes.

My cheeks flushed as I nodded, my mouth dry at his sudden closeness as I hastily grabbed my bag of textbooks.

Oliver swung his door open and slammed it behind him, but before I had a chance to climb out into the rain, struggling down out of this high beast of a machine, Oliver was at my door and opening it. He offered his hand, and I accepted the help down from the big cruiser.

Oliver grinned as he intertwined our fingers, dragging me after him to the house. My breath hitched at his touch, a warm tingle shooting through me as my stomach knotted. I doubted he even knew what effect his touch had on me. It'd been ages since I'd had a partner, since I'd had the touch of a man. I'd forgotten just how nice it was, even just to hold hands. Not to mention Oliver was incredibly cute, and my cheeks burned as my mind brought up the vivid picture of him naked on my bed. Damn, maybe I'd forgo saving for a car and get a good vibrator first. That sounded like a good idea.

Skip was cursing as he tore after us, but then the rain suddenly stopped.

I came to a stop as I looked around dumbly. The rain was still falling, but it seemed to be bouncing off a bubble surrounding us.

"Guess Lucas is home," Oliver stated as he squeezed my hand.

My eyes dropped to our joined hands, and a smile spread across my face. He had a firm but soft grip on me, and I caught those mischievous amber eyes as they lit up.

Did he feel the same interest too, that little spark? I returned my gaze to the protective bubble around us, grinning stupidly at the magic that vibrated in the air. I could actually feel it, like when I crossed through the wardings. It tingled against my skin, making the hairs stand up on end.

"C'mon, he won't want to shield us forever," Skip said as he drew up behind me. His hand touched my lower back, and I quivered at the soft touch.

What was it with these damn attractive men? Were they trying to make me swoon for them? Hell, they seemed completely oblivious to how they were making me feel. Maybe this was how they treated all their female friends.

Friends, yes, I felt like it was safe to call us that now. They seemed genuinely nice, and fun to be around. Living with them would be good, although, maybe falling for them was a bad idea.

My eyes landed on the strikingly handsome man on the verandah, looking out at us with an arched brow and a soft smile. His arms were crossed, but that was not what drew my eyes. It was the lavish black suit and crew cut, the front styled in a side sweep. He was breathtaking in a charming way, that crooked smile making my chest tighten.

Damn, what was with the men in this house? How was I supposed to not think about them? Maybe Lucas cast some magic on them to make them all irresistible. That seemed the most likely.

"Luke!" Skip called out, his hand leaving my back and making me nearly pout. I caught myself, internally scolding my body for reacting to his touch. Hell, I was still secretly warmed by Oliver's hand holding mine.

These men were too much, it was like they'd known me longer than just a day. I felt close to them already, which was weird. But I liked the company of Oliver and Skip, they were uplifting and fun.

The closer I got to the verandah, the more I could appreciate Lucas' devilishly handsome features.

His hair was a golden blond now that I was within better visual range, the kind of hair you'd expect from someone who loved to sit out in the sun for hours bleaching it, and his skin was a gorgeous sun-kissed color. As I climbed the steps to the verandah being dragged by Oliver, I could see the flecks of vibrant green lighting up that deep forest green hue in his eyes. His five o'clock stubble was sexy as hell too.

He nodded at me, and I spied the ear piercing in his left ear, a dazzling diamond-like stone glinting at me. Hell, his whole aura screamed wealthy, from those polished black boots right up to the dark crimson satin tie. It wouldn't surprise me if that earring was a real diamond.

"Well, it's nice to finally meet you in person," Lucas said, and I caught the slightest hint of satisfaction in his eyes as he glanced at Oliver clutching my hand.

Guess he was hoping Oliver might have a chance.

Hell, I was interested in the lot of them, all sexy and

charming and friendly. Except Marcus, he was just a delicious piece of eye candy as long as he kept his mouth shut. Once that opened, his attractiveness couldn't salvage his shitty personality.

"Likewise," I finally said, realizing I'd been ogling him for a few moments. Damn, that smile was perfect. Skip's smile was warm and friendly, even flirtatious, but I got a whole other feel from Lucas.

"Well, the weather has taken a shitty turn. Guess you won't be mowing the lawn," Lucas said as he glanced at Skip, who had climbed the steps behind us. I only now realized that he was standing awfully close behind me.

If I just stepped back, I'd feel that bare, ripped chest against me.

"We should watch a movie. See if Ally likes the same stuff as us," Oliver suggested.

"Bee Sting here might want to settle in still, she might not want to sit with a bunch of guys just yet," Skip warned him, although the devious smile on his lips made it clear he didn't dislike the idea.

"Bee Sting? Really?" I rolled my eyes at the pet name.

"It suits you." Skip chuckled, but his skin was prickling out here on the verandah, the rain pounding down around us and the sudden wind whipping it our way.

Why he hadn't grabbed a shirt still baffled me.

"Well, I'm going to make hot milos, and I intend to watch the next few episodes of Game of Thrones. Whoever wants to join me, can," Lucas shrugged.

"Hot milo sounds good," I nodded, pulling my bag of textbooks to my chest as the cool wind chilled me. I really wanted to change into something warmer. A dress had been a terrible idea as my legs were covered in goosebumps, and the wind was threatening to blow it right up and give the boys a lovely look at my old, worn panties. I seriously needed some new ones.

"Well, let's get inside where it's warmer." Lucas stepped aside, the door swinging open on its own.

I grinned as I felt the magic once more. I knew it was Lucas' doing, and it exhilarated me. I could see that it had the same effect on Oliver and Skip as they brushed past him into the house, their movements light and practically tingling with electricity. I liked the feel of Lucas' magic; it was both welcoming and yet exciting all at once.

I headed inside, sighing as the cool air gave way to a warmer interior. I wondered if he had the reverse cycle on or a fire, but then just summed it up to magic. Damn, he was good with it.

I followed Skip through to the kitchen while Oliver flopped down on one of the red lounges, sprawling out like the cat he turned into.

"Thanks for carrying those," I said as Skip set my two grocery bags on the center island.

"Don't mention it," he waved me off. "I'll start putting it away, do you want any of it labeled?"

"Just the chocolates," I said after a moment of deliberation.

"Of course," Skip snorted.

"Hey, I need them," I defended, and he just gave me a cheesy grin.

"Go take your books upstairs, little pixie," he shooed me away.

I turned up my nose playfully, which he just chuckled at, before I tromped up the stairs.

I dumped my bag of books on my bed and abandoned my sandals at the foot of the bed before slipping on some dull pink socks. They'd faded a lot over the years, and I was in need of some new ones.

I glanced back at my sandals, my worn joggers set beside them. Maybe I'd invest in some heels, I was sure my housemates would like them.

I groaned at myself. God, I was already hooked on these boys. It wasn't hard though; they were caring and funny, and I already had an intriguing feeling about Lucas. There was just something about him that fascinated me.

Too bad Marcus was a jerk. Otherwise I'd have the perfect bunch of housemates. Not to mention the house was surprisingly tidy considering that four men lived here.

I hurried back downstairs to find Skip had already put away my groceries, and a quick look in the fridge revealed my bag of Freddo's were stuck in the door. 'Bee Sting' was scribbled on it in permanent marker. I just grinned at the nickname. It was certainly an interesting one. But it made me crave some delicious bee sting. How I wished we'd stopped at the bakery in Maleny now to try out the slice they had.

I eyed the blue cooler on the bottom shelf, frowning at Marcus' name plastered on it. Curiosity won out, and I unzipped the cooler to peek inside.

I recoiled at the sight of blood bags.

Of course.

"How many sugars in your hot milo?" Lucas asked, and I jumped as I turned to spy him over by the kettle. I quickly zipped up the cooler, grateful that he was facing the kettle still. How long had he been there?

"Two, please," I said as I straightened. I caught my breath as Lucas waved his hand and the teaspoon rose from the sugar jar and dropped sugar into the row of mugs while Lucas grabbed the milo from an overhead cupboard.

"Wow, that must be extremely useful," I breathed.

"It is." Lucas gave me a devilish grin as he flicked his hand towards me.

I jumped as the milk rose from the fridge door that I was still holding open.

"Marshmallows?" he asked.

I was mesmerized, watching dumbly as the milk container opened itself, floating in mid-air as it poured into the mugs.

"Haven't seen witch magic in action before?" Lucas asked, grinning as I finally dragged my eyes away from the floating milk bottle.

"Um, no, I was, well, I guess sheltered, from supernatural stuff, went to a mainstream human school," I mumbled, moving to the side as the milk whizzed back and set itself back in the door.

"Wow, that's strange." Lucas frowned as he leaned against the counter and folded his arms.

I was still stunned that he was wearing a suit.

"Not as strange as your suit," I shot back.

"This? Well, I like suits, sue me." He shrugged, giving me that dashingly crooked smile once more.

Damn, he was swoon-worthy.

"Wait, you wear them all the time?" I said in disbelief.

"It's my brand." Lucas posed for me, causing me to giggle. "I grew up with rich parents and an equally rich lifestyle. Which meant that my parents were always dressing up, and that meant me too. I kinda kept it when I inherited this house, it's just a part of me," Lucas said nonchalantly.

So I was right, he was a secret millionaire. Could this deal get any better?

"So, you're a pixie wolf?" he asked, cocking his head to the side as the kettle boiled and began pouring hot water into the mugs. The teaspoon dove down in perfect sync after it, mixing the hot milo's.

"Yeah, that's me." I pursed my lips.

"Cool, interesting mix."

"A witch looks like more fun," I remarked as the kettle set back down and the dishwasher opened up as the teaspoon dove in.

Magic. Now this was a real step up from my old life. So much better than mischief magic.

"You didn't answer earlier, do you want marshmallows?" he repeated his earlier question as he pushed off the counter and rummaged through an overhead cupboard.

"Sure."

"Okay, go sit, I'll be out in a minute," he said.

I did as told and headed out, my bright grin dropping as I spied Marcus entering the living room on the other side.

Great. The vampire had risen.

"Morning," Marcus droned as he slunk through the living room, only giving me the barest of glances before slipping past.

Probably seeking out his breakfast in the cooler.

The thought made me shudder. Did he just drink it cold? Did he pour it in a glass or just suck it from the blood bag? Or did he microwave it?

"You watched any Game of Thrones?" Skip asked. He was relaxing on one of the lounges, which had been pulled away from the wall to angle towards the TV better. Oliver had done the same with the other one.

"A little bit," I murmured.

I flicked my eyes between the two lounges, debating where to sit.

Oliver was grinning, and I knew he wanted me to sit next to him, whereas Skip was just getting the show ready. He seemed to be using a PlayStation remote, and it took me a moment to realize that we must be watching it through the console.

I joined Oliver, who moved to give me room to sit beside him.

"We just started season four, we're onto episode three. We've already watched it before, but it's an awesome series worth rewatching," Oliver explained as he pulled his legs up to huddle into the arm of the lounge.

Skip quietly cheered as the TV sounded off, the Game of Thrones theme music playing as he reached the menu.

"Hot milos all around," Lucas declared as he strode in with two mugs. The other two were floating behind him, as if being carried by an invisible person.

He slumped down beside Skip on the other lounge, handing him one mug as the two floating ones drifted over to Oliver and I.

"Extra marshmallows for our little pixie if she so desires," Lucas grinned, and I giggled as the bag of marshmallows floated into the room and set down on the coffee table.

"Are we waiting for you, Marcus?" Skip called out over his shoulder.

"I'm coming," Marcus muttered as he entered the living room, glancing at me finally then looking longingly at the other lounge. Lucas was spread out though, his feet propped up on Skip's thighs. Something that struck me as odd, but I didn't question it.

Marcus sighed, eyeing the vacant spot beside me.

"Do you mind?" he asked, his voice low, as if it was something he hated to ask.

"Do you?" I shot back instantly, and he scowled. "Whatever, sit." I rolled my eyes.

He made a soft grunt as he sunk down beside me, distancing himself as best he could from me.

I ignored him, instead shuffling closer to Oliver, who seemed pleased that I was now pushed up against his side a bit.

I imagined any other girl would feel out of place and maybe even intimidated in this roomful of young men, but despite it only being my first day here, I felt at ease.

Besides, ever since I'd started being able to shift, I felt like I could better defend myself if needed.

Skip played the show, and I sighed as I sipped my hot milo, grateful that Lucas had left a teaspoon in it for me to stir the marshmallows in.

I tried to refrain from asking questions, but I slowly caught on to what was happening in the show.

The immediate forced sex with the brother-sister pair at the funeral was a little strange, and I couldn't help but glance around at my male companions. Thankfully, they seemed to be all immersed in the show.

Good.

It wasn't until the scene with Oberyn and Ellaria and their companions that my body began to react despite my inner scolding. The sensual scene, with multiple lovers, both male and female, made me shift uncomfortably as I throbbed. God, I hadn't been laid for ages, and this was just plain cruel, watching this scene with a group of sexy guys. I tried to keep my cheeks from flushing in their presence, as Skip murmured in approval and Oliver leaned forward to take in the delicious scene.

I knew instantly that Marcus had sensed my slight arousal as he sucked in a breath, and I clenched my jaw as I flicked my hooded eyes to him.

His frosty blue eyes were struggling to stay on the TV, and his jaw was set as his fingers dug into the arm of the lounge. My body ached, desperate for the touch I'd gone so long without. I could feel the tension in the air around him, and I glanced down to his jeans, curious to see if it had caused a reaction.

Goddamn.

"VB," Marcus growled.

I turned to him, frowning. "What was that?"

"Vampire Bait," he muttered, flicking his eyes to the coffee table. "Your magic."

I followed his gaze and groaned as the marshmallow bag shuffled and barked.

It full on barked, a tiny, soft sound.

"What was that?" Skip asked, pausing the show as he sat up straight.

Lucas had a curious smile playing at his lips as he sat up too, removing his legs from on top of Skip's.

Oliver laughed as a little marshmallow bounded out of the packet, soaring across to the lounge in one giant leap.

How its tiny little legs had managed that was beyond me.

Skip was laughing now, leaning forward and clasping his hands as the four legged marshmallows spewed from the packet, rushing in all directions.

I looked back to Marcus, who seemed to have relaxed now that something else had our full attention. My throbbing had died down too as I watched in horror as the marshmallows barked and ran around.

"They're puppies?" Oliver chuckled, freezing as the first marshmallow leapt onto his lap. They had no faces, just little legs, but each time they made that strangled bark, a soft hollow would appear in the end of the marshmallow. It was utterly freaky.

"Mischief magic, always entertaining." Lucas grinned, flicking his twinkling green eyes to catch mine.

"Um, why's it doing that?" Oliver murmured, frowning at the marshmallow.

The marshmallow that was humping his hand.

"I'm so done with this," I groaned, covering my face as my cheeks flushed.

"Does it have anything to do with the scene we just watched?" Skip asked, struggling to contain his soft snorts of laughter.

I lurched off the lounge, darting out of the room and bounding up the stairs in embarrassment. I couldn't bear to be around them when they figured out why that had happened.

I threw myself on my bed, scowling and groaning into my pillow as I heard the men downstairs trying to deal with the marshmallows.

Lucas was a witch. Surely he could handle it considering he made stuff do his bidding all the time.

After a few minutes had passed and downstairs fell silent, laughter bubbled up inside me and I let it out, utterly disbelieving this whole situation.

"It was pretty funny."

I rolled over, giving Lucas a soft smile as he leaned on the doorframe. His suit was a little ruffled since he'd been sprawled on the lounge, but he looked quite entertained as he gave me that crooked smirk.

"Did you get them under control?" I asked, biting my lip as he chuckled. I should've helped deal with my mess.

"Yeah, I dealt with it. Although, Ollie ate that one marshmallow that was having fun with him," he snickered.

"I'm sorry," I grimaced.

"Don't be, Oliver told me that apparently you never got taught how to control your magic. Your mischief magic reacts to your emotions, although, being horny, that's rather interesting, isn't it?" He grinned as he folded his arms and cocked his head.

My face felt like it was on fire as I averted my gaze, instead glaring down at my pink socks.

"Hey, relax, we're pretty open with that kind of stuff here," he said gently. "Although, you did spark a response from Marcus. He even called you vampire bait," he snorted at the term.

"Yeah, well, he better not get any ideas," I said instantly as I played with the hem of my dress.

"You're safe here, we're like a family, and hopefully, you can slot right into that. I got a sense from you that you'd fit well with us here."

I didn't want to tell him that I felt more at home here than I'd felt with my Aunt and my cousin. There was no feeling like I wasn't equal here, and Oliver and Skip had made me feel quite welcome and at ease.

"Hey, I meant to give you this, too." Lucas straightened as he pulled out a small charm bracelet from his pocket. He crossed the room and sat down at the end of my bed. "I'd appreciate if you could always wear it. Oliver can't control his shifts, and when he changes, well, it's the only way we can communicate with him," Lucas said softly.

"He doesn't like to talk about that, does he?" I said as Lucas offered me the silver charm bracelet. It had a cat, stars, and hearts hanging from the chain. I held out my wrist, and he happily did it up for me, his warm fingertips brushing my skin and making it tingle.

"He has his reasons for not wanting to talk about it," was all Lucas shared. He didn't say it like he wished I didn't ask, more like he knew it wasn't his tale to share. But he knew more than me, I knew that instantly.

"Thank you for accepting my application, too, I was

really running out of time to find a place. When do you want me to pay rent?" I asked as Lucas' fingers lingered on my skin. It was hard for me to not focus on those warm fingertips, how he was rubbing soft circles into the back of my hand automatically. It looked like he didn't even realize he was doing it as he looked out my window in thought.

"Whenever is easiest for you, you said you had some work starting here, so just after your payday, I guess," he said.

I relaxed as he massaged my hand, my mind flicking back to Marcus' reaction. I wouldn't deny that his reaction had excited me.

Even if he was a tool.

That's how long it had been since I'd been laid. Even a tool excited me.

"Sorry," Lucas said as he quickly pulled his hand away and gave me a sheepish grin. "Habit."

"Who's the lucky girl?" I asked with a smile, although a sharp twist in my gut made me purse my lips. I had no right to be jealous. Hell, I hadn't even considered that my housemates were probably not single like me.

The thought made me deflate a little. Such sweet guys like them, I doubted they were single; they were probably comfortable around me because they were taken.

"No one right now," he said.

"Oh, that's a shame," I said, but my heart fluttered. So he was single.

No, Ally. He's your landlord.

That was a no-no.

"Such is life," he said with a lopsided smile. "So, you want to come finish the episode with us?"

"I think I might just chill up here for a while, I'm a bit tired actually," I said. I didn't want to tell him that I was not up to seeing Marcus again right now. I felt strange about him after that episode. He'd seemed so uninterested in me, like I was just a nuisance, and yet he'd reacted to my moment of horniness. Not to mention I could just picture the grins Oliver and Skip would give me, and I wouldn't be able to hide the reason as to why the marshmallows had become horny little dogs.

"Okay, but if you change your mind, you're more than welcome to join." He smiled as he patted my knee.

"Thanks," I murmured as he stood up and headed for the door.

Once he'd shut the door behind him, I rolled over and reached for my iPod in the bedside table. Some music sounded good right now.

5

I groaned, rubbing my eyes as I sat up groggily. I'd drifted off, and my iPod had died at some point as I listened to the Evanescence albums.

A glance out the window revealed it was still pouring with rain, and I rubbed my arms as I pulled my jacket tighter around me.

I wondered how long I'd slept for?

I tugged my earphones out and set the iPod down on the bedside table as I stretched. I glanced down at my bag of textbooks I'd moved to the floor when I'd curled in bed. I should really check my schedule. I only had one more day off before uni started.

I straightened out my dress, which had ridden up and crinkled thanks to my nap, and moved to perch on the end of the bed as I dug through the bag.

It was a little booklet with my temporary schedule, teachers, and a map of the University. I'd organize my proper schedule on my introductory days.

I loved the insignia for the uni, the shield with the phoenix in it. A symbol of magic and hope.

My schedule was pretty basic. My veterinary science lectures were first up Monday morning with an introductory lecture, followed by a fae magic class in the afternoon.

My first semester's study units were animal management for veterinarians, animal and veterinary biology, and veterinary professional foundations.

I had Fridays free, where I would work my new cafe job, along with Saturday and a short Sunday shift.

I needed to check with Lucas if it was still okay to borrow his laptop for study, and maybe ask if it was possible to borrow it for my classes and lectures if needed.

I sighed as I set down my schedule after glancing over the map of the university. It was a rather large uni, but I shouldn't have expected anything less considering it was the only supe university in this area. There was one down at Caloundra, but it didn't offer the Veterinary Science degree that I wanted to do. Not to mention it was a little too close to home. I wanted a fresh start away from where I'd grown up.

The next one was down at Caboolture, and then Brisbane had not one, but three of them.

I checked my hair quickly, running my hands over it to find the ponytail was rather loose. My mirrored wardrobe gave me a full view of my look, and I sighed at my reflection. My hair needed fixing, as it looked how I'd expect it to look after a nap. I redid it as I stood, and then headed out into the hall.

I spied Oliver in his room, the door wide open as he read a book. Predatory cats biology. It made me smile as I stopped in his doorway and knocked on the doorframe.

"Hey." Oliver's face lit up as he sat up on his queen bed. His room was rather sparse, a desk to one side with a chair, a bookcase stacked to the brim with books and DVDs beside it, and a set of drawers and a bedside table on the other side. The sliding door wardrobe was closed, and it had one mirrored door as well, set at the end of his bed with a window above his drawers.

"Sorry about earlier," I murmured.

"The marshmallows? Don't worry about it." He waved it off.

"So, you nervous?" I asked, stepping into his room when he patted the bed for me to join him.

"For uni? Nah, the first week shouldn't be too hard. Lucas is into his third year, he told me the first week will be pretty laid-back, introductions, a proper schedule. The one they gave you is just a rough guide, the actual timetable will have all the workshops and practical days. They have an on campus veterinary center, so that's a bonus." He sat up, crossing his legs as he set his book down beside him. I sunk down on the edge of the bed, noting how he had a creamy peach colored bed set. Probably helped mask the ginger and white cat hair when he shifted.

"I wonder if we'll share classes since we're both studying the same thing," I mused.

"I can make sure we are. Actually, Lucas suggested I make sure we can be in the same classes. Just in case I have… issues," he chewed his lip as he looked out the window. The rain had eased a little, and I hoped it cleared up for my first day.

I wasn't entirely sure what to expect on Monday.

"What kind of issues?" I asked, but I instantly played with the charm bracelet Lucas had given me.

"If I get stuck in cat form. The tutors and professors have all been informed of my… problem, and they'll be understanding if I miss days. I can just study off you if we share classes." He grinned hopefully.

"Sure, I don't mind," I said easily. Having him sharing

my classes made me relax a little. At least I wouldn't be alone in a strange, unknown place.

"I'm already getting Fridays off, so it'll just be selecting my line-up of lectures, prac and tutorials," I said.

"Cool." He nodded. "I can show you to class Monday, that'll be fun."

"Have you ever been to the university before?"

"Well, no." He frowned.

"So we'll both be just as equally lost finding our first class then," I arched an eyebrow at him as my lip pulled into a smirk.

"Well, no, Lucas has class too, Skip doesn't start till later in the day, and Marcus takes the evening/night classes with the other vampires. Luke can show us where to go," Oliver retorted.

"What's Marcus studying?" I asked.

"Bachelor in game design. His class is one of the most normal ones actually. Our Veterinary science classes will have special days where we focus on our magic and/or abilities to help us in the practical and hands on stuff. Lucas' classes focus on Business Management and Sorcery and Magic. Only witches can do sorcery and magic," Oliver explained.

"He must be really good at it, especially if the bracelets work," I said as I eyed the silver charm bracelet.

"They do work, and he is really good, he comes from a long line of strong magic-wielders," Oliver said.

"You're lucky you ended up living here with him, somewhere else might've been harder, especially with your shifts." I glanced at him, wondering if he might let me in a bit more and tell me more about this curse of his. He just frowned down at his hands for a moment.

"I've known Lucas since primary school, although not in

the same grades. Our families both live here in Maple Grove, and they're quite close, hence why we became good friends. Even Skip and Marcus went to primary school with us, and we became friends in roughly grade four," Oliver said. "I was only in grade one, but they didn't mind."

"Marcus lived here before he got turned? What was he before he became a vampire?" I asked, curiosity winning out. Only supes lived here in Maple Grove, which meant there was more to Marcus than I knew.

"He was a witch," Oliver said, but I could see his uneasiness surfacing at the subject. No one had told me anything about how Marcus had been turned—it made me worry. What were they all hiding?

"Skip left the high school after grade eight to go work on his parents' farm. He was living with his grandmother here while he attended the supe schools. Maple Grove has a primary school, a high school, and a University," Oliver explained, dodging the topic of Marcus. I'd have to touch back on that later, I had a few questions I wanted to ask about it, but I could sense Oliver didn't want to talk about our vampire housemate.

"How'd Skip get into uni then?" I asked, but I guessed the answer. The same way as me, considering I'd ditched school before completion to work, and yet here I was.

"He applied for a pathways program, where they test you to give you a ranking. He got in," Oliver said as he fiddled with the arm of his jacket.

Same as me. I'd had to apply for the pathways program too, and try to do it all online or over the phone. That had been a struggle, but they'd made the exception for me.

Now here I was.

"Do you know what Skip's goal is with his studies?"

"I think he wants to become a conservationist or something along those lines. Find solutions to environmental problems, protect the wildlife and ecosystems," he said with a shrug. "That's about all I know."

So there was more to Skip than I thought as well. That laid-back, easygoing nature hid an interesting man.

"Is his grandmother still here?" I asked.

"Nah, she died three years ago. Thankfully, Lucas was in need of housemates, so Skip got in early. Marcus was next, he's in his second year of study too. I moved in way before the other two. Lucas inherited the place when he was just sixteen. I moved in with him at his request, he didn't want to be alone in this big 'ole house." He chuckled.

"So you would've been, what, fourteen?" I did the quick maths.

"Yeah, I finished high school while living here with him. He started uni almost immediately out of school."

"Your parents didn't mind you moving in?" I frowned. He'd not mentioned his family at all.

"Nah," he murmured, shifting uneasily. I recognized those walls slamming up. I'd done it so many times myself.

There was more to this sweet little shifter than I thought. Something he was hiding. Something about his family.

"Hey, you two hungry?"

I snapped my head round to spy Marcus slouched against the doorframe like a heavenly God. Lucifer reincarnated with his divine godly looks.

Yep, that was his personality. I mentally slapped myself. What the hell was up with me? I'd only known these guys for a day and I was already swooning over all of them. Even the arseholey vampire.

"Not if it's what you're sharing," Ollie retorted.

Marcus just rolled his eyes and smirked.

"Red's making burgers, figured you and VB would want some for a late lunch," he said as he crossed his arms.

"What's the time?" I asked. How long had I slept for? When I'd last looked at my iPod before falling asleep, it was a little after eleven in the morning.

"Two," was the blunt reply.

"You know, I'm not a beer, VB isn't my name," I growled.

"No, but you are vampire bait, little pixie halfling." Marcus smirked, those icy eyes trailing over me and making me warm up. Too bad he was a prick. I just scowled at him in return.

"Well, if you want them, you better head down now and let him know," Marcus said lazily, as if it had been such a pain for him to relay the message.

He pushed off the doorframe, disappearing silently down the hall. I heard his bedroom door open and close, the only sound of his movements.

"I could go for burgers," Oliver said as he stood and offered me his hand. "What about you?"

"Sounds good, I'm starving."

Turned out that Skip was a pretty good cook. Oliver informed me that he and Lucas were the main cooks of the house, with Skip specializing in meats.

"He works as a chippy while he studies, bet you didn't know that!" Oliver declared as he rested his elbows on the table as we dug in to our burgers.

Skip was sitting with us, finally wearing some form of clothing, although the singlet left little to the imagination considering how tight it was and how much it dipped under his arms.

"Huh, that I did not know." I nodded as I bit into the mouth-watering burger.

"Homemade rissoles, I make them every fortnight," Skip said proudly. "I freeze some of them to use throughout the week."

"They're amazing," I said through a mouthful of burger. Mine had the standard salad filling, the rissole, and I'd gone with barbecue sauce, while Skip and Ollie had chosen tomato sauce.

"You should do a roast tonight, she'd love that," Ollie said, flicking his head my way as he spoke to Skip.

"I think Lucas wants to do pizza since Richo and Issac are coming over. What kind of pizza do you like?" he focused back on me as he took a hefty bite from his burger and downed it with some coke. How he was still ripped despite his love of coke was beyond me.

"Pepperoni, but don't worry about me, I can make myself something for dinner." I shook my head.

"Nah, it's on us, consider it our official welcome dinner." Skip grinned, the dimples in his cheeks making my stomach flip.

"I can put some money in at least," I offered, but Skip shot it down.

"We like to head into Maleny for our pizzas, there's this fucking awesome wood-fired pizza place," Skip emphasized with his hands as he leaned back in his chair at the table.

"Hey, language, there's a lady present," Oliver scolded him.

"I've heard it all before." I chuckled.

"Yeah, shithead, she's used to it. Living with us, you'll get used to the swearing. Hate to say it, but we're a little bogan." Skip winked as he clasped his hands behind his head.

The small move only made his biceps flex, making me nearly bite my lip at the sight.

"What he's trying to say, is that *he's* bogan," Oliver rectified.

"Whatever," Skip grumbled as he closed his eyes, having polished off his burger and almost all his glass of coke.

I sipped my orange juice, watching Oliver mirror me unknowingly with his own glass of juice.

"So, you play pool?" Skip asked, not bothering to open his eyes as he cleared his throat.

"Here and there, I guess," I said.

My aunt's second boyfriend had a pool table in his house, which we'd all moved into not too long after they got together. It was only five minutes from our old place, but a bit of an upgrade.

I'd played pool with him a few times, but I pushed those memories down. I didn't want to remember my aunt, or him. Especially him.

"Lucas and his two mates tend to put money down, so if you're good, you should try your hand at it," Skip suggested.

"They're all witches though, so I'd butt out," Oliver warned me.

"What's that got to do with anything?" I frowned.

"Tricksters, Lucas and his mates are big tricksters. Using magic to warp the game, although if you were to play, they'd use no magic," Skip said as he finally opened his sweet blue eyes and gave Oliver a look.

"I'd be more inclined to watch, I'm quite curious now." I chuckled. Tricksters. I'd enjoyed seeing Lucas' magic in action, and I was quite intrigued by it.

"I'm sure you can do that," Oliver said as he demolished the last bite of his burger.

As if he'd heard us talking about him, Lucas appeared in the doorway.

"Where's mine?" he pouted as he stared at the measly crumbs left on our plates.

"I asked, you said you didn't want one," Skip groaned.

"I'm just kidding." Lucas grinned and waved him off. The movement made me do a double take. The way he said it, I was starting to suspect maybe he was batting for the other team.

"Huh," I murmured, wondering if my suspicions were correct.

"What?" Oliver glanced at me.

"Nothing." I shrugged. I wouldn't say anything, I wouldn't jump to conclusions. But Lucas and Skip had seemed close while we were watching Game of Thrones, and there was definitely a different vibe in the air between them than with the other guys.

And yet, Skip seemed very… straight. Well, I was being very stereotypical there. Lucas had seemed straight until this moment, and I'd been a little curious with how he laid with Skip on the lounge.

I might ask Ollie later. Although, to be honest, it wasn't any of my business. No, I wouldn't ask. They were my housemates, their sexual orientation wasn't something I needed to worry about. Although, it was a bit of a bummer. I had liked them. And God knows I'd been single long enough.

Ah, Ally. I mentally sighed. These were my housemates, getting into anything with any one of them was a bad idea. We could only be friends. *With benefits,* my mind whispered.

Lucas pulled out of the fridge with a platter of fresh fruit. I had not seen that there earlier.

"Using magic to conjure up food is unfair." Oliver pouted, eyeing the array of fresh fruits. Kiwi fruit, mango, strawberries, pineapple, passionfruit, melon. Damn, it did look delicious.

"I have the fruits there first, I don't just conjure them from thin air. Most of it is kept in the bottom drawer, you're all welcome to the fruit, some of it's grown right outside, we've got fruit trees, so go pick it yourself." Lucas carefully walked past holding his plate out of reach as Oliver looked longingly at it.

"What kind of fruit trees?" I asked.

"Mandarin, grapefruit, lime, lemon, mango," Skip listed them off.

"Help yourself to them, Cupcake." Lucas grinned before striding out of the dining area and into the living room.

"Why are you all giving me nicknames?" I gaped. "At least Ollie just uses Ally, is that so hard?"

"Nah, Bee Sting, it's so much more fun to give you a name that suits. We all have different names for each other, it's just tradition," Skip chuckled.

"You've only called Lucas, Luke, and Oliver, Ollie," I said blatantly.

"Sometimes I call Ollie, Cat, and Luke has other names, while Marcus can be Arses, it passes." He grinned and then slapped his thigh. "Hah, that rhymed."

I just rolled my eyes, but I did crack a grin as Ollie chuckled.

"So, what's your plans for the afternoon?" Skip asked as he downed the last of his coke.

"I'm not sure, with this rain, I'm not too keen on heading out into town, since I would've liked to see my new place of work, Dingo Diner," I said as I pondered it. "I did tell them I'd try to pop in before I started uni to pick up an apron and to speak with them about when I can work. Definitely weekends, but they're flexible with my other days, whether it be just short afternoon or morning shifts around uni."

"You know, Maleny used to have a Dingo Diner, wonder if there's any relation," Oliver mused as he gathered up the plates for us and loaded them into the dishwasher.

I cringed at how he didn't rinse them first, something I'd always done.

"That sucks that you'll be working weekends, we won't be able to do any fun stuff." Skip sighed.

"I didn't realize that you wanted to," I raised an eyebrow at him.

"You're living with us, we need to be friends. Which means doing stuff. Sometimes I take that old girl out there for some four-wheel-driving out in the forestry down at Beerwah and Glasshouse, or find some other tracks." Skip grinned. "Would've been fun to have you tag along."

"I've never been four-wheel-driving before," I said, interested in the idea.

"I'll take you sometime, it'll be fun!" Skip lit up at the prospect.

"Usually he gets one of his mates to come along, as you aren't meant to go alone, but if Lucas tags along, then it's fine. He can magic us out of any situation." Oliver gave me his trademark boyish grin.

It made my chest squeeze when he did it. He was so freaking cute, in an attractive way.

Ugh.

"Do you play PlayStation?" Skip asked excitedly.

"No, sorry." I gave him a sheepish smile. "I used to play a bit with my cousin as kids on the old PlayStation 2, but I haven't played in a long time."

"Oh man, you are soooo missing out." Skip laughed.

"We're taking turns playing through Metal Gear Solid 5:

Phantom Pain. It's epic!" Oliver said as he bounced on his toes by the counter.

"Come watch, you can even have a go if you want," Skip offered.

Well, I didn't really have any afternoon plans anyway, and spending it sitting around with these two sounded good.

"Isn't Lucas in there?" I asked as Skip leaped up and led the way.

"Nah, he'll be in the library studying or outside practicing his magic," Skip said.

If he was practicing magic, I'd definitely be up for watching that. What exactly could a witch do? I'd seen him make things do as he wished, and he didn't need a wand like in Harry Potter.

"I think she'd rather see what magic Lucas is up to if he's practicing," Oliver noted when he saw my face with a look of intrigue. He gave me a tender smile, and I bit my lip. Damn, he was cute. Shorter than the other guys, with Lucas and Marcus being almost the same, and Skip the tallest. "Well, we can go watch him for a bit before we play PlayStation? We've got all afternoon free," Skip said, those bright blue eyes falling back on me after he looked over his shoulder.

"I think that'd be awesome." I grinned. I really did want to see more magic, I'd never known much about it, hell, I knew very little about the supe community than what I would've liked. My aunt and her need to send me to mainstream school and dampen all my magic with that pendant had shut me off from the world I was meant to be a part of.

I knew so little, I just hoped that the university would open it up for me.

"You said your aunt had a pendant made so you couldn't use your own mischief magic. Did that mean you also didn't know much in general about supes? I remember you saying something like that with vampires bursting into flames." Oliver cocked his head as we all now stood just before the doorway into the kitchen.

It was like he'd read my mind. "Well, I knew about faes, as my aunt was my mother's sister, so she was a fae. Half sister. My mother's father was a pixie apparently, hence my mischief magic. And vampires, since my cousin dated an older vampire when she was fifteen. He was nineteen, like Marcus, although I think he was technically older than that, but he only ever told us his turning age. She's a year younger than me. I left pretty soon after he moved in as well," I shared.

"So you never knew about witches? Shifters? Other supes?" Skip now turned fully around, frowning as he searched my face for answers.

"No, not really. I knew a bit about shifters, too, since I knew one. As for the others, I heard them mentioned here and there, but I didn't go to supe school, had no supe friends, and I wasn't allowed to talk about them. I could google at the library though, but I doubt what's out there on the internet is actually true. The vampire stuff wasn't, and it's all so conflicting." I sighed, my shoulders slumping. I'd accepted I may never know much about the world I was a mere shadow of. How I'd desperately wanted to know about it, but my Aunt forbade me from asking too much.

"Damn, that's so sad. Why was your Aunt such an arse to you? What a bitch, keeping you from the truth like that," Skip growled. "You're a supe, you need to know these things."

"Hey, that's her Aunt you're talking about," Oliver chided him.

"No, he's right, Ollie. My Aunt wasn't a nice woman, and I have no good feelings for her. She didn't like me because I was simply my mother's daughter, and they never got along.

My mother was apparently the spoiled child, the better woman, blah blah blah. The only reason she took me in was because of the money she'd get in it," I explained as I waved off Ollie's sad look. I didn't want them feeling sorry for me.

"Well, you're better off here, far away from that cunt," Skip spat.

"Skip!" Ollie threw his arms up.

"Swearing is fine, I attended a public school and worked in retail and as a barista. You hear it everywhere, it's part of the Aussie language now." I chuckled as I patted Ollie's arm, grateful he was trying to protect me from such language. He was many years too late though.

"We should teach you. How about you ask us anything you want while we go see if Lucas is practicing magic?" Skip suggested.

"I'd love that!" I grinned. Finally, some answers to all the questions I'd stored in my head for when I started here at uni. I'd doubted I could just ask them in my magic classes, but at least now I had friends to ask.

"He's so lucky, being able to shield himself from the weather," I remarked as we sat out on the verandah. The rain hammered down on the roof, but there was nothing out before us where Lucas stood, shielded by an invisible bubble.

He was conjuring fire and water on the spot, hurling them and honing his attacks.

It made me wonder why he needed to know this. Was he expecting an attack? Or was it customary? God, what I wouldn't give to just know the basics of supes.

"Yeah, bloody warlocks," Skip muttered as he slouched into the cushioned wicker chair.

"Wait, I thought he was a witch?" I frowned.

"A warlock is the highest type of witch, we just say witch to most people as warlocks are quite rare, and some are still scared of them," Oliver explained as he sat beside me on the wicker lounge. He was bouncing his leg as he watched Lucas wield his elemental powers, his amber eyes watching the magic intently.

"What's so different between them?" I said as I watched Lucas create a mini tornado. Damn, that was some epic power to have. I could only imagine just what he was capable of.

He flung it forward, the small tornado tearing up the lawn as he focused on it, flicking his hands to make it change direction.

"When it comes to elements like what he's doing now, witches can only harness one, whatever their affinity is, and they need the element available in order to use it. Say you have a fire witch, they need an open flame in order to wield it. They can't just conjure it up like a warlock," Skip said.

"Although, there are elementals too, usually of another supe species. Having supernatural blood can sometimes contain a gene for the elemental ability. So during the magic classes at uni, you'll be tested to see if you have an elemental ability. It's like a witch, you have to have the element there, like water in a bottle or an open flame, but you can be of any species," Oliver elaborated.

"So what's the difference between a witch and an elemental?" I shook my head. God, how I wanted to jot all this stuff down.

"Witches have other abilities, depending on their bloodlines and specialties. Some are psychics, others can create potions infused with magic, others can wield their magic. Some can do all of the above. There's more to it, whereas an elemental can only wield one element and then they have the abilities of whatever species they are," Oliver explained.

"Okay." I chewed my lip. So much information, but I think I was getting it.

"Can witches do the thing where Lucas makes stuff do what he wants? Like the teaspoons?" I asked, picturing the sight of when he was making the hot milos.

"Some witches, the stronger ones. But all warlocks can," Skip said.

"What else can warlocks do?" I asked. Was there a limit to their power?

"Almost anything, depends on the warlock, and what they train themselves to do. There've even been some who can control the very weather," Oliver said, clasping his hands together. "There've been warlocks in history that have caused earthquakes or floods."

"Damn, they must be considered dangerous by some people then." I frowned. Lucas was now making the grass around him twist and grow, reaching up as the small tendrils quivered and snaked around him. It was utterly amazing to watch all of this magic in action. He really knew what he was doing.

"Yeah, that's why they're all tracked and watched," Skip said, his brow furrowing.

"Wait, what? Is that legal?" I scowled. Lucas was being tracked? How did they do that? And they watched him. "So what, they keep an eye on him, twenty-four seven?"

"As a child, once it's discovered that they're a warlock, a High Council member, a warlock from the Supernatural Council, comes out and marks them with a tracking spell. It's a safety precaution. They check in here and there, home visits, but you know they're always watching, like in some crystal ball or some shit," Skip grunted disapprovingly at the idea.

"How's that not a violation of privacy?" I murmured. Poor Lucas. He was being watched simply for what he was. How was that right? He didn't get to choose what he was. I mean, I wouldn't choose otherwise considering those wicked abilities, but still. It must be tough always knowing you're being scrutinized.

I watched him sadly as small dandelions began sprouting all around Lucas as his hands glowed a soft green. He looked so content, his eyes closed as he focused on his power. Still in his suit, of course.

"It is, but they don't care. Warlocks are considered a danger to all. Remember Hitler?" Skip turned to me, and I snorted.

"Who doesn't know about that psycho?"

"Well, supposedly, a family member of his was a warlock. As a child, Hitler succumbed to a fever and died, but was brought back by this warlock. You can see what followed. Nothing good comes from black magic like that, and warlocks are the only ones capable of bringing back the dead," Skip explained.

"Damn," I breathed. Imagine how humans would react if they found that out? That Hitler was a zombie type thing. They'd lose their shit.

"You know, mischief magic can be wielded properly and used," Oliver piped up.

"What can it do?" I asked, still thinking about this whole thing with warlocks being tracked and watched. I felt sorry for Lucas. What kind of life was that? Knowing you were always looking over your shoulder and making sure you never broke any of the rules. What were the rules anyway? What would make them class him as a danger?

"Well, you can actually use it whenever rather than just with emotions. It seems your natural affinity is for food, so your magic targets food when your emotions trigger it. But you can animate other things, objects and such. Mischief magic is a unique magic, and has many strange uses," Skip said as he thought about it, tapping his chin with his forefinger.

"My sister's boyfriend had an affinity for electrical stuff, but if he focused, he could use it on anything."

"Of course it's food for me," I snorted as Oliver chuckled.

"I will admit, it's pretty entertaining when your magic goes haywire. At least there's an easy fix!" Oliver laughed, and I remembered him watching me jumping around the living room eating the flying pasta.

"Lucas can get it under control too if it plays up," Skip assured me. "But I'm sure we can all manage."

"So, what can I learn to do with it? How can I wield mischief magic?" I asked, curiosity winning out. Could I actually do more with my magic?

"Well, um, people can use it to animate objects, so if you're getting attacked, you can animate something nearby to defend you. Or you can even mess with people's clothing and such. I'm sure there's more, but I don't know many pixies." Skip shrugged as he rubbed his arms, a cool breeze sweeping in from the far end of the verandah.

I shivered as the rain grew heavy, and Lucas looked to the sky coldly.

"Can Lucas control the weather?" I murmured, watching as Lucas started heading back our way.

"Nah, and even if he could, it would be forbidden," Skip shook his head.

"Having fun watching?" Lucas grinned as he jumped up the steps onto the verandah and smiled down at me. I couldn't help but return the grin, and nodded when I remembered he'd said something. Those forest green eyes were bright and alert, and he held my gaze for a few moments longer than I thought was normal before he turned to Skip.

"Bee Sting here knows very little about supes, her Aunt kept her from supe schools and learning about them," Skip said with a frown.

"Huh, that's absurd, why would she do that?" Lucas pursed his lips as he gave me a concerned look.

"Cause she didn't get along with her mother, so Ally caught the brunt of their sibling rivalry," Oliver jumped in.

"Still, that's not a good enough reason to deny someone the chance to learn about what they are, their abilities and other races," Lucas grumbled as he crossed his arms.

"Yeah, well, never too late to learn," I said, wanting to move away from the subject. I didn't want them asking any questions.

"That's true. I've got some history books in the library, proper books on the different species," Lucas informed me.

"Oh, that'd be wonderful! I guess it slipped the minds of these two." I raised an accusing eyebrow at Skip and Oliver. Ollie just gave me a sheepish grin while Skip shrugged dismissively.

"That's because they'd rather play PlayStation than read," Lucas said distastefully.

"We'll read when uni starts, why bore ourselves before then?" Skip groaned.

"Because, knowledge is power," Lucas stated.

"Whatever." Skip waved him off as he stood up. "We were going to get Bee Sting to watch us play some Metal Gear Solid, we've only got another day before we have to knuckle down, might as well enjoy it."

"Exactly my point," Lucas scoffed and shook his head

with a smile. "Feel free to check out the library whenever and explore the house properly. I'd assumed Marcus gave you a tour, but…" he cocked his head, noting my thin-lipped smile. "I guess he didn't."

"Nope, too much hassle." I shrugged as I stood up.

"I'll show you while Skip gets the PlayStation set up," Oliver jumped at the opportunity as he stood up and slung a warm arm around my shoulders.

"Good, Richo and Issac will be by in a few hours, we'll be ordering pizzas, so make sure Cupcake here chooses her pizza from the menu. They've got some delicious selections." Lucas grinned as he unfolded his arms. He watched Skip head inside with an odd look, possibly affection? I didn't dwell on it.

"C'mon, I'll show you the library," Ollie said, his warm breath brushing my ear as he turned his head to be heard over the rain.

I couldn't help but notice the sly smile Lucas gave me as Ollie dragged me into the house.

6

OLIVER

Ally was gorgeous. Too bad when I'd first met her I was stuck in cat form. I may have taken advantage of that, but I wasn't going to admit to it. And the scolding I'd gotten was well worth the chance to see her partially undressed. She had nice boobs, that was something I'd learned quickly.

And burns. They littered her sides and back, some looked to be cigarette burns. The other scars, it was hard to tell. Almost like someone had held a lighter against her skin.

That was something else I'd noticed. But I kept my mouth zipped about that. I got the feeling she didn't want to talk about them.

She was lively, and I enjoyed talking to her once I'd shifted back, after our awkward moment when she saw me naked. I was a little embarrassed that she'd seen me on full display, not to mention I had morning wood.

I couldn't help it, and to be honest, I was getting worried that I wouldn't shift back until after uni started. I was glad that wasn't the case.

Now, I was showing Ally around the house fully, showing her the games room with the pool table, dartboard, and a second TV and lounge set up. As you walked in, there was a small bar to the right along the wall, then the pool table was set up with the lounges on the far side set up around a coffee table with a flat-screen TV on the wall opposite the doorway. It was the designated drinking and football night area, we never brought the PlayStation out here.

Then we were onto the library, which Ally awed at. I guess she liked reading, something Skip hated. I quite enjoyed it, but I tried to read in private as Skip would sometimes poke fun at me. I'd been a bit insulted when Lucas had said I didn't read, he knew I did. Guess it was words in the moment, even though I'd read a lot when we were younger, and he knew that. I had cut back, more-so because I was having more troubles with my shifting than before.

Ally walked around the library room, the ceiling-high bookcases jammed with assorted tomes. All sorts of spell-books Lucas had inherited, history books, and normal fiction books. It'd had most of these already when we'd moved in a few years ago. Lucas' grandfather loved reading and learning, too bad he'd not used potions and magic to prolong his life. He came from Lucas' mother's side, a standard witch lineage, so he didn't have the same abilities as Lucas, which stemmed from his father's side. He'd still invested in a heap of Sorcery books, as if he knew Lucas would be living here eventually.

I'd liked the old man, I'd spent many nights having sleepovers here with Lucas. Usually when Lucas ran away from home to avoid his snobbish, uptight parents.

"This room is gorgeous," Ally murmured as she twirled around the room, taking in the plush red lounges and armchairs set up in the corner. There even a tidy, old wooden desk in the center of the room where I'd studied on occasion.

"Yeah, Lucas spends a lot of time in here, studying magic.

He wants to start up a big magical shop one day." I grinned.

"So that's why he's studying business then," Ally murmured as she ran her hand over the world globe sitting on the desk. "There's no dust in here," she remarked as she rubbed her fingers together and inspected them.

"Lucas uses magic to keep the place tidy all the time. Skip can get messy," I said as I flopped down onto one of the red armchairs to watch her take in the beauty of the library room.

"I'm sure it's only Skip," she snorted softly, still gazing around the room.

I loved how mesmerized she was by it, and I was so glad I'd been the one to show it to her.

I liked her. She was funny, and we all clicked so well together. Well, except for Marcus, but he was always the odd one out since he got turned.

Who could blame him after what happened? I'd want to keep everyone at arm's length, too.

"So, what do you do in your free time?" Ally asked as she moved around the room, inspecting the various books on the shelves. I watched quietly as she pulled one out after the other, flipping through them, her eyes bright and excited as she began setting some out on the desk. Mostly history ones.

"I read a bit," I said, unable to take my eyes off her. I did have a hobby, but I didn't want to share it. She might laugh at it.

"That's all?" Ally mused as she selected out an old red leather-bound book to add to her reading stack.

"I play PlayStation with Skip, I used to play it with Lucas, but he's turned into a party guy now," I scoffed. We'd been so close for so long, but he'd changed a lot lately, and I kept to myself more. I hoped that with uni starting back up that things would return back to the way they were.

Maybe Ally could help bring everyone back together more, she'd managed it already. Skip was fascinated with her, I could tell by the way he watched her. So was I, she was beautiful, doe-eyed and sweet, but with a bit of fire underneath.

The thought made my face flush, and I was glad she was too busy looking at the books.

"So Lucas is a partier, is that where he was last night?" Ally mused as she skimmed through the red book.

"Yeah, last Friday night thing with his group of friends from uni. Tonight he's catching up with some of his friends from our high school days. I don't know them too well, I was a few years down in the grades, so I mostly hung out with him outside of school thanks to our families," I said, but then I bit my lip as I played with the hem of my jacket.

I hoped she wouldn't ask about my family again. I really didn't want to talk about them.

"Skip was at a party too, right?" she continued, breezing past my mention of my family. I knew she'd caught it though, because she'd flicked those chocolate eyes my way before focusing back on her book.

She perched on the desk as she became fascinated with it, and I leaned forward to try to read the cover.

Supernatural Encyclopedia by the looks, one of a few. She'd have her reading cut out for her if she was intent on reading all about the different kinds of supernatural creatures and everything about them.

"He was out drinking. I was meant to go but then I got stuck as a cat, so I got left at home," I grumbled. It hadn't been planned. I hated this curse so much. "You might notice he likes to drink. He comes from a rather bogan family out at Gympie. They've got a cattle farm out there."

"Right." Allison nodded, but I could tell her mind was elsewhere as she turned the pages of the encyclopedia.

"Whatcha reading?" I asked as I rested my chin on my hand to stare at her.

She was bent over the book as she sat on the edge of the desk, her short dress riding up to show her thighs. Damn, those long legs were perfect. So smooth and flawless, not a freckle in sight.

Her brown locks were falling free from her ponytail, a few strands framing her face as she frowned at the book.

"Pixies. Just wanting to know more about what I am, I guess," she murmured, entranced as her eyes flicked over the pages.

"Learning anything?" I asked, unable to keep my eyes from gliding over her, soaking her up in this moment of beauty, caught in a state of utter concentration, her lips parted ever so slightly. I wondered how soft they were? What would they feel like to kiss?

"We like sweets, I knew that, we have mischief magic, I also knew that, but nothing about my ability to sense when things are wrong with animals. But apparently I can—" she stopped immediately, her cheeks blushing crazily as she did everything not to look at me.

Okay, now I was curious as hell.

"You can what?" I pushed, standing up as I cocked my head at her.

"Nothing," she mumbled, unable to look me in the eyes.

"Let me see it?" I stuck out my hand, but she pulled the book close to her chest as she shook her head timidly.

"Really? You're going to play this game?" I chuckled.

Now I had to know. I darted forward, snatching at the book, but she turned her body away, her legs not moving fast enough as I stumbled into the table.

"No." She giggled as I tried to grab the book, her legs pinned by my thighs as I reached over her.

"I will find out." I grinned, reaching for the book as she held it over her head to avoid me. She was leaning back in her attempt to keep it away from me, and I leaned over her, stretching to get it.

My breath caught as her body pressed against mine, and I froze, realizing I'd pinned her to the desk.

Those chocolate eyes were just as surprised as mine, our faces inches apart as I still had my hands out, although I'd momentarily lost interest in the book.

Damn, those eyes were so beautiful, up close, you could see the small golden flecks in them, a reminder that she had a bit of wolf in her. I'd never met a werewolf before, they were uncommon here in Australia.

Her lips looked soft, and she was drawing in sharp, shallow breaths as her eyes flicked between mine.

I wondered what those lips would taste like? If she'd taste as good as she smelt, like honey and flowers.

Her body was pushed up against mine, and I knew mine was starting to react to her warmth, her curves melding nicely against my own. So soft and petite, but those boobs were pressed against my chest, and they were a perfect size for her. They'd fit perfectly in the cup of my hand.

"Wow, don't let me intrude."

I snapped back like someone had hit me with a bucket of water, scowling at Skip who stood in the doorway with a grin ear to ear.

"She's hiding some pixie ability, she read it in the book!" I defended myself, already feeling the heat rushing to my cheeks.

And not just there, I could feel something else had come

alive, and I angled my body away from Skip and Ally to avoid further embarrassment.

"What was it?" Skip asked, glancing between us curiously.

"Nothing," Ally shot back quickly as she sat up and straightened her dress. It had ridden up even more in our little moment, and I'd caught the sight of her black panties.

"Obviously it's something if you two were going at it like that." Skip laughed, and I flicked my eyes apologetically to Ally, who just groaned and clutched the book to her chest.

"It's nothing you two need to know," she muttered as she slid off the desk.

"Technically, that belongs to Lucas, so we have just as much right as you to read it," Skip retorted with a gleeful grin as he strode over.

I glanced down at my denim shorts, grateful that my body was calming down. Still, it wasn't going away fast enough.

Damn, she'd smelled so good, too.

"C'mon, it can't be that bad," Skip smirked as he held out his hand. "Don't make me take it, I'll be much more capable than the kitten," Skip snickered.

Ally's shoulders slumped in defeat as she thrust the book at him before crossing her arms and pouting like a little child.

"What page?" Skip asked as he opened up the book.

"I'm not saying," Ally muttered as she turned away.

Skip sighed as he flicked through the book, before clicking his tongue when he finally found the section.

"Some stuff here about wielding mischief magic to create distractions or even offensively, the ability to animate almost anything, huh, I didn't realize you could animate anything. Does that include buildings?" Skip mused. "Why's that so bad, I don't see why— oh." His face lit up as he grinned at me.

"Damn, you nearly got yourself into a pickle there, Ollie," he sniggered.

"What, why?" I frowned, snatching the book off him.

I chewed my lip as I read the paragraph, and then read it again to make sure I'd gotten it right.

"Is it true?" I practically whispered, and Ally just scowled at me.

"Is it?" Skip asked with a smile as he spun the globe on the desk.

"Yes," she mumbled as she looked away, her arms crossed over her chest protectively.

Holy hell.

I had not known such a thing.

"You used to be a playboy, you should've known this, surely you've been with a pixie," I muttered at Skip, who burst into laughter. I felt more embarrassed for Ally. I felt bad for pushing now, it was a personal thing to discover.

"Look, it's not that big of a deal," Ally groaned as Skip pulled himself up to sit on the desk.

"Your orgasms are sparkly and taste like honey," I said, miraculously keeping my face straight. Now that was certainly news to me.

"And if it gets on something, it infects it with mischief magic," Skip snorted as he slapped his thighs. "That is pure fucking gold right there!" He laughed.

"I'm going to my room," Ally declared as she spun away from us.

"Aw, c'mon Bee Sting, we're only messing with ya, how about we tell you some of our weird sex things?" Skip called out just as she reached the doorway. She froze, turning back slowly with a bewildered look.

"Do I want to know?" she asked with an arched eyebrow.

"Different supes have different... specialties," Skip said carefully.

Ally glanced at me for confirmation, and I sighed and nodded, still coming to terms with this new revelation about her.

I was still pondering about the whole infected with mischief magic. Could it affect a penis? What happened when she cleaned herself down there afterwards?

God, I wanted so badly to ask, but I was afraid I'd only embarrass her more and end up forcing her into her room to avoid us.

"All right, tell me." Ally stuck up her nose as she marched over to plant herself before us. She was adorable in her little blue dress, pretending she was annoyed at us but really she was intrigued by what our weird sex stories were.

"Well, fun fact, the whole down under thing came from kangaroos, because their dick is under their testicles," Skip started with.

I couldn't contain the laughter that bubbled up my throat. What an opening.

Ally looked horrified as her eyes dropped to his nether region in shock.

"I said kangaroos, not kangaroo shifters," Skip waved his hand in front of his crotch to draw her attention away.

"Well, that's not a weird sex thing then, just a weird fact." Ally puffed up in defense, her cheeks reddening as she cracked a smile.

"But, due to female kangaroos having not one but three vaginas, their shifter counterparts have maintained the unique ability to have an embryo in reserve while they're carrying one baby to term. So right after birthing, they can have another baby growing immediately," Skip stated.

"What?" Ally just gave him a dumbfounded look.

"It's called embryonic diapause, and it also means that no kangaroo shifter can have twins, they only birth one child at a time." Skip looked mighty pleased with himself as he crossed his arms and leaned back.

"Okay," Ally muttered, shaking her head as she processed this.

"Kangaroos also have two pronged dicks," he added. "Which does carry over to the shifter side to extent. When aroused, a small second head forms and it rubs the g-spot, it's why the ladies love us." Skip shrugged as Ally's mouth dropped open.

I just rolled my eyes, it was not the first time I'd heard this.

Wait for it, there was more.

"Male kangaroos also grow substantially larger than their female counterparts, especially the red kangaroos, which is my shifter form, and that carries over in... other ways." He winked, and Ally practically choked as her face turned beet red.

Yep, I'd seen that one coming a mile away, Skip always loved to brag.

"Don't worry, wait until you hear Ollie's secret weapon, you'll be wishing you never opened that book." Skip chuckled.

Ally turned to me, a hesitant look on her face.

"Depending on what my most recent shift was, I take on the characteristics of that shifter," I said with a defeated sigh, glaring at Skip.

"And due to being a true shifter, he can legit grow his dick," Skip tossed out there.

Ally just looked between us like she was caught naked in front of the whole school. Poor thing, she looked so freaked out and lost. It was adorable.

"Since he turns into a cat only for now, his dick has barbs." Skip cocked his head.

"All right, I'm done, I can't deal with this." Ally threw her hands up in defeat as she squeezed her eyes shut.

"It's okay, Lucas and Marcus have normal penises." Skip grinned.

"And you know that how?" Ally shook her head in disbelief. "Wait, I don't want to know."

She sighed, her shoulders slumping as she collected up a few books.

"Aw, don't go honey-buns, I thought you were going to watch us play the PlayStation?" Skip pouted, and I rolled my eyes at him. Of course he threw in honey-buns.

"Maybe later," Ally shot him a displeased look with the new nickname as she hurried out of the library.

"Sparkly orgasms, I'll never get over that one," Skip snickered.

"Do you think the mischief magic does anything to the penis?" I asked in a hushed tone.

"Dunno, guess you might find out if you keep up that little act." Skip smiled as he slid off the table.

"What? No, I would never," I growled.

"She's pretty hot." He shrugged. "If you won't, I might."

"Don't, she's not just another one for you to mess around with," I warned.

"Well, that's up to her, but I'll hold off, there's no rush, besides, I wouldn't want to scare off our new house mate too soon," he said. "Makes you wonder though, when she cleans up down there, what happens? Does the mischief magic affect everything it touches?" he said as he rubbed the back of his head.

"I have no idea," I said honestly.

But man, was I damn curious.

7

I groaned as I sunk onto the end of my bed with my stack of books.

I'd learned so much... more... about my two companions in the last twenty minutes than I was comfortable knowing so soon. To be honest, they knew something about me, too.

I had known about my mischief magic down there, that was the whole reason I made sure to wear my pendant nearly all the time when with a partner. If things got heated, the pendant went back on.

Let's just say a flying, honking, pink vibrator is not something you want to have to deal with, especially when it's covered in sparkly fluids.

I'd had to beat it to death with a book. Thankfully, it had been my first ever toy, and cheap. My next one was a little more, so the pendant stayed on, and we had no more freaky occurrences when I finished.

I was just lucky my housemate hadn't been home. Doubt I could've explained that one. Although, I was in a warded area at the time, so it would've been warped in her eyes. I did sometimes wonder what she would've seen instead.

I made sure to be careful with my next one, although it had died a few months back now. Guess I may have been using it a little too much between tinder dates.

I glanced down at my tattered black handbag that I'd discarded beside the bed. I reached down, rummaging through it until my fingers curled on the chain. I pulled out the small green agate stone pendant, pursing my lips at the heart-shaped piece.

I could feel the magic in it. Even after running away and getting a witch to break the spell on the clasp, I'd worn it always while out and about, almost constantly, as I didn't trust my own magic. But being able to remove it meant I'd learned a little about it in my own spare time.

And this honey tasting orgasms? Well, let's just say my two partners hadn't been too keen on giving me that finish. I'd used a toy mostly, too bad they kept dying on me.

I wasn't even sure my orgasms would taste like honey anyway with my pendant on, considering they weren't sparkly when I wore it.

I ran my thumb over my pendant. I'd decided to take it off now that I was in warded area, and I knew that my magic classes at uni would need me to be at my full ability. I didn't want to live in fear anymore, but maybe I was being too quick to think I could do this. I'd already had two episodes of issues with my mischief magic.

"Hey."

I looked up to spy Ollie standing at my door awkwardly.

"Sorry for getting you mixed up in that," he said with a lopsided smile as he fumbled with his jacket zipper.

"Not your fault, I kinda walked into it," I admitted as I stuffed my pendant back into my purse.

"Skip likes to brag about... well, you know," Ollie said, his amber eyes frustrated with his housemate.

"It's fine, I just, well, I got more information than I bargained for." I gave a short, sharp laugh.

"Yeah, that you did." Ollie nodded, running a hand through his mess of brown hair.

"What causes your shifts, anyway?" I tried to move the subject away from our interesting little conversation.

"Um, well, if I get stressed, scared, upset." Ollie shrugged as he stepped into my room. I moved to sit on the edge of the bed and patted beside me, and he happily joined me.

I couldn't help that our moment on the desk was still fresh in my mind, and I was wondering if that was indeed his interest I'd felt against my thigh. It had certainly heated me up.

And to think he could actually grow it at will.

Stop. I scolded myself.

"It can also just happen randomly too," Ollie said unhappily. "It's really freaking annoying, actually. You know how shifters have to be naked to shift, otherwise the clothes get all caught up on you? I got stuck in my jean pant leg once, it was torture. Only Marcus was home too, and he didn't want to help me for ages," he said as he threw his arms up at the memory.

"Aw, you poor thing!" I grinned, unable to keep the light, humorous tone out of my voice as I squeezed his shoulder.

"It sucked. He eventually helped me when I kept crying out. He ripped my jeans apart to get me out, I was too big." He chuckled. "I try not to wear jeans too often now if I can help it, not until this curse is lifted."

"I can understand the precaution." I chuckled as I leaned against his arm, imagining the sight of him as a fluffy cat stuck in his jeans. Soft giggles tore through me and he chuckled with me.

"I still can't believe you don't know much about your

own kind, your own magic and such." Ollie shook his head once our giggles had died down. "That's so sad."

"Well, never too late to learn."

"You're part werewolf, too, but your nose doesn't work?" Ollie frowned as those amber eyes settled on me. The pupil was narrower than usual, and I wondered if that had anything to do with his cat side.

"Nope, I can shift into a wolf, though, although I've rarely done it. It's not easy to hide, I have to be in a warded zone, otherwise people will freak out. But all the extra senses I'm meant to have, the great hearing and sense of smell, I got nothing. I can just turn into a brown timber wolf if I want to. Which, I also only discovered after getting my pendant off," I scowled.

"Wait, so how long have you been able to shift for?" Ollie cocked his head, his smooth baby face confused.

"Three years. I only found out that I was part werewolf when a shifter found me at work. He was a dingo shifter, and he smelt what I was. He helped me learn a few things about myself, and taught me to shift," I explained, my mind falling back to the memories.

"You really have no idea?" The tall guy frowned, his arms crossed as he leaned against the counter. He was devilishly handsome, with his dark hair, dark eyes, and five o'clock shadow. Not to mention that singlet was showing off all those tight muscles.

"A werewolf?" I snorted, glancing around the shop to make sure no one had heard us.

"And fae," he added. "But I've not met many werewolves in my time."

"Well, there's nothing to tell." I pulled back, cleaning the front desk. It was nearing the end of my shift, and I was quite eager to get home and kick back. Although this shifter, as

he'd called himself, was intriguing. And calling me a were-wolf? Well, that was new.

"My father was one," I murmured. I'd never actually known if I had werewolf in me. My aunt had never told me anything.

"Have you ever tried shifting?" the man asked as he rested his arms on the counter, watching me as I worked. I was glad no one else had come into the small clothing store after him, although I doubted he would've continued this conversation.

"What if someone hears you?" I hissed.

"They won't, I've got good hearing, I'll know if anyone can hear us, just talk quietly," he said softly.

"To answer your question, no, I haven't tried shifting," I muttered. "Today's the first I even considered having were-wolf in me."

"It's in your blood, why wouldn't you think you had it?" He frowned.

"You're asking a lot of questions for a stranger," I smirked as I finished wiping down the area.

"Derek, Derek Manning." He grinned, revealing a set of perfect, white teeth as he offered his hand.

"Allison, Allison Smoak," I said with a roll of my eyes as I shook his outstretched hand.

"I already knew that." He chuckled.

"How?" I frowned. Had he been stalking me?

He grinned as he pointed at my shirt, and I mentally slapped myself as I glanced down at my name tag. Right.

"Well, when do you get off, Allison?" he asked as he straightened.

"In twenty minutes. Why?" I cocked my head at this inter-esting man.

"Because, I'd like to learn more about you. And maybe

teach you about yourself," he said, a smile tugging at the corners of his mouth.

"Really? Just some random girl you just met?" I scoffed.

"Why not? You're intriguing," he breathed.

"Fine," I said as I spied another customer heading in. I wanted to appear casual, but to be honest, his interest excited me. A shifter too. I had so many questions for him.

"So this dingo shifter, why didn't he tell you more about your kind, about others?" Ollie asked, tugging me from the memory of when I'd met my first ever boyfriend.

"Turns out he didn't really care," I mumbled as I played with the hem of my dress.

"Oh, well, too bad for him." Ollie pursed his lips.

"He ended up being my first boyfriend, actually. Didn't last too long," I admitted.

"Oh," Ollie said as he shifted uneasily. "Why not?"

"He wanted me more for the bragging rights, a werewolf halfling. At least I learned how to shift, but when my mischief magic played up once at my place, he got a little weirded out. He didn't really know many pixies, apparently they're not common down on the coast," I murmured. "We broke up after... well, some personal stuff. We were only together exclusively two or three months." I did not want to get into that. That meant opening up a whole other can of worms. And I was not too eager for that. Derek had been anything but the charming man I'd thought he was when I'd opened up to him. He'd changed dramatically once we were together.

"What an arsehole. Pixies and fae are pretty uncommon, pixies more-so. There'll be a few at the uni, though," Oliver said, trying to focus my mind away from my ex. "So, no other boyfriend?" Ollie asked offhandedly as he pretended to only be casually interested. I could see right through it, and it brought a delighted smile to my face. He was so bloody adorable.

"No, After Derek I met Keith, but that didn't last either. He was human, and I wanted to feel normal, I guess. Derek had kinda made the whole supernatural world less likable, but it never stopped me from wondering more about it," I said as I bounced my foot on the floor. "And since I didn't have a good nose, I couldn't really find other supes to try to befriend. Not until I caught wind of this university anyway. I called my cousin's supe school after biting the bullet. I wasn't sure what to say, 'oh, I'm a pixie werewolf and I have no idea what my powers are or much of anything to do with our own kind. Is there a forum or weekly meet-up for supes?' so I asked if there were any supe Universities. They sent me out a whole brochure on Universities in the region, and a special website and code to access the specific supe University guides and towns. Most of the Universities are set up in supe only towns."

"Oh, cool." Ollie nodded, but his mouth was curving upwards slightly at this information. From the looks of it, I wasn't the only single one here. "It must have been so strange, having to hide what you were and not knowing who was like you. You know, you'll be able to use your magic to sense others, that'll be something they'll teach you at the magical classes. Every supe can sense others like themselves, other supes. No one taught you how, that's all," Oliver assured me with a gentle nudge of the elbow. "It's good you reached out to the supe school, I bet that opened up so much for you."

"It really did, that's also how I found out about the other supe schools in my area that my Aunt could have sent me to," I muttered. "I found Lucas' listing for a housemate through the site, too. I was so excited to finally embrace what I was, rather than be stuck between the two worlds."

I groaned as I laid back on the bed.

"I really fucking hate my Aunt. My life could've been so different, I could've learned so much if she didn't cut me off from it all, forcing me not to talk about anything supernatural, hiding my powers. I felt so alone for so long. I was just lucky that after I met Derek I found that witch through him to get the stupid pendant off. She moved right around the time when we broke up, so I lost my only chance at knowing more about the supernatural world," I growled. I'd been so lost, knowing I was different but having no one who understood or who could help me. I'd met a few of Derek's friends who were shifters, but none of them would speak to me after our break-up, and I had to accept I'd lost my link to the supernatural world once more. There was no way in hell I would crawl back to my aunt.

"I'm so sorry, Al," Ollie murmured as he squeezed my knee sadly. "No one should've had to live like that. It's all going to change now. You've got us, and we'll teach you everything you need to know. How about you get started on this reading? I'm sure you're excited to." He smiled as he patted the stack of books on the end of the bed.

"Thanks," I mumbled as I pulled myself back up to sit beside him. "You're so sweet, thank you. Moving here, finding out about this town, it's been amazing. I grew up at Maroochydore, which has some warded areas, but not entirely for supes. It seems there's different wardings for different areas. Like here. From my understanding, no humans know this place even exists, we're meant to tell people we're from Maleny or Conondale instead, right?"

"Yeah." Ollie nodded.

"So the postal guys who handle this area must be supes

then. And the wardings actually reject humans?" I clarified. I hadn't quite understood the terminology on the website.

"To those passing the outskirts, all they see is old farmhouses, only supes can see the real thing. And if people try to drive into those farmhouses, they forget and end up back out on the road again. I don't fully understand the magic behind it, I just know it works," he said.

"It was so strange, knowing that there was this other side of the world all around you, but having no idea how to see it or connect to it. That's now changed. I dunno why I didn't reach out to her school sooner. I should've," I said as I balled my hands up into fists. I'd spent so long not knowing about all this, teetering on the edge of the human world, but not quite falling into the supernatural world. Until now.

"Hey, relax, why don't you bring a book down and sit with us while we play PlayStation? You can ask any questions you want," he suggested as he patted my arm.

"Okay," I breathed, forcing my fluttering heart to slow. I'd gotten a little worked up thinking about my stupid, cruel life. I'd not dwelled much on my lack of knowledge and understanding of the supernatural world due to dealing with other life issues. Other dramas.

I pushed the ugly memories from my head that tried to surface as I stood up. I picked two books from my stack, struggling with the choices, but settled on the encyclopedia and a historical one. Ollie led the way, and I relaxed a little. These boys were too good, and I was mighty glad I'd met them.

Oliver was a lifesaver.

"What's a skinwalker?" I asked as I turned the page to the grotesque creature pictured. It looked like a man, but it had shriveled skin and its limbs were twisted as it crawled across the page. Such a lifelike illustration that it was actually frightening.

"Very, very rare, pretty much non-existent here in Australia. They're kinda like us true shifters, although they have the ability to control others and turn into people, not just animals. Not a nice bunch actually," Oliver said from his perch beside me on the lounge. His eyes never left the TV though, where Skip was playing as some guy called 'Snake' and taking out some base or something. It was actually a little interesting to watch.

"Not creepy at all," I murmured as I decided to fold the corner of the page for future reading. I was more interested in supes I might run into.

"Don't let Lucas see you doing that." Oliver chuckled. "He has a stash of bookmarks in the library for anyone to use."

"Sorry," I cringed. I'd always just folded the corner of the page, it was easy. Bad, but easy.

"So are mermaids a thing?" I asked as I moved onto reading about sprites. Another form of fae that was relatively uncommon. The general fae were the most common, but sprites, pixies and others were offshoots, having some form of lesser abilities than the main fae. Putting it nicely, I'd lose in a magical fight with a fae. Fae, who could actually hurl magic, unlike pixies.

"Yes, there's even some down on the coast, mermen too," Skip spoke up. "All the ocean shifters live down there. I cannot tell you how many shark shifters I've met who are named Bruce, I've met three so far. I swear their parents thought it was the greatest thing," Skip groaned as he tapped away at the buttons aggressively. An explosion occurred on the screen and he did a soft cheer.

"Damn, poor guys, guess their parents loved Nemo too much," I murmured.

Skip paused the game to shuffle down the lounge to stare hard at me.

"Are you serious?" he stared hard at me, that smirk reaching his eyes as they lit up.

"What?" I frowned.

"Damn, she has no idea," Skip gaped as he looked to Oliver.

"That's sad." Oliver sighed as he slouched against the arm of the lounge, giving me a sad smile as he tutted and shook his head.

"What? Is this some kind of inside joke?" I growled. What was I missing?

"You've never seen Jaws?" Skip raised an eyebrow.

"I've heard of it. I wasn't allowed to watch things much until I moved out, and then I was working my arse off to afford to live on the coast," I crossed my arms defensively.

"Bruce is the all famous shark from Jaws, I can't believe you've never seen it," Skip let out a long groan of distress.

"I don't do horror movies," I muttered. I'd heard about Jaws, but it wasn't on my to-watch list. I was more of a Netflix TV show gal or Disney girl. I liked my fun, action packed movies. Not scary movies.

And I was terrified of sharks.

"It's not a real horror," Oliver snorted.

"Look, I didn't swim at the beach, do you know what's in our waters? We've been getting box jellyfish now, and then there's the sharks. Do you see fins or flippers on me? Webbed feet? No. I was not born to swim, I'm a land girl," I retorted.

Skip just broke into a wide grin at this, amused by my deep distress about the ocean.

It was a terrifying thing, so much of it was unexplored

and unknown. I'd prefer to be on land where I knew where I stood.

"We will get you to watch it with us one time," Skip promised as he clapped his hands.

"Don't force her," Oliver groaned.

"I won't. But you're not a true Aussie unless you watch it," he said as he turned his nose up.

"So, you've met mermaids?" I tried to switch the subject.

"Yes. Not as amazing as you'd think. They're mostly surfer people, they can control the water around them to a degree and apparently communicate with all aquatic life. They tend to shift when they're alone, but they're lucky, their magical abilities obscures it from humans. Humans don't see their tails and webbed hands, or the gills on their necks. They just see people in full body surf suits, if they happen to come across them," Skip said.

"That still sounds pretty amazing," I admitted.

"They're surfer people. All they care about is the ocean, and they love to sleep around. Fun fact, they can only impregnate their own kind. Not any other supe or human," Skip added.

"Speaking of, what happens if you were to sleep with a human? What would they see?" I asked, unable to keep the picture of a penis with a second one growing out of it from appearing in my mind.

"To be honest, from my understanding, all things like that with supes just get seen and felt like a normal penis to humans. Like if a male guy went down on you and made you finish, he wouldn't taste the honey orgasm or see the sparkles. The mischief magic though, that one's uncertain, depends how well you know how to wield it. You'll be taught how to conceal it, mask it from humans. It will mean it gets distorted in their eyes, like reality is warped. Say you make a muffin turn into a dog and bark at someone, all they'd see is a muffin that has fallen off the table and is rolling around. It's best to learn to control it so it doesn't happen in public though," Skip explained. "Your magic will already conceal it a bit, but it needs honing to become a better camouflage."

"Huh, okay," I said as I took it all in. So not only could I learn to control my abilities, but I could cloak them? Damn, I was learning something new every passing hour.

"So, I'm going to get some more beer, that one carton won't be enough for us all, you want anything, Cupcake?" Lucas appeared in the doorway, suited up like he was going to prom.

I wonder how others took him, or did he alter how they saw him too? Damn, magic and all this new knowledge about supernatural stuff was mind-boggling.

"I don't drink, thanks," I said.

"You sure? I can grab some wine, spirits, cocktail ingredients? I can make specialty cocktails?" Lucas offered with a lopsided, charming smile.

"I'm sure." I nodded sweetly.

"Well, toodles then, Cupcake. I will be back shortly." He bowed, drawing a soft laugh from me.

"He can be a bit over the top." Oliver chuckled.

"Rich people can be over the top," Skip snorted.

"I'm not," Oliver argued.

"You're no longer as rich as you were, besides, you were always the black sheep," Skip snickered.

"Least I wasn't given a stupid name like Skippy," Oliver muttered as he scowled over at him.

"Least I'm not cursed," Skip shot back.

"Enough!" I rolled my eyes as I looked between the two. "Now, why don't you go back to playing PlayStation, and Ollie, anything I should know for when I start at uni? Any supes I should study up on or something?" I asked as I chewed my lip, hoping this would distract the pair.

"Whatever," Skip muttered as he turned back to the TV.

"Um, well, it'll mostly be shifters and witches, they make up most of the students. You'll have some elementals thrown in, you won't really deal with the vamps unless you take night classes, um, there'll be fae, and then you'll get a scattering of other supes," Oliver shrugged.

"What's the most common shifters then?" I asked.

"Up here? Natives mostly—koalas, kangaroos, wallabies, dingoes. You'll have some dog, cat, and bird shifters too, no exotics really, like you. No panthers, tigers, or wolves. At least, not that I'm aware of. You're the first exotic in Maple Grove since Gregory the panther moved down south to meet up with the other panthers down in NSW. There's a couple of them there, black panthers," Ollie said as he mulled it over thoughtfully.

"Gregory?" I cracked a smirk at the name.

"Yeah, he studied up here a few years ago, I remember him," Skip murmured as he focused on his game once more.

"Great." I let out a raspberry in annoyance. I doubted an exotic supe would slip under the radar easily.

"Don't worry, everyone is quite nice up here, laid-back and casual. You'll be fine," Oliver reassured.

"I hope so," I murmured as I focused back down on the pages of my book.

I wanted to learn how to use my abilities and help animals more. I'd always loved them growing up, they'd been much nicer than people, much more loving and sweet. My Aunt had had a dog for years, little Maisy, a tan staffy. She'd comforted me more than any of my so-called family over the years. I took over caring for her since my Aunt did very little to look after her.

When she passed, I came to the conclusion that I preferred the company of animals over people, and vowed to leave my Aunt's home and become a veterinarian or run a rescue or something.

And coming to this University, I could also learn more about the world I was a part of. I could be taught to what extent my abilities could help me.

Strange though, because for the next hour or so, I couldn't find anything under any of the fae lineages or sub-species about sensing illness or fatal issues in animals.

How peculiar.

8

I sat on the lounge in the games room with Oliver as Skip and Lucas versed Richo and Issac in a game of pool. They were split into teams, and Skip and Lucas were winning. Skip hadn't been too big on playing until Richo and Issac told him they'd promise not to use magic. Lucas would monitor it, too.

I bit into my pizza, a pleasant change from my usual pepperoni. I'd seen their menu and decided to choose the BBQ Chook, a pizza topped with chicken, bacon, red onion, barbecue sauce and cheese.

And it was bloody amazing.

"So, Ally, you're from Maroochydore?" Issac asked as he stood back with his pool cue while Lucas took his turn.

Issac was tall and broad, easily standing over the others. Sadly, he swung for the other team it seemed, and had been talking about how he was going to see his boyfriend tomorrow before he went back to uni. Not that I would've even guessed he was gay, considering how he reminded me of a Rugby player. Maori descent too, which was obvious by his thick kiwi accent and indigenous appearance. His chin and cheeks were covered in a dusting of stubble, like he'd recently shaved. It suited his more rounded face, and his solid frame made me wonder if I was correct in thinking he may have played Rugby. Although the man bun was throwing me off.

"Yeah." I nodded through a mouthful of food.

"Musta bin noice, living near the beach." He smiled. I struggled to understand most of his words, as they sounded vastly different with his accent. Even beach almost sounded like bitch.

"Nah, I didn't swim," I said as I finished up my slice of pizza and glanced over at Oliver beside me. I wondered if he struggled to understand the kiwi as much as I did.

"Right, shame dat," he clicked his tongue. "Well, least ye can enjoy the greenery up 'ere den."

"Yeah," I nodded.

"Issac grew up in New Zealand but moved here, what, six years ago?" Oliver clarified as I looked over my shoulder. The lounge was set up so you had to turn to look over at the pool table.

"Yip, moved 'ere to study sorcery, New Zealand doesn't offer very good sorcery classes," Issac said as he moved over to the bar to sip his bottle of beer on the countertop.

Skip was perched on a stool while he waited for his turn, swigging from his beer too.

"Do you miss home?" I asked as I dug into another piece of the heavenly pizza.

"Sometimes, but it's bin good 'ere, learning the full extent of my abilities, what I can do. Not as good as this 'ere bloke, though." He raised his bottle to Lucas who just smirked and nodded in appreciation.

"So Ally, what made you decide to put in your application to join a house full of guys? Surely that was a little intimidating?" Richo said as he took his turn, hitting the white ball and watching as it connected with a red one and sunk it.

Richo was a similar build to Lucas, and wore the same kind of lavish suit. It made the rest of us stand out like sore thumbs. Richo had a buzz cut though, and a strong jawline with a short beard. Those blue eyes were dark like the ocean, nothing like Skip's bright sky-blue eyes.

Skip and Issac looked quite out of place with the two elegantly dressed men, while they were both in singlets, shorts and thongs.

A quick glance revealed that Issac had actually abandoned his thongs over by the bar now.

"I lived with my cousin for ages, went to a non-supe school, decided girls were arseholes. Bitchy, backstabbing cows most of the time. Men are easier, they're normally straight to the point, and if their intentions aren't pure, you know pretty quick. Like how Marcus doesn't like me, he didn't pretend to," I muttered the last part.

"Oi, be nice to that fanger, he can't help it. Especially with ye being a fae, he's got his reasons," Issac scolded me with a wave of his pool cue.

"Marcus doesn't not like you, Cupcake. He's just an acquired taste, and untrusting at first," Lucas said as he indicated at Skip that it was his turn.

I pursed my lips at this. Everyone seemed to know something about Marcus that I didn't. What was being hidden from me?

"You know what, I don't get this whole being fae thing being an issue for him. My cousin dated a vampire witch, she was fae, he handled it fine," I said as I reached for my glass of lemon, lime, and bitters. Lucas had made it for me when he'd offered to make up everyone's drinks. Most of the boys had been easy with beers, but Oliver had wanted some midori and lemonade, and I asked for anything non-alcoholic. It seemed the bar was rather stocked with cocktail ingredients, and yet most of them preferred beer. I was with Oliver on that one, it tasted like piss. And I wouldn't touch alcohol with a ten-foot pole anyway.

"He's got his reasons, it's not a general fae thing," Oliver murmured as he leaned closer so I could hear him.

"Maybe try talking to 'im, don't let 'im push ye away, it's his go to move. Doesn't like to let anyone get close, even deez guys, who he's grown up with," Issac said as he waved his hand at the group.

I frowned at Issac as Skip strode over to sit on the lounge across from me.

"Don't take it personally, trust me, Marcus went through some bad crap, but it's not my place to tell you. Just know that he's the way he is for a reason, he may be a jerk, but he's not actually that bad." Skip gave me a smile, revealing those dazzling teeth. How did they stay so white with all the alcohol and crap he ate?

"Fine," I said as I sipped my drink. I did wonder what Marcus had gone through. Maybe I should ease off on him. Not that I'd been rude or anything. He didn't join us much, and I hadn't seen him since our Game of Thrones moment. When he'd reacted to my arousal.

Damn.

I focused on my food as Skip rejoined the guys for their game of pool. I sat quietly with Oliver, talking here and there about things I'd read, supes that I had learned interesting facts about. I couldn't believe the amount of empty stubbies that were piling up on the bar, and they moved onto cans once they'd drank through the two cartons. They were onto their third game now, and my over listening had informed me that

Richo had a girlfriend, whom he'd been with since early high school. Lucky lady.

Skip paid him out for this, baffled at the idea of settling down so soon. It was quite obvious he was a player, and yet I couldn't deny I was still attracted to the rather bogan roo shifter.

"You know, Jane says your sister is starting uni this year, too," Richo said suddenly when the conversation had died down.

I frowned as Lucas tensed his jaw, tightening his grip on his pool cue as he focused on the table as Skip sunk another ball.

Now I was intrigued. Was there some issue between Lucas and his sister?

"Why would he care, bro? What's the point in telling 'im?" Issac said, seemingly unhappy with Richo's announcement.

"Just in case he runs into her, don't want him caught by surprise, that's all," Richo said.

"Thanks, but you needn't worry," Lucas growled, his demeanor unsettling. I'd thought he was laid-back like Skip, but he looked mighty displeased with this news.

"Okay, I just thought, y'know." Richo shrugged as he pursed his lips.

"Well, we stopped talking years ago, I moved here, much to my family's pleasure, and things have been better than ever," Lucas said coldly as he watched Issac take his turn.

So, Lucas was estranged from his family? I'd had my suspicions about Ollie, since he was so tight-lipped about his family, but I wouldn't have guessed with Lucas.

"Okay." Richo nodded, looking like he'd wished he'd never brought it up.

"How long have you known Lucas, Richo?" I asked,

wanting to relieve the tension a bit. He looked thankful as his shoulders relaxed a little.

"Jeez, since mid high school, when I met Jane. She was friends with Lucas' sister, they hung out a lot, and I happened to run into him when I dropped her off one time. Hit it off, been friends since." He smiled, but it faltered when he flicked his gaze to Lucas, who was silent as he took his turn. He looked like he was boiling just beneath the surface as he struck the ball with more force than necessary and sunk the white along with a colored. He cursed softly at this, and Richo shot me a look as he bit his lip.

"Well, it's been nice hanging with you guys, but I think I'm going to have a shower and maybe do some more reading before bed," I said, wanting to escape the uneasiness in the room. I'd glanced at the clock over behind the bar which informed me it was eight-thirty. I really wanted to have a shower before bed tonight.

I stood up, glancing at Ollie who looked like he wanted to slink off with me but decided against it.

He certainly wasn't going to sneak into the bathroom again, that was for sure. The memory made a smile play at my lips even as I cringed.

I left the boys to their game and drinking as I already imagined the warm water washing over me. It had cooled down considerably with the rain still hammering down on us, and climbing the stairs only made it grow louder as it belted down on the roof.

I slipped into my room and gathered up my pajamas and a pair of clean underwear before heading out to the bathroom and locking the door behind me.

I stripped down and climbed into the shower and turned the water on. As much as I would've liked to have a soak, I didn't feel like it was my place to do so. I'd have to check to see if the place was on town water or tank water.

The warm water washed over me and I relaxed as I warmed myself up. This was so much better than my shower at my old rental, with its pathetic water pressure and broken fan, which meant I had to leave the window open instead. Thankfully it was a two-story so no one could peer in, but due to it being a more modernized bathroom, the shower had no door or curtain, and the cold air seeping in over winter had made showers horrible.

Nothing like this one, though. The fan was on this time, and I could enjoy this shower much more than last night's one now that I felt more at home after having met everyone and getting to know them.

I soaped myself up, humming softly to a tune of AC/DC as I wondered about my housemates. Three of them were charming and sweet, and Marcus, well, now I knew that there was more to him being a jerk. I wondered if he'd ever tell me.

I wouldn't pry, just like I didn't want them to pry about my family life. I thought I'd avoided the topic of my family fairly well. They knew about my Aunt, but not her boyfriends. I'd like to keep it that way.

I clenched my teeth as a wave of inner pain washed over me.

"Little girls need to learn their place!"

The sharp pain of the belt striking behind my knees made me cry out as I fell against the table, clutching frantically at the edge of it to stay upright as my legs stung from the hit.

"This is not your home, you learn to speak only when spoken to!"

I winced at the incoming strike, gritting my teeth against the pain.

I shook my head at the horrid memory, trying to push it from my mind. It was only one of many similar incidents.

"You're nothing. Not even your own mother wanted you," *my Aunt spat as I sat huddled in the corner of my room, only* *twelve years old.*

I gasped as the tears sprung forth, sniffling as I wept softly. Why had those memories flared up so suddenly?

I ended my shower early, my body trembling as the horrid words and beatings sliced through my mind as if it was just yesterday.

I grabbed my towel from the rail and dried off, trying to rein in my upset emotions as I tried to think of something else. Anything else.

"Tell me, little one, how does it feel, how does it feel for *your flesh to burn?"*

I growled as I pulled my underwear on, tugging on my pajamas and hanging my towel back up as I dried my tears and sniffled.

I'd gotten away from all that. I was free. I had to remind myself of that.

I drew in a deep breath before flicking the fan and light off before stepping out into the hall.

I froze as I spied Marcus stepping out of his room, those icy eyes falling on me.

His jaw tightened as he took in my face.

I could only imagine how puffy my eyes were. Great. Just what I needed right now.

"What?" I hissed, annoyed when I had to sniffle.

Marcus' eyes softened a little, and he stepped forward, like he wanted to say something.

Then those eyes shut down as he sighed and averted his gaze.

Just like I thought. I wasn't worth the effort.

I knew my mind was still fraught and I shouldn't have thought it, but I still did as I stormed into my room and slammed the door behind me.

Marcus wasn't the only one with things that haunted him. I thought I'd gotten good at hiding it, forcing it away. Guess I'd lowered my guard and gotten too comfortable around the boys today.

I headed straight for my bedside table, groaning when I remembered my iPod had died. I tugged the drawer open and pulled the charger out, popping it on immediately. I needed to drown out everything.

I climbed onto my bed, ignoring the pile of books I'd set down on the floor beside it as I curled under the blanket.

A soft knock on the door made my throat tighten.

"Ally? It's Ollie. Can I come in?" the muffled voice asked.

I sighed, swallowing as I forced myself to smile.

"Of course."

Ollie slowly opened the door, giving me a sad smile.

"Marcus said you seemed upset, that you could use someone to talk to," he said softly.

"Marcus should mind his own business," I snapped, but then closed my eyes as I sucked in a breath.

"Are you okay?" Ollie asked after a moment as he sat down on the end of the bed.

"Why does Marcus avoid me so much?" I asked, wanting to divert the question.

"Skip said it wasn't our place to tell, but I can tell you this, he had a problem once with a fae girl, people got hurt. So I think being around you reminds him of that," Ollie murmured.

I sat up as I cocked my head at this. People had gotten hurt? Did he mean he hurt her? Because of what he was?

"Well, I guess that's somewhat understandable then," I mumbled, feeling a bit guilty for being so annoyed with him now. Never assume. That was something I tried not to do, but it wasn't easy, especially with how cold Marcus had been.

He'd looked genuinely concerned though when I'd come out of the bathroom, and for a moment, I thought he might let his guard down. Seemed he was better than me at keeping himself protected.

"So, why were you upset?" Ollie asked gently as he pulled his legs up to sit cross-legged.

I pulled the blanket up to my chin as I sat with my knees up in front of me, resting my arms on them.

"Just some crap that happened in the past, remembered it a bit," I said, my throat tightening as I frowned.

"Do you want to talk about it?" he asked with a soft smile.

"Not really, we all have things we'd rather not share," I said, and he nodded understandingly.

"Yeah, but sometimes, eventually, it helps to tell someone. When you're ready," he said as he played with the frayed ends of his denim shorts.

"Did it help you?" I asked.

He chuckled as he cocked his head at me. "Lucas was there for me, he knows everything that happened. I find it hard to tell others about the issues with my family, we all have secrets here, all of us. I know you do too, I saw those burns on you the other day, figured I wouldn't mention it," he murmured. "But if you ever want to get it off your chest, you can talk to me."

"You barely know me," I shot back with a small smile.

"I feel like I do." He shrugged. "I know it's only your second day here, but I feel like we already know each other."

I understood that. I wasn't sure why, but I felt the same

with most of them. Like I belonged already. Maybe it was because I'd never felt so welcome before, even at the house I grew up in.

"Why are your eyes that color? Were they always like that?" I asked, wanting to move to an easier topic. Ollie seemed to understand this, and didn't try to pry.

"Well, since I got cursed, they got stuck like this. When I'm about to shift, they turn into slits. I can sometimes change them to slits too if I want to try to see things better. Cats have good eyesight," he explained.

"Huh, cool. What color are they normally then? Before this happened?" I asked, intrigued by this tidbit of information.

"To be honest, I'm not sure anymore, green I think, although the boys say they were more hazel. They've been this way for so long, I've actually forgotten a bit," he said with a soft laugh, but his brow was furrowed at the struggle to remember.

"That must be weird," I murmured.

"I got used to it. Hey, would you like to have some ice-cream? Ice-cream makes everything better." He gave me his boyish grin, and I softened. "We can maybe watch a movie in the living room, I'm guessing the others will be out in the games room for most of the night."

"Sure, sounds good," I said. God, he was so kind and understanding. And I was forever grateful that he didn't demand answers from me. He understood that sometimes we needed to hide things, to protect ourselves. I might tell him, one day, if I felt like I needed to.

"Do the others know I was upset?" I asked as I pulled myself out of bed.

"No, Marcus found me in the kitchen when I was raiding

the fridge… I might have stolen one of your Freddo's," he said sheepishly with a light smile.

"Well, since you're getting me ice-cream, I'll forgive you." I chuckled. So even with my name on it, it might still get raided. I didn't mind though. Ollie was too adorable to be mad at, and it was just food.

"We can find something on Netflix, maybe a comedy. I think that'll be a good choice," he suggested as he led the way out of my room.

I followed after the shifter, my heart squeezing at his kindness. I'd really won the lottery getting this room. Not only were my housemates all attractive, but the majority of them were charming and sweet. No bad intentions anywhere.

Well, Skip was debatable, I'd seen him checking me out a few times, but I enjoyed it, taking it as a compliment. I'd just make sure not to fall too much for him. Although, after my last boyfriend, I had become a bit of a one-night stand kind of girl.

No. You don't need that, Ally. Not with your housemate. You'd have to live with him, for as long as my course took, which was several years.

Yeah, no. If things turned sour, that would make it hard, and finding another rental would take time, making it awkward.

"So, you said your second boyfriend was human. Guess that didn't last for obvious reasons?" Oliver asked as we entered the kitchen and he went for the fridge. It was one of those two door fridges, with a freezer on one side with an automatic water and ice dispenser set into the door.

"We were together for a year, and it was quite good, but I felt like I was lying, hiding a main part of me for so long. We had our occasional fights like anyone, but eventually I realized I couldn't live like that, hiding who I was. And it's forbidden to tell humans about us," I said as I sat down at the table. I didn't mind talking about Keith, he'd been good. A tradie who spent most of his afternoons in front of the TV with a beer, but he'd never hit me. Sure, we'd fought, we'd yelled, I'd broken down. Even he had never known the extent of my childhood issues. It would be too difficult to explain while keeping quiet about the magic.

Sometimes, I wondered if it was the wedge that divided us too much. He'd been a few years older than me, but the lead up to our break-up had been sad. I knew he was beginning to question us too, he knew I'd been hiding things from him. But he wasn't like me, he was a strong man, hiding his emotions all the time, using anger instead of sadness. It was something I'd disliked about him, sometimes I'd wished he'd just cry when he got upset rather than yell.

But he'd never hit me, and he'd apologized.

We still drifted apart though, and I knew it was my fault. I couldn't ever open up to him properly. We were different.

After that, I avoided relationships. I didn't want to form such a personal connection to someone to tie me down. I was young, and I wanted to explore my sexual side.

If only my memories would stop haunting me.

"That sucks. There are some supes who've made it work, but it's so much easier to be with another supe, you don't have to hide anything," Oliver said as he struggled to shovel out the ice-cream.

I watched in amusement as the spoon bent and he scowled.

"That's why you use the ice-cream scoop like you're supposed to," I pointed out.

Oliver just shot me a deadpan look before sighing in defeat and rummaging for the scoop in the middle drawer. I'd opened that when looking for cutlery, it seemed to hold all the other odd utensils.

He served up the vanilla ice-cream with a hefty amount of milo sprinkled over the top, and then we were heading out into the living room.

I smiled softly at Marcus who was perched on the lounge, and he gave me a brief glance as I sat on the other red lounge with Oliver.

"Sorry I snapped at you," I said as I tried to give Marcus an apologetic smile.

"It's fine," he said gruffly as he focused back on his screen with his headphones still on.

I turned to Oliver with a raised eyebrow, and he just shrugged.

Guess it was a step in a good direction. Maybe.

I pulled my legs up and nestled back as I began eating my ice-cream while Oliver got Netflix up.

"Have you seen the *Good Place*?" Ollie asked as he sat down on the lounge beside me with the PlayStation control in hand.

"No, I haven't," I admitted.

"It's pretty good I think, I've seen a few episodes but no one else would watch it with me. It's funny. " He shrugged, but I could see the hope in his eyes as he waited for my response. God, those amber eyes were so unique.

"Sure, we can watch it, from the start though," I added. I liked to see things right from the beginning, that way I knew what was going on.

"Awesome!" He grinned as he sat back, sifting through the shows on the screen until he found it.

I glanced over at Marcus, his feet resting on the coffee table as he focused on the laptop in front of him, the faint glow lighting up his face.

It made him look deathly white, not the attractive white that he normally had, this was duller, more lifeless. I felt a little sorry for him. What secrets did he have? Why was he so withdrawn from people?

I knew the feeling a little bit. I'd withdrawn from people after Derek, but then I'd met Keith, who'd helped me find myself again and open up just by being good to me. Sometimes, I wished he could've been a supe, so we could've made things work.

But that was the past, a relationship I'd had while I was seventeen and eighteen. That had ended over nine months ago. And despite having spent a year of my life with him in it, it had been a clean break-up. We'd both known it wasn't working anymore, and we'd agreed to be friends.

Not that I'd stuck to that. I wanted friends who I could relate to on a deeper level.

I had a bunch of one-night stands in the few months after that, and then my hours got increased at work and my social life died. Goodbye Tinder. Hello constant tiredness.

And then I decided it was time to learn more about myself and pursue a real career. I hated retail and hospitality. I wanted more.

I finished my ice-cream and set the bowl on the table as I settled in for the show.

Oliver was right, it was a unique show, and funny.

We spent the next hour watching a few episodes since they only ran at around twenty minutes each, and even Marcus had been sucked in, removing his headphones to watch.

It was a nice, quiet evening with the soft sound of rain outside.

And for the first time in a long time, I felt like I belonged.

Like I was right where I was meant to be.

9

The slap knocked me to the floor, and I whimpered as I scrambled to get away.

"You're all useless, the lot of you!" the man roared as my Aunt tried to avoid his wrath. Too bad my cousin had walked in right then.

"Where have you been?!" he screeched, and I watched from the floor as my Aunt stepped in, taking the harsh blow intended for her daughter.

"Why do you even have this pathetic child? She's not even yours!" he shouted as he turned on me once more.

I closed my eyes as I leaned up against the wall, waiting for the next slap.

Then the scene changed, and I was crying out as I was held down.

"Tell me, little one, how does it feel, how does it feel for your flesh to burn?"

I shot awake, gasping for air as sweat soaked through my top, and I groaned as I slumped back against the pillows.

Another nightmare. Well, were they still nightmares if they were memories?

I rolled over, watching as the morning sun filtered through my open curtains. I'd left them open last night, forgetting to close them after staying up with Oliver watching Netflix.

I smiled softly at the memory. Such a perfect man.

I sighed, fully awake now, and reached for my iPod to check the time. Not even seven in the morning.

Well, never too early to shower, and these clothes would be added to my dirty clothes pile in the corner. I'd ask someone to show me to the laundry room later.

I climbed out of bed, stretching and wiping my sticky hair from my face. I wiped the sleep from my eyes and headed out into the hall, yawning.

I froze as I caught the sight of someone at the end of the hall, standing just outside the door on the verandah over-looking the backyard.

I blinked, waiting for my sleepy eyes to focus as I headed down the hall.

"Marcus?" I murmured as I stepped through the open door and onto the verandah.

He gave me a confused look, giving me a once over before smiling softly.

"You get nightmares too?" he murmured as he looked back out across the backyard.

"Vampires sleep?" I scoffed, avoiding the question.

"That we do, normally during the day though. Nighttime is when we can move around easiest. We're more tired during the day too anyway, although some of us still do things during daytime, but we mostly try to get some sleep," he murmured. I just nodded as I looked out at the morning sight.

To our left, the same side my room was on, was the glow

where the sun was slowly creeping over the horizon. The backyard was covered in a soft fog, and just past the estate homes beyond the back fence was the rolling farmland as far as I could see, all covered in a fine foggy haze.

"It looks so serene after a rainy night, foggy like this," Marcus said, his voice barely audible.

"I think this is the most you've ever spoken to me," I stated as I stepped up to stand beside him.

"Hmph," was the only response I got from him.

"Do you miss it?" I asked quietly, enjoying the cool morning air on my clammy skin.

"Miss what?" Marcus frowned, his arms crossed, but his mouth set in a knowing line. He was wearing gray shorts and a black t-shirt with a skull on it and the text 'The Punisher'. I'd seen some of the TV show before I'd cancelled my Netflix subscription to save on bills. I'd enjoyed what I'd seen.

"The sun, being out in the daylight," I said. He knew that was what I meant.

He just gave me a look, a sad, pained look that made me shiver.

"Well, I'm off to bed, have a good day," he said, and I could see those walls slamming back up as his face turned stoney once more.

He turned and flitted inside, disappearing into his room with barely a sound.

Well, I hadn't expected that this morning. And to say seeing a vampire flit for the first time was pretty cool. They could move at incredible speeds if they wanted to.

I stretched, letting the cool morning air hit my sweaty armpits. I gave them a sniff and gagged. Yep, definitely needed a shower. And a shave. Hopefully Marcus hadn't caught a whiff of me, it might have scared him off if he did.

No, I knew it was something else. He'd dropped his walls down, even if only for the briefest moment. And I finally got to see the real Marcus, the one that hid behind a cold exterior.

And to be honest? I kinda liked him. Maybe I'd catch more glimpses of him.

"Morning," Lucas greeted me as I strode into the kitchen. He was wearing a purple suit today, and it suited him surprisingly well, even with the red tie. It was still quite a sight, but he'd said it was his brand, so I'd just have to get used to it.

"Hey." I gave him a soft wave as he stood before the stove cooking up breakfast. A glance in the pan revealed pancakes, which made my stomach groan.

"Hey, how many drinks did you have last night? And you're perfectly fine? No hangover?" I asked as I padded over to the fridge. I'd thrown on my blue dress again for today after eyeing the clear sky outside. Today was probably going to be a warm one. And it wasn't dirty, I'd only worn it once. Dresses could be worn more than once before washing in my books. Besides, I only owned the two dresses. I'd buy more once I had more money. I did love dresses, but I'd lost most of them when I'd broken my lease. Let's just say my housemate had not been too happy with my desire to pursue a better life, and a fair few dresses had wound up tossed when I hadn't packed them soon enough. It was a real shame, since I thought we could've remained as somewhat friends, until she went all Godzilla on me.

"I don't get hungover." Lucas chuckled as he turned to me. "How many pancakes would you like? Consider it your formal breakfast welcome."

"Um, three?" I frowned as I double checked the size of

the pancakes in the pan. Easily a medium plate size. "And why don't you get hungover?"

"Magic, because of what I am. Skip, on the other hand, will probably be regretting those drinks last night. Luckily for him, I've got a potion in the cupboard above the fridge to help relieve them faster than anything else," he said as he flicked his hand at the fridge. I was now standing at the table pouring myself a juice to get me started for today.

"So, what are your plans for today?" he asked as he began serving up the first few pancakes.

"Well, I'd like to maybe check out Maple Grove a bit, go see Dingo Diner and chat with them," I said as I sat down at the table.

"I'll drive."

I turned to spy Skip in the doorway, slouched over in nothing but a pair of boxers as he groaned and rubbed his face.

"I want to get you a slice of that bee sting from the Maleny bakery," Skip said, groaning again as he closed one eye against the sunlight filtering in from the window over the sink.

"Top cupboard." Lucas indicated at the overhead cupboard with his spatula, and Skip dragged himself over there.

"I'll come too, would be nice to show you around," Lucas said.

"Cool. Hey, do you ever not wear suits?" I asked, trying to keep my eyes off Skip, who was too tempting on the eyes. That gorgeous, golden, toned back was being arched and stretched as he rummaged in the cupboard for the potion. He grumbled, but then relaxed when he pulled out the small bottle with a hand-written label.

"Suits are my thing, but sometimes I might wear swimmers, I guess," Lucas said thoughtfully.

"What about jeans and a shirt, or a singlet?" I asked, unable to stop myself from rolling my eyes over Skip's bare chest as he leaned on the counter facing me. He poured some of the potion into a medicine cup and downed it quickly.

So chiseled and perfectly defined, they should all try to get jobs as models to be honest. Or strippers.

Lucas and Marcus were the only ones who I hadn't seen with their shirts off, and I doubted they wouldn't be the same as their companions.

"No singlets!" Lucas said as he held up his spatula. "I'm no bogan."

"Hey," Skip warned as he put the potion away.

"I wear singlets," I said as I sipped my juice.

"Singlets are not my style," Lucas said as he turned and cocked his head at us.

Skip pushed off the counter and sunk into the dining chair beside me.

"Dress looks nice on you, can see why you're re-wearing it," Skip remarked as he slumped his head down on his arms on the table.

"Thanks," I murmured, surprised he'd taken note of it yesterday. *You'd look good in nothing at all*, I thought.

"Pancakes, Skip?" Lucas offered with a smirk at our hungover friend.

Skip groaned but nodded weakly.

"All right, well, Ally's are nearly done," he said as he flipped the next batch.

"Can I have some, too?"

I turned and smiled as Oliver strode in, stretching and yawning in his batman boxers and iron man shirt.

"Aren't they different universes?" I asked. I may have enjoyed my superhero movies.

"Huh?" Oliver frowned.

"Batman and Iron Man," I specified.

Oliver's face broke into a broad, boyish grin as he plopped down on the chair off to my other side.

"They are! So you like your superhero movies too?" he asked, the excitement reaching his eyes.

"Yes, which are you, DC or Marvel?" I asked, my mouth curving up at his cheeriness.

"How can you both be so awake right now?" Skip groaned.

"Don't make me choose, I love them both." Ollie pouted.

"DC," Skip muttered. "Because Batman."

"Marcus is into superhero movies too, he watches the TV shows on Netflix. Jessica Jones, Daredevil, Gotham, Arrow, you name it. I've watched most of them, too." Oliver grinned as Lucas set down some pancakes before me.

I drew in the warm aroma of them, and giggled as the fridge opened and the cream floated over to sit on the table, followed by the real Canadian maple syrup in a glass jug and some cutlery. I could tell it was real from the label plastered across it.

"Want any berries or anything on top?" Lucas asked as he focused on finishing the next batch of pancakes.

"Mmmm, berries sound good," I said as I went to push my chair out.

"Stay, I got it," Lucas gave me his charming, lopsided grin as he waved his hand.

I froze as a knife shot out of the cutlery drawer, hovering mid-air over my plate.

Then some strawberries floated out of the fridge, and the floating knife sliced the tops off and then quartered them before they drifted down to sit on my pancakes. Some blueberries joined them, and I just shook my head in utter amazement as the knife floated away and the leafy tops of the strawberries floated into the composting bin at the end of the counter.

The rest of the pancakes were served quickly, and only Lucas and I chose to have berries with ours. Oliver went with just cream, while Skip had an equal mix of syrup and thickened cream on his.

"We should've whipped it first," Oliver mumbled through a mouthful of pancakes and cream.

"Too late now," Skip said as he finished off the second of his pancakes already.

"So, guess we're checking out your new place of work today," Lucas said as he delicately ate his pancakes, making sure to cut everything to a nice portion, nothing like the massive chunks Skip and Oliver were shoveling into their mouths.

"You don't have to come," I said, but Lucas waved me off as he straightened his red tie.

"No, it'll be good to support a local business. I applaud them for opening it in this dreary town of supes. Hopefully the other locals will join in and support them as well," Lucas said.

"It'd be good to see Mr. and Mrs. Melvin again," Oliver piped up. "I haven't seen Mr. Melvin for ages."

"He was your old neighbor, right?" Skip clarified as he held his fork out.

"Yeah, my parents' place," Oliver said, and I noted how his smile faltered.

"So, you can make a mean coffee then?" Oliver changed the subject. "You said you used to work as a barista?"

"Yeah, I guess I make a decent coffee, my new position is

barista and waitress," I said as I sipped my juice to wash down my first pancake. God, they were good. Lucas sure knew how to cook.

"Awesome, I know where I'll be getting my coffees from now on," Skip said, his voice muffled through his food.

"Well, we might as well show you around the rest of the town, and give you a proper tour of Maleny while we're at it," Lucas said.

"Sounds like a plan." I smiled, flicking my eyes around at the three guys. They sure were a sweet bunch.

"Well, this is Dingo Diner," Skip stated as we pulled into the small six bay carpark out the front of the small cafe building.

"Who even says diner," Oliver murmured as the old Landcruiser rumbled to a stop.

"They've done well, actually, it's only been open a few weeks, but they're getting a decent amount of business," Lucas said as he climbed out of the backseat. I was in the front with Skip, while the other two were in the back.

I smiled as Lucas held open my door for me and did a little over the top bow with a cheeky grin.

I just rolled my eyes as I climbed out of the cruiser, and readied myself to meet my new employers.

"C'mon, it'll be fine, they'll love you! We do," Oliver assured me as he popped up beside me and wrapped an arm around my shoulders. "Mr. and Mrs. Melvin are really nice, you'll see."

"Don't crowd her, Oliver." Skip chuckled as he rounded the bonnet of the cruiser to join us.

"I'm not, am I?" He pouted and turned to me with those big amber eyes looking thoroughly concerned.

"No, you're not." I gave him a sweet smile and he relaxed, not removing his arm from around my shoulders.

"We should order, you know, to support their business here," Skip said as he eyed the big painted sign across the top of the building. A dingo was sprawled out with the shop name over it, the scenery of Ayers Rock behind it.

"We literally just ate," Lucas said as he shook his head.

"We could grab a milkshake each? I could go for one?" Oliver suggested as he started forward, pulling me with him.

I eyed the cafe, taking in the unique orange window frames and orange trimmings. Even the glass door had a thick sandy orange strip. The dark orange made me think of the outback, or even the hide of a dingo. Guess that was the intention.

It was a small building set up on the corner of the main street of Maple Grove. To be honest, there wasn't much to the main street at all. A corner store on the other end of the rather short street, a barbershop, a real estate, a healer for supes, and an old-looking bookstore with the sign faded and peeling above it. Oh, then there was the small complex about midway down the street, set in an old brick building. It homed a solicitor's and lawyer's office, specifically for supes, and an employment agency, which Oliver said consisted of two ladies who helped supes find jobs in supe businesses.

We pushed through the glass door, and I sighed at the cool air-conditioned building. It was hot and muggy outside, and I was beginning to sweat already, feeling sticky and yuck.

"Welcome!" a cheery voice rang out, and my eyes fell on the older blonde woman behind the counter. Her hair was cut short, pixie style, and she wore a white apron over a navy shirt that had 'Dingo Diner' embroidered over the right breast, and her name over the left. She had her elbows resting on the counter as she stood patiently at her post.

"Hi, Mrs. Melvin!" Oliver waved, and the older woman's hazel eyes lit up.

"Ollie! It's been so long, how've you been? Henry! Ollie's here," she called over her shoulder.

The cafe was small inside, booths lining the walls and the kitchen easily visible over the counter, only a steel bench with a high back blocking the view of the stoves and fryers.

Mr. Melvin—Henry—appeared from behind the steel wall, obviously having been by the stove or fryers. He had short brown curls tinged with gray, and those blue eyes looked pleased at our arrival.

A few of the booths were occupied with patrons enjoying breakfast, and I was glad to see that they had some business going on a Sunday.

"Ollie! Is that Lucas too? And Skip? Damn, I still remember when you three were this small." Henry beamed, indicating waist height. His rounded belly stuck out from his navy shirt as he made the size reference. He was clean shaven and a large man, someone I could picture happily sitting down after a long day to watch some footy and down a few beers. The belly certainly indicated as much.

I wondered what kind of supe he was? Shifters had trouble gaining weight thanks to their genetics. "Yeah, that's us." Skip laughed as he stretched and held his hands behind his head. He'd thrown on a red singlet today, but wore his trademark board shorts and thongs.

"Well, what do we owe the pleasure?" Mrs. Melvin said as she wrapped one arm around Henry's waist as he drew up beside her.

"Well, this here is Allison Smoak," Lucas began, but Mrs. Melvin jumped in before he could finish.

"Oh, so you're Allison! We spoke on the phone! It's so

lovely to meet you," Mrs. Melvin said as she rounded the counter to stride over and greet me.

"Likewise." I smiled brightly.

"Well, I'm Gina, and this is Henry, how about we head out back and discuss everything. Your resume said you've worked as a barista before, and done some waitstaff work?" Gina confirmed as she indicated for me to head behind the counter.

Oliver released my shoulders, and I shot them a delighted look before letting Gina lead me out the back.

"Yes, I've been a barista for almost two years, I did waitressing too," I said as we headed down the short hall and into the office on the left.

"Toilets are right across." Gina indicated at the door opposite the office with a male and female sticker on it. "So, you've just moved here to study right? Veterinary science, right?" Gina checked as she closed the door behind us.

"Yes, that's right. I'm actually living with Lucas, Oliver, and Skip. Well, Marcus as well," I added quickly.

Gina's smile faltered for the briefest moment, but I caught it.

"Sit, that must be interesting, living with those four, although, I guess you only just moved in," Gina said as she walked around the desk and sunk into the red executive office chair on the other side.

I sat down in the small black office chair, resting my worn handbag on my lap.

"Yes, it's been interesting, but they're all quite lovely," I said. Well, mostly. Marcus was an odd one to decipher.

"They are, they've been good boys most of their lives, Oliver has had some trouble, which I'm sure you're aware of." Gina pursed her lips as she tried to gauge how much I knew about my housemates.

"His curse, yes." I nodded.

"Yes, well, that'll pass when he reaches a certain age from what I understand. So, have you found out what days you're free?" Gina moved onto business as she shuffled some paperwork around on the desk and picked up a pen.

"Friday is my day off, and then the weekend. My schedule is only a temporary one for now, the introductory classes are this week which will determine my true schedule, but Friday will remain my free day," I explained.

"I understand, how about we don't start you until Saturday then? Give you your Friday off to get used to everything, and then get you started Saturday? We can do half shifts, we have another girl who works some days a week, and I'm sure she can do half shifts if you'd rather have some time off over the weekend to study?" Gina's hazel eyes landed on me as she held her pen poised over a form.

"I'm happy to do a full day either Saturday or Sunday, but maybe a half shift on the other day?" I suggested.

Gina nodded and scribbled it down.

"Fridays we'd love to have you from nine in the morning till three in the arvo, would that suit?" she asked, not taking her eyes off the paper.

"Yep, sounds great," I said, refraining from fiddling with my handbag strap.

"Okay, so, we'll get you in for the same hours Saturday then, and do a half shift on Sunday. And once you find out your true schedule, maybe we can get you in for some morning or evening shifts? We stay open until seven at night each day, we found it draws more customers who want a professionally made coffee later on in the evening, and take-away dinner." Gina grinned as she focused back on me. "Now, I'll need your tax file number and bank details for pay, and I've got a shirt made up for you. You said you were a size twelve, correct?"

"Yes, that's right." I nodded firmly, and Gina stood up to move over to the filing cabinet to the side of the room. She pulled the plastic bag off the top and handed it to me.

"There's two shirts in there, and an apron. I'll give you my phone number, and have you got your bank details and tax file number on you now?" she asked as I took the offered bag.

"I do." I reached into my purse, grateful I'd had the sense to write it all down.

"Great!" Gina grinned, her short hair bouncing around her face as she bobbed her head. I handed her the piece of paper and her eyes crinkled as she smiled. It was obvious her hair was dyed to be such a perfect bleached blonde. And the soft wrinkles in her face that were visible from this close position proved she was older than I'd initially thought. She'd have to be if she'd known the guys since they were kids.

"Well, I think that'll do us for today, it was very lovely to meet you, Allison," Gina said as she held out her hand.

I shook it as she grinned widely at me.

"Now, let's go see what those trouble-makers are up to?" She winked.

I knew I was going to like her already.

"So, how's Marcus doing?" Henry asked as he handed Oliver a milkshake.

I rounded the counter as Gina joined her husband, and was surprised when Lucas offered me a milkshake.

"Vanilla malt?" he said questioningly, and I gave him a grateful smile.

"Actually, it's my favorite," I said with a frown. Had he

known? No, he looked genuinely pleased at himself for getting it right as he turned back to Henry.

Maybe he just got lucky.

"Yeah, he's good, studying now," Oliver said as he slurped his milkshake. Skip had taken up a position at the closest booth, perched on the edge facing the counter as he drank his own milkshake.

Even Lucas was sipping one.

"That's good to hear, I'm glad he's getting himself out there again." Henry sighed with a soft smile.

"So, you're starting uni this year, too?" Gina asked as her eyes settled on Oliver. I took the chance to join Skip at the booth, sitting down across from him.

"Yep, I'll be doing Veterinary Science with Ally." Oliver beamed.

"Great! You'll be wonderful at it." Gina smiled happily as she clasped her hands together.

"I hear yer sister is still studying, what was it again?" Henry frowned as he glanced to his wife for assistance.

"Beauty," Oliver said, although I could hear the pitch in his voice. I didn't even know he had a sister.

Not that he'd told me anything about his family.

"Right, that's right. I thought it was more of a Tafe course, but I guess Corviticus offers shorter qualifications, too." Henry shrugged.

"She should've finished it by now, she's been studying it for two years already, it's not that long of a course." Gina frowned.

"She puts her social life first and her studies on hold," Oliver stated, his voice flat.

"Right," Gina murmured, chewing her lip as she sensed the subject was bothering Oliver. "So, you going to show Ally around tomorrow?"

"Yeah, well, I'll try, I'm only starting too, so y'know." He shrugged sheepishly.

"Well, if you're both studying Veterinary Science, then you'll probably have a few classes together." She smiled warmly.

"That's the plan, we'll try to organize our schedules to match, as I'd like Ally's help if I have some… issues." His smile faltered.

"Of course." Gina bobbed her head.

"Well, we best let you guys go," Henry said as the door-bell chimed when some new customers walked in.

"You have a good day." Oliver waved as he turned back with his milkshake in hand.

"See you Saturday, Allison!" Gina gave me a brief wave before plastering on her bright smile to welcome the new patrons.

I nodded and waved back before following the others outside to the cruiser. I was glad Lucas had thought to get takeaway milkshakes.

"All right, so you've got your uniform, you've seen the tiny main street of Maple Grove, now let's get you into Maleny, the proper town of the area." Skip chuckled as he climbed into his beast of a vehicle.

"Maple Grove will get there," said sighed as he held the door open for me. "M'lady." He bowed his head to me.

"I'm no lady," I scoffed, drawing a snort of laughter from him as I climbed into the passenger seat.

"Well, we'll give you a tour of Maleny, then we'll stop in at the bakery,. Skip grinned as he started up the engine. The cruiser sputtered and grumbled as it struggled to life.

"Why the bakery?" I asked, but I had a feeling I knew the answer already.

"Some bee sting for our little Bee Sting." Skip winked as he turned to look over his shoulder to reverse.

"Right." I chuckled.

"It's so good," Oliver moaned. "I swear it's the first time I've ever heard of it as a slice."

"Yeah, the baker there thought it'd go over well," Lucas remarked as he slurped his milkshake. Skip was the only one who had completely downed his before leaving the cafe.

I sighed as I looked out the window, content despite the rather hot and muggy weather. My new bosses seemed nice, my housemates were sweet and lovely, and tomorrow, I'd start my studies.

Life was finally looking up.

10

"Okay, you were right, this is just as good as the bee sting cakes, maybe better," I mumbled through my third bite of my bee sting slice as we sat at one of the small tables outside the bakery. The sweet buttery cream filled my mouth, and the honey coated almonds topping it were the perfect mix with the pastry on the top and bottom. Not too sweet, but delicious nonetheless. We had a perfect view of the bustling main street, and I'd discovered there were a quite a few op shops here. Four to be exact. Quite a handful for the rather small town.

Lucas had informed me it had grown to be a very big tourist town, and the airbnbs were huge here.

But the locals were still a friendly, cheery bunch, and the tourist visits were good for business.

I leaned back in my chair as Oliver polished off his piece.

"You should try the crepes next time from Maleny Alley," Skip said as he eyed some women striding past. Their short skirts were no help at all, and Lucas scoffed at Skip's lack of subtlety.

I wouldn't deny it, they were hot.

"Yeah, but the Greek stall is pretty epic," Oliver shot back.

That was what we'd gotten for lunch. Maleny had a small area past the IGA where a wide alleyway had been converted to a food market, with stalls lining both sides and a row of tables down the center. There was a stage at the end with live music—a guitarist had played us some acoustic blues while I'd devoured a haloumi wrap at Lucas' urging. I was just grateful Lucas was taking it upon himself to shout me today. I had some money, but it was going to have to get me through the week until I started my new job.

"They had Indian there, too, and a pie specialty stall, not to mention those doughnuts," I said as I ate the final bite of my slice.

God, that sweet, creamy goodness was perfection.

"Mmmm, those doughnuts are reeeaaally good," Oliver practically moaned.

"Oi, Skippy, do you mind? We have a lady with us," Lucas growled as he slapped the table in front of Skip.

"You know I hate it when I get called that," Skip groaned as he focused back on us, rather than the blonde catwalk model that had just pranced past.

What I wouldn't do to have a bust like that or legs that perfect. Uh-oh, there was my self-conscious side creeping up again.

"So, anything else I should see here?" I asked as I glanced across the road at the IGA. It was entertaining to watch the drivers struggle with the parks in this street. It was poorly designed, and it was obvious it had been a much smaller town and was struggling with a population growth.

"Not really." Skip sighed.

"Does anyone police this? Look at that guy, he just cut in front of him to park straight on into that park. They're reverse angle parks only, right?" I shook my head in utter disbelief.

"They get parking inspectors in here relatively often, but not often enough," Lucas said as he followed my gaze to the impatient older gentleman who'd cut in front of the incoming traffic to park head first on the opposite side of the road.

"This main street is chaotic for parking. You're best off parking behind the IGA and walking," Oliver stated.

"Crazy," I muttered as someone honked their horn impatiently while a woman struggled to park. For some reason she didn't get that it was an angle park, not straight.

"Did you want to do any shopping or anything while we're here?" Lucas asked, drawing my attention away from the drivers.

"Nah, I'm a bit tight on cash, but thanks," I gave him a warm smile.

"Oh, hi!" Oliver chuckled as a border collie prodded him in the leg gently with its nose.

"Dogs have a fascination with shifters, especially true shifters," Lucas said softly as he leaned forward.

"Jack, leave him alone," an older gentleman scolded as he jogged up to us. The border collie was not the first dog I'd seen in the main street off-leash.

"Oh, it's fine." Oliver waved the gentleman off as he bent over to ruffle the dog's black and white fur. "Jack's a nice name," he cooed.

Jack turned his head to me, lolling his tongue out, and I melted at the sight of his one blue eye and one brown one gazing at me expectantly.

I broke, reaching out to pat him since his owner didn't seem to mind.

"He loves his attention, but he must really like you guys to have just come up to you like that," the older man said. He was a slim man, and his skin was weathered from many years in the sun working the land. I could picture him and Jack working sheep or cattle in the blazing sun.

But my mind couldn't focus right now.

Because uneasiness had washed over me as soon as I'd touched Jack.

"How old is he?" I asked, noting that he didn't seem to have any gray around his face.

"Turned eight recently," the man said, resting his hands on his hips as he shook his head at his dog, who was reveling in the attention from Oliver and I.

"When was his last vet visit?" I asked, glancing at Oliver who was frowning, too. He said he could sense issues in animals as well, and I think he'd sensed it now. Not immediately, but maybe his ability worked differently to mine.

"A few months back, why's that?" his owner asked, and I noted the sudden defensiveness in his voice.

Damn.

"He's got some slight muscle tremors. We're studying to be vet students," Oliver jumped in.

Skip was leaning forward now in his seat, his hands clasped together as he glanced between Oliver, I, and the owner.

"Muscle tremors? You sure?" The owner's voice instantly changed to uncertainty as he knelt down. He looked to be in his sixties, and the worry evident in his eyes for his loyal friend made me purse my lips.

"I think you should take him to the vet," I said, running my hand along Jack's sides as I tried to understand what the issue was. When I'd sensed cancer in my colleagues Labrador, I'd sensed growths, deadly growths inside him. But with Jack, I sensed something painful, something attacking his organs, his kidneys.

"Ask them to check for poisoning," I said, suddenly understanding the sensation I was receiving.

"Jesus, are you sure?" his owner murmured as he patted Jack on the head.

Jack looked completely at ease, but I could feel his elevated levels, his tension and unease. I could sense it all.

"Yes, you'd best make sure he gets checked soon if possible," I said with a firm nod.

"Oh, of course, we'll head over right now! Thank you." The man stood quickly, giving a sharp whistle as he turned away.

Jack shot after him, and he jogged alongside his worried owner, who walked briskly with jarred movements.

"What was that about?" Skip asked once the man was out of earshot.

"Ally can sense illnesses in animals, hers seems to be stronger than mine. How'd you know it was poisoning?" Oliver frowned.

"I don't know, I just got a feeling," I said softly, hating how all three of them were solely focused on me now, scrutinizing me.

"I've never heard of such an ability in the fae before, only true shifters, and not even they can distinguish exactly what it is," Lucas remarked as he cocked his head, chewing his lip as he stared at me, as if the answer would reveal itself.

"Does it work on people?" Skip asked.

"I don't know, I don't even know what it is, just that I've felt it in animals. It started with a colleague's Labrador, then a cat at my last rental. I decided to go into Veterinary Science to put it to good use and to help animals," I said, shifting uneasily under their heavy gazes.

"Interesting," Lucas murmured, those green eyes flashing with intrigue and curiosity.

"I hope his dog's okay, I mean, something is wrong with him, but hopefully they can fix it," Oliver said sadly as he looked off in the direction they'd headed. "We should've gotten his name so we could've checked in with him."

"Well, we know the dog's name? Maybe we could call the vet later and ask?" Skip suggested.

"It'd be confidential, they wouldn't be able to tell us." Lucas waved the idea off.

He had drawn quite a few gazes in his lavish suit, so I could safely assume he wasn't masking his appearance with magic.

"I can't wait until I get taught how to sense others like me, other supes," I murmured as I rolled my eyes over my companions. They looked like a trio of regular guys hanging out, well, except for the eccentric one who looked like he'd stepped out of the seventies.

I'd never have known any better.

"They'll teach you in your magic classes, but most supes already know how to from a young age. But since your powers were masked with magic, then you wouldn't have had full access to your powers. I could show you, if you'd like?" Lucas offered.

"What? Right here?" I frowned as I glanced around at the people drifting past, conversing and laughing.

"Yes, don't worry, it won't reveal your magic or anything," Lucas assured me.

"It's pretty easy once you learn it, you'll start doing it automatically," Oliver said with a boyish grin.

"There's a few supes here in Maleny, they come over from Maple Grove, but there are some who reside here," Skip added.

"How?" I murmured as I leaned forward, resting my elbows on the table as I played with the end of my ponytail.

"Close your eyes," Lucas commanded.

I frowned, and he rolled his eyes.

"Trust me, I'm here, if anything goes wrong, I can handle it," he said with that deliciously charming, crooked smile.

I sighed and closed my eyes, biting my lip as I heard Oliver drag his seat closer.

"Now, imagine your power, your essence and energy, is flowing through you, feel it, and acknowledge it," Lucas said.

"How?" I groaned. They weren't exactly proper instructions.

"You said you can feel when your mischief magic is coming on when you're not in warded zones? Well, imagine it, the sensation you get when it comes on," Oliver coaxed me.

Okay, now that was more informative.

I imagined it, that tingling, electric spark that churned my gut as it washed over me.

"Now, once you feel it, imagine it reaching out, brushing over all those walking around you, all those in your vicinity," Lucas murmured.

I focused, the tingling shooting through me as I clasped my hands together.

"You want to feel for the same thing inside others, start with me, can you feel me, sense me?" Oliver asked from my left, his voice extremely close.

I arched my eyebrows in shock as I felt it. It was like I could feel his outline, his presence, amongst all the other walking shadows. He was a speck inside my mind of utter vibrancy and rainbow colors.

"Rainbow." I chuckled.

"Yep, that's a true shifter." Lucas clapped his hands, pleased with my realization.

"Skip, you're a yellow, although tinged with orange," I

murmured, focusing on his presence in my mind, my eyes still closed.

"Yellow is shifters, and depending on what they are, you'll get a mix of other colors in there," Skip said, and I could hear the delighted smile in his voice.

"And Luke, you're purple," I snorted, grinning at the obvious color. "Although, it looks like a galaxy really."

"Warlocks are galaxy-like, normal witches are plain purple," Lucas said.

"Can you sense others?" Oliver asked softly, his warm breath washing over my ear and making a shiver of warmth run through me.

I could.

As I reached further, I could feel others walking in the street. Mostly shifters. I could sense a witch inside the IGA.

I opened my eyes, my mouth falling open at the slightest tinges of color around my three companions.

"When you focus, you'll see it." Lucas grinned, knowing exactly what I could see. It was incredible, like a galaxy was swirling off his body.

"This is awesome," I breathed.

"Welcome to the underworld, baby," Skip said and chuckled as Oliver shook his head with a laugh.

"What color am I?" I asked curiously.

"You'll be a pink with a little yellow and gray, at least, I think wolf shifters are gray," Skip mused.

"Amazing," I murmured.

I let my senses fall back to normal, watching in amazement as the colors radiating around the edges of my companions faded away.

That hadn't been too hard.

"Sensing others is one of the first things we're taught as children, so it's not too difficult," Skip said.

"Oh."

"Still, you got it pretty quickly," Oliver said as he shot Skip a look.

I had been pretty chuffed about myself.

"He is right," Skip said quickly, and Lucas just shook his head and sighed as he stretched.

"Well, let's go for a drive, we've still got plenty of daylight, might as well show Ally just how beautiful this area is," Lucas said as he pushed his seat out and stood.

I tried to pretend I didn't feel let down by finding out my quick on-the-spot learning wasn't as epic as I'd thought it was. Hell, I'd still believe it was great for my first time.

I played with my silver charm bracelet as I stood up with the boys, and we headed off across the street to make our way back to the cruiser.

The sun beat down on us, and I was more than happy when we slipped back into the shade. I'd thought it was hot the other night, nope, today was a scorcher. We'd barely gotten a storm yesterday, just heavy rain and the occasional flash of lightning. We'd definitely get something tonight, no doubt about it.

Being the lone girl with three dazzling guys earned me a number of looks from those walking by, including a group of schoolgirls who ogled my three companions and giggled as they whispered to one another.

A pang of jealousy washed over me, and I nearly tripped on the sidewalk at the sudden sensation.

I had no right to feel that way. These were my housemates.

Not to mention the jealousy wasn't specific to any of my three companions.

Ohhh boy.

I tried to busy my mind, instead focusing on the thought of my new job.

Gina and Henry were friendly and nice, and the cafe offered air-conditioning, which was a step up from my last job.

"Hey, what are Gina and Henry?" I asked as we traversed the gentle sloping sidewalk down to the carpark behind the large IGA building. It was covered so that shoppers wouldn't be doing mad trolley runs in the rain down the slope, but the carpark itself was uncovered.

"What do you mean?" Skip asked as his arm brushed mine, sending a hot tingle through me which I squashed down.

"Supes? Everyone is supes in Maple Grove, right?" I clarified.

"Yep! Gina is a shifter, a koala actually, and Henry is a shifter too, crocodile I believe. Get him riled up, and he can get scary," Oliver said as he walked out in front, leading the way back to the cruiser.

"A koala," I murmured. Interesting to know.

"Yeah, every now and then as a kid, I'd see her shifted. They have a few eucalyptus trees out the back of their place, and she'd go sit in one, sleeping and eating. It'd drive Henry mad, but it apparently really rejuvenated her and gave her a heap of energy. She wouldn't sleep much after a day or two of being shifted and she'd get so much done." Oliver laughed at the memory.

"Well, considering koalas sleep for eighteen hours a day, I can understand that." Lucas chuckled.

"If you're wondering, reptile shifters can put on weight easily. They're a little cold-blooded and slow like their counterparts, and yet they still eat and drink like a normal person. Snakes and crocodiles don't eat often, snakes vary from once a week to once a month average, sometimes even longer between meals, and crocs are similar, I think. So that's why he's a bit on the bigger side," Skip explained.

"Do they have kids? And what would a child end up being anyway?" I asked.

"They have a daughter, she ended up being a crocodile shifter, she lives down in Brissy now," Oliver said.

"With shifters, the child has a fifty-fifty chance of being the same as one of their parents. But if only one parent is a shifter, they're more likely to be whatever the non-shifter parent is. Seventy-five percent chance of not being a shifter," Lucas added.

"So, if a shifter ended up with a witch, the kid would be a witch most likely?" I checked.

"Yep, but in rare cases, like, quite rare, they can be both. A shifter-witch, or like you, a wolf-fae halfling," Skip stated as we reached the cruiser.

I shielded my eyes from the sun glinting off the bonnet, and mulled over this.

So I was a rarity then? Halflings weren't too common by the sounds of things.

Guess that made me special.

"So, how about we head up to the lookout out at Reesville? Or check out Gardners Falls?" Skip suggested as he unlocked the cruiser.

It didn't have central locking, so he had to climb in and reach over to unlock my door and then the back door.

"No, definitely not Gardners, it'll be crowded as hell today." Lucas shook his head firmly. "Lookout will be good. And we'll just drive around the back streets, explore."

"There's some really nice places tucked away out on the back roads, you'll love them." Oliver beamed as Lucas held my door open for me yet again.

Such a gentleman.

I climbed in after thanking him, and the cruiser sputtered to life as I rolled down the window to let the breeze in.

"Still wish we had a way of finding out about Jack." Oliver sighed as we pulled out of the carpark.

"He'll be okay," I said, but I did wonder. His owner seemed quite stressed by the possibility that his furry friend was sick, so surely he was at the vet now getting it sorted.

I hoped.

"It's a shame Marcus can't come out with us," I said as I rested my arm on the window frame, the cool rush of air caressing my skin as we pulled out into the main street.

No one said a word at that, and I glanced back at Oliver and Lucas to see if I'd hit a button.

They both looked a little saddened by my comment.

"He used to come out with us, before he got turned," Oliver murmured as he rested his head back, the wind blowing through his open window ruffling his messy brown locks.

"Marcus used to paint and draw a lot, he'd always bring a sketchbook with him wherever we went. Such talent." Lucas smiled as he gazed out the window, playing with the cuff of his suit. How he wasn't overheating was a mystery to me. Magic, I guess.

I frowned at this.

Marcus was an artist? I couldn't picture that really. I mean, maybe the dark, brooding artist type, but he'd only ever tucked himself away behind his laptop whenever I saw him.

"He used to?" I said softly.

"Yeah, he stopped when he got turned," Skip said as he focused hard on the road. No one seemed to want to look at me now.

"His pieces were so realistic sometimes, you'd think they were photos." Oliver's mouth tugged into a small smile. "He just focuses on his gaming now, and game design."

Hiding himself away. That's what Oliver was really saying.

Marcus was avoiding everyone, keeping to himself and holding everyone at arm's length.

How was that any way to live?

My mind wandered back to how they said someone got hurt. Did that have something to do with this? I didn't doubt it.

The cruiser fell into silence, and I sighed as I looked back out the window.

Maybe I'd try to talk to him tonight.

I relaxed under the warm spray of water, flinching when another crack of thunder tore overhead.

I'd been spot on. We'd spent the better part of an hour driving around, and then sat at the lookout for a while just chatting about TV shows, arguing about which superhero was the best in the Avengers movies. It was interesting hearing the differing arguments by the three men. It seemed all of them enjoyed the Marvel movies, although only Ollie and Marcus were big on catching them as soon as they released.

And we watched as those dark, ominous clouds rolled in over the acres of farmland. Our perfect view all around from the lookout was amazing, and I could see the Glasshouse Mountains with ease, and even the coast way in the distance.

We decided to head home once the rain started, and I spent the remainder of the afternoon watching some more 'Good Place' with Oliver until the power went out. Lucas offered to use magic to get it all going again, but I wanted to catch a nap.

Now I was in the shower, the warm water washing over me and waking me up properly after my nap. Apparently, either the power had come back on, or Lucas had sorted it out.

Either way, I was grateful, otherwise I'd be showering in the dark.

Thunder rumbled and snapped outside as the rain hammered down on the roof, and I focused on scrubbing myself.

I shuddered as a loud thunderclap rattled the house, and I resigned myself to hurriedly washing.

I knew it was an old wives' tale to not shower in thunderstorms, but getting dressed and into my cozy pajamas sounded good, along with a hot milo.

I finished up quickly and clambered out, sighing at the warmth washing over me from the heat light overhead.

I wrapped the towel around me, grumbling at the fact that I'd forgotten to grab my clothes this time thanks to my groggy state.

I headed for the bathroom door, flicking the switches off as I unlocked it and stepped into the hall.

Lightning flashed outside, lighting up the hall and making me jump in fright as a shadow caught the corner of my eye.

"Jesus, you scared me," I gasped, willing my heart to calm down as I looked at Marcus, who stood outside his door.

"Sorry," he apologized, catching me by surprise.

I wouldn't have expected an apology from him.

"Hey, are you going to come join us downstairs? I think Skip was going to make a roast tonight, although, I guess you can't eat it..." I trailed off as I rubbed my arm nervously. Stupid. He was a vampire, of course he didn't eat.

He gave a soft half laugh as he smirked, those frosty eyes trailing over me as the lightning lit up the hallway once more. I was tempted to cross over to the wall to flick the hall light on to better see him, but I resisted.

"I was already coming down to use my laptop," he said, his smooth voice almost drowned out by the pounding rain and another rumble of thunder.

"Oh, good." I nodded.

"You better get dressed before you catch a cold or something," he said, his smirk fading as his shoulders rose back up.

Again, the walls were slammed back up.

"Right." I sighed, dragging my eyes away from the dark vampire as I crossed to my room. I didn't even see him flit past, just felt the slightest whoosh of air.

"Hey, I'm on a local Facebook group, and you won't believe this, but that guy just posted wanting to thank the 'two vet students' he met in the main street. He says here that '*Jack must have ingested some rat poison over the last few days without my knowledge, and without their quick diagnosis, he could have wound up a lot worse, but thankfully, with the help of the vet, he's on the road to recovery*'," Lucas said as he joined us in the living room while reading his phone screen.

I'd just sat down beside Oliver as Skip played some Metal Gear Solid. Lucas had been in the library until now.

"Oh, awesome!" Oliver grinned as he nestled into the lounge cushions with a blanket wrapped around him.

"I'm glad to hear that," I said, a part of me relaxing at the news. I had wondered about little Jack.

"I've been doing some research, trying to understand

why you have this ability. Being part 'wolf, I thought maybe it was that, but apparently your shifter wolf side is not the dominant gene, the fae side is. Something to do with how it was your mother who was the fae, and how they're a more powerful gene than the shifter gene." Lucas waved it off. "I haven't come up with any explanation yet, but I'll keep looking into it." He gave me his charming lopsided smile.

And for a change, he was now in tracksuit pants and a plain black top. And he looked fine as hell out of a suit, so much so that I was struggling to keep my eyes off him.

"How's the roast coming along?" he asked as he turned to Skip on the other lounge.

"Good, it's in the oven, it'll take another half an hour, I set the timer," Skip said, focused on the mission he was battling his way through.

"I thought Marcus was coming down here?" I frowned.

"He was, he's in the library now," Lucas said as he flicked his head over his shoulder.

"Well, I'll get a round of hot milos sorted, who wants one?" Lucas asked the room.

"Yes, please," I said with a smile as Oliver nodded and Skip grunted in approval.

"Right," Lucas said with an eye roll directed at Skip. He strode off, and I chewed my lip.

I knew I should go see Marcus. Ever since this morning, I'd softened a little towards him.

There was more to why he was an arse at times. And I wanted to see that other side of him more.

"I'll be back," I murmured to Oliver as I stood.

He just nodded, his eyes not straying from the TV as Skip cursed softly while he struggled with his current mission.

Boys and their toys.

I padded into the library, pulling my old gray jacket tighter around my shoulders.

Marcus sat at the desk with his laptop set up before him, and from my position, it looked like he was working on a character concept perhaps?

"Hey," I said softly as I strode over to the desk and leaned against the edge of it.

He grunted in acknowledgement, not drawing his eyes away from the screen.

"What are you working on?" I asked.

"Stuff," he muttered.

"What kind of stuff?" I urged, folding my hands into my lap.

"Game stuff."

"What kind of game stuff?" I pushed, not willing to let him force me away.

"You're persistent, aren't you?" He gave me a smirk as he finally pulled those icy eyes away from the screen to look at me.

Damn, he was godly beautiful to look at. The porcelain skin only added to his tempting features.

"Well, I don't think you're the big mean vampire you pretend to be." I shrugged.

"I don't try to be," he said, his mouth still curved up in that devilish smirk.

"Well, you certainly act like a dick sometimes," I said bluntly.

He just looked away and sighed before focusing on me again.

"You should be careful with vampires, we're dangerous," he murmured as he leaned forward.

"I don't think you are." I shrugged nonchalantly.

"You barely know me," his voice was almost a whisper.

"I know your friends, and they're sweet and kind, and you've known them for most of your life. I can only assume that underneath that cold exterior, you're like them, too," I said, surprised at my own confidence as I leaned forward to stare at him.

His eyes narrowed as he stood slowly, those cold eyes sweeping over me once again.

"I'm not who I was when I grew up with them," he growled softly. Now I was looking up at him, and he was dangerously close, only the smallest of gaps dividing us.

"Why? Because you're a vampire now?" I asked quietly, searching his eyes for answers.

What was he hiding?

"Partly." His mouth pulled back into a scowl. "You should be mindful, little pixie."

"I'm not little," I shot back instantly.

I gasped as he moved, closing the gap between us as his face dropped down to my neck.

A shiver of fear and uncertainty tore through me as I froze.

"You have no idea how tempting you smell to vampires," he purred, his cool breath washing over my neck.

"Are you going to bite me?" I asked, not trying to sugar-coat it.

"No," he growled as he pulled back, but he paused by my cheek as he drew in my scent. "You'll be courted by other vamps, those wanting to turn you into their own personal blood bag," he stated.

"I'll be careful." I frowned. He sure was acting weird. Really weird.

"Why do you push everyone away?" I blurted, hating the strange tension that had settled over us.

He drew in a sharp breath as he looked away.

"You ask a lot of questions," he muttered.

"Well, I'm living here now. We're going to be running into each other a lot," I said.

"Doesn't mean we have to talk."

"You seemed a little more talkative this morning," I reminded him, trying to shake off our peculiar moment.

"Don't get used to it," was his instant reply.

"I liked the you from this morning better than this you," I snapped. There he was again, the prick.

"This me is the real me," he retorted.

"I don't think it is, I think the real you is hiding under this arseholey version of you," I said as I pushed off the table. "And he's a lot better, the real you."

"The real me is gone," he murmured as I strode away, so softly that I almost didn't hear it.

11

LUCAS

"Look at you in that gay get-up, trying to impress someone," Cathy sneered from her perch on the luxurious blue lounge in the living area.

"Oh, sweet Cat, you wouldn't know how to be impressed," I shot back as I gave her a sarcastic curtsy.

"Lucas, put on something more appropriate, purple is not what you want to wear," my mother huffed as she breezed into the room in her perfectly fitted baby-pink ballgown dress. Her golden hair was sculpted carefully in a perfect updo, a few locks falling free in lovely curls to frame her face. Cathy was just a younger version of her, her hair done up in a bridal style bun. She wore a baby-blue dress, a similar design to our mother's.

They could've passed for sisters if Mother was younger.

"Where's Father?" Cathy asked, and I cringed at the snark in her voice. She knew he'd fume at my attire.

"He'll be along shortly," our mother replied.

"Did Lucas tell you who his date was?" Cat said, seemingly bored as she checked her hair with light touches, *straightening her dress as she bounced one glittery silver heel on the polished white tiles.*

"It better be Sarah, or so help me." My mother turned on me, fear and distaste flashing in those emerald eyes.

"Oh, no, it's not Sarah." Cat's face broke into a devious grin. I scowled at her, at her desire to fuck things up for me, always.

"Lucas, please, tell me you didn't." My mother's pained eyes fell on me.

I gritted my teeth at the utter grief I saw there, the shame she had for me.

"Why would he bother anyone?" I snapped, folding my arms as I glared hateful daggers at my troublesome sister.

"Because, it's not right!" my mother huffed, frazzled at this hiccup in her plans.

"No, I'm not right, that's what you mean," I hissed.

"No." My mother closed her eyes as she drew in a calming breath.

"Oh look, daddy's here," Cathy sung out.

I tensed as I sensed him coming up behind me, the terseness ringing out clear in his voice.

"Get changed, now!"

"No! You know what? Screw this stupid event! You can count me out!" I snapped, fuming as I stormed to the door. I could feel my father's disapproving gaze burning a hole into my back, not bothering to say a word as I walked out the front door.

Too bad it would be one of my final times.

I caught myself, dragging my mind from the memory as I flipped through yet another book with my hot milo in hand.

Even at sixteen, I knew I was different, not gay, but not

straight either. Bisexual, apparently. And at only sixteen, I'd met my first love.

Daniel.

Too bad it was too good to be true. The struggle with my family had fractured us, and despite me moving into the house left to me by my grandfather at his passing, we fell apart.

I smiled as I ran my fingers over the old book of supernatural creatures. Rarer creatures, lesser known specimens of our kind.

I was hoping to find something to help me understand just what Allison was. No fae could sense issues in animals like she could, but it was the dominant side of her, rendering the abilities that her 'wolf side had useless. She could still shift, retaining the basics of her other half side, but her senses were of no use, which was strange for a halfling. Most shifter halflings still retained their basic traits, but additional abilities, like sensing illness or whatever the supes specialty was, would be nullified. Maybe something was different with her. The ability stayed, but she lost her wolf senses? No, I hadn't found anything like that, but I was starting to think she was just some utterly bizarre occurrence, a one-in-a-million thing.

Definitely not normal, and nothing I'd ever seen before, but I couldn't rule it out as a possibility.

I flipped back to the title page, sighing at my grandfather's handwriting.

'To my dearest Lucas, you are special and perfect the way you are. You may feel like a rarity, but you're not, you are one of many.'

It was his way of accepting me just the way I was, and he'd gifted me the book to prove that just because it wasn't known or recognized widely, didn't mean it wasn't real.

He'd known since I'd hit puberty apparently, and he'd

taken me in countless times when my parents had troubled me with their harsh words. They refused to accept me for the way I was, but I couldn't deny it.

I spent many days and nights, even weeks, in this house. Even Oliver stayed over when his parents caused him trouble.

Two troubled boys, hiding away with a welcoming adult figure.

My grandfather had been good to us, all of us.

This home, all four of us had spent time here over the years, accepted fully by my grandfather until his death. I'd been forever grateful that he'd passed in his sleep, a peaceful death, rather than something worse. I hoped I'd pass the same way one day.

I sighed as I closed the book and laid it back down on my desk. I'd rather be in the library, but Marcus was in there, and Allison had gone to speak with him briefly before returning to slump on the lounge in annoyance.

We'd had the delicious roast dinner, but she was lost in thought for the most part, probably after some weird interaction with Marcus no doubt.

She wouldn't understand the way he was. He was still hurting, still broken inside.

And she, being a fae, made it more painful. She drew him like a moth to flame, whether she knew it or not, and he fought it every step of the way.

I didn't question whether he'd hurt her. He still had witch blood in him, and he was not a young vampire anymore, he'd been turned for a few years. He could control himself around a fae.

But I knew it still pained him.

He pretended he had no regard for her, but he'd asked something of me tonight.

Just a small favor to help her out.

It made me smile softly to myself. The Marcus I'd grown up with, the sweet, artistic, kind Marcus, he was still in there, hiding beneath that icy mask, trying to protect himself from more harm.

Oliver had told me Allison had burn scars that looked to be cigarette burns, amongst others.

I guess this was a house for the broken.

No one here didn't have a story behind them, a past that they battled with in some way.

I sat back, holding my hands together as the magic flickered from my fingers.

"Sleep well tonight, Allison. Sweet dreams."

12

I awoke to the alarm sounding off on my iPod on the bedside table.

I fumbled for it, peering at it with one hazy eye to tap the snooze button.

Just five more minutes.

Five more minutes of blissful sleep. I'd had no nightmares plaguing me for a sweet change, and I wanted to cling to the peaceful slumber.

Except today was my first day at uni.

I sighed, rolling onto my back as I forced my eyes open.

Excitement coursed through me, along with an uneasiness that churned in the pit of my belly.

Magic classes. Why was I so worried about them rather than my actual degree?

Well, because Lucas was just as confused by my abilities.

Not to mention everyone else probably had a family that had taught them about themselves.

Me? Nope. I'd had a dingo shifter teach me how to shift into a wolf, but no one had taught me about my fae side. When my aunt had bothered teaching my cousin, I was told to stay in my room, and it was hard to overhear anything from there.

I dragged myself out of bed, deciding I'd change now before heading downstairs. I went with a pair of dark jeans and a teal shirt, and decided to grab my old gray jacket just in case. A glance out my window revealed it was overcast, but not raining. I wouldn't take my chances with throwing on something less warm.

The weather up here was so unpredictable. Scorching one day, freezing wet the next.

I tromped down the stairs, finding a barely alert Oliver slumped at the kitchen table while Lucas poured some cereal into a bowl.

I'd bought myself Nutri-grain the other day, a staple of my diet.

"Morning, how'd you sleep?" Lucas asked as he flicked his hand and the fridge door opened to allow the milk to float over to him.

"Good, really good," I said as I grabbed myself a bowl and the Nutri-grain box from the cupboard.

"That's awesome." Lucas nodded as he served up some Weet-bix for Oliver.

"Thanks," Oliver said with a yawn.

I reached for the milk on the counter, but froze as it floated up and poured over the top of my Nutri-grain for me.

Lucas was giving me his charming smile, and I just rolled my eyes.

"Skip starts late today?" I checked as I joined Oliver at the table.

"Yeah, doesn't start until ten today. You two start at nine, same as me, so I'll show you to your first introductory lecture. Oliver said it's room 309. I can show you to it," Lucas said as he sat down with his own bowl of Weet-bix.

"Thanks, hey, is it still okay for me to borrow your laptop? I'll have to wait another few weeks, I have some money saved up, but the move and everything ate up a chunk of it, I'll need to save for a little while before I'll be able to afford my own," I said with my spoon poised over my bowl.

"It's fine, I've got an old one you can use." Lucas waved me off, his navy blue suit an intriguing sight.

"You sure? Maybe I can buy it off you later on if possible?" I suggested.

"Yeah, sure, if you want. It's not being used anyway. Got an apple ID?" he asked before taking a mouthful of his Weet-bix.

Oliver had propped himself up on one hand as he ate, his brown mop of hair a disheveled mess.

"Yeah, why?"

"It's a MacBook."

Damn. I'd never owned a Mac before. My last laptop had been an Acer, second-hand from my cousin, which I'd had to buy off her. It had died after only a year, but it had done the job for my schooling, and a few weeks after, I was working, so had no need for one.

Thankfully, my second job after my retail position, working as a barista and waitress, also consisted of light bookkeeping duties, which they had a small MacBook for. So I'd learned the interface of the computer already.

"Well, I'll get it set up after breakfast for you and you can take it today," Lucas said.

"Oh, thank you, you're amazing," I said warmly. God, he was a lifesaver right now.

"That's me," he said with a scoff. "Amazing and dazzling."

Oliver chuckled through a mouthful of food at this, and I just grinned.

I'd been stressing about needing a laptop for my studies, and had been trawling ads online at the library for second-hand ones before I moved.

Having my own laptop and way of googling and such would be a godsend.

Next would be a phone.

"So, you know your rough schedule?" Lucas asked.

"Not really, just the introductory lectures today, and then I'll adjust my schedule accordingly. I need to try to match it with Oliver to help him out," I reminded him as he nodded and his green eyes flicked to our tired companion.

"Thanks, that means a lot." Oliver gave me a small smile.

"You okay? You seem pretty tired?" I frowned.

"I'll be fine, just had a moment where the curse nearly kicked in. If I focus my breathing, sometimes I can stop it from taking over and forcing a shift. I really didn't want to be stuck as a cat on my first day." He sighed.

Lucas gave him a sad smile as he patted his shoulder.

"That sucks, I'm sorry," I murmured.

"It's fine. I'll wake up properly once I get changed and get ready," Oliver said with a shrug. He was wearing a spider-man top and blue boxers, which made me smile.

"Anyone ever told you that you look like Tom Holland?" I said with a grin.

Oliver's face lit up and Lucas groaned.

"Yeah, if only. Spider-man is pretty cool, the actor does most of his own stunts, too, he's a dancer and gymnast." Oliver beamed, chuffed at the lookalike compliment.

"I think he played one of the best spider-man's. Actually fit the age bracket," I said, causing Oliver to clap his hands as he bobbed his head.

"Yes! Right?" He shot a look at Lucas who just rolled his eyes.

"Look, I'm not saying he isn't good, I'm just saying I liked the Andrew Garfield movies *as well*," Lucas emphasized.

"Wasn't a fan of his aunt, though. Too young," I added, causing Ollie to pout. At least he was suddenly awake now.

"Well, Cupcake, would you like to accompany me to the library after breakfast and we'll get the MacBook set up for you before we head off?" Lucas cut Oliver off just as he opened his mouth to respond to my unhappiness with the aunt.

"That'd be awesome, thank you again, you're a lifesaver." I sighed as I shoveled more cereal into my mouth.

"I aim to please." Lucas chuckled.

I focused on finishing up quickly, glancing at the clock on the microwave which read seven forty-five. Hopefully an hour was easily enough time to get it set up.

I couldn't help but be a little excited at the prospect of having a MacBook. I'd finally be able to google again, and do research and online reading. And back up my ancient iPod touch.

It certainly needed it.

I gripped my laptop bag strap tightly as I stood before the lecture hall with Oliver, grateful for his comforting presence beside me.

Lucas had set up the MacBook with me, downloading pages and the other free programs that would be useful for my studies. He'd even given me a laptop bag, saying it was mine to keep, since the only other bags I had to use were my gym bag and my pathetic little handbag.

I'd checked my emails quickly, then decided to deal with that later considering the massive number of unread emails.

I pulled a photo from the google storage drive I had set up with my Gmail account, and set it up as my screensaver. A picture of my real parents on their wedding day, posing under a white archway.

They looked so happy and perfect. I was glad I'd uploaded all my photos to my google drive from my old laptop. I'd found the photos when I'd borrowed my Aunt's laptop for an assignment once when mine played up.

She'd unhappily allowed me to use it for school, and I was surprised to find photos of my mother and father. So I'd quickly emailed them to myself, grateful she'd always left it logged in, and then deleted them from the sent folder.

Lucas had asked if I had Facebook, and I'd laughed. I'd never had a reason for it, I barely had friends growing up. Hard to make friends when they weren't part of your world. Technically I'd made a fake one for Tinder, but I'd never done anything with it, and when I'd deleted said dating app, I'd deleted the profile too.

I was jealous of the boys upbringing, being part of the supe community. They were lucky. Me, not so much.

He'd suggested I get it, especially since I might make friends now and it was an easy way to stay in touch. Not to mention I could search for family.

Family.

A touchy subject.

"Well, you ready?" Oliver asked as another student pushed through the door and into the hall, while we remained outside.

I'd expected more when we got here, more magic, maybe shifted shifters, some hurled spells, anything. But no, it seemed like a regular University.

How'd I know that? Well, I'd gone to one on an excursion in high school, paid for by myself, of course. As soon as I'd turned thirteen, I'd found an afternoon job at a pizza hut to make some money to afford a phone and to buy the laptop off my cousin. Amongst other things. I even hung out with kids from school, but I'd never go so far as to say they were friends. They never knew the real me.

"Guess so," I said.

Oliver took my hand, giving it a gentle squeeze, before pulling me into the lecture hall with him.

I relaxed when I realized it wasn't so bad.

At least Lucas had brought us to it, otherwise we would've been lost.

But the atmosphere was quiet and calm as students chatted quietly and got their notebooks out. I'd brought a notebook to jot things down in, along with the recommended textbook.

I'd seen the email briefly for my login details for the campus website, so I could do some lessons and lectures online if I chose to, and to check schedules and rooms. I'd make sure to check it all out later.

We found a spot off to the side, the red-cushioned seats rather comfy as I sunk into mine. I pulled the little fold-out table over my lap and got out a notebook and pen from my laptop bag.

The high ceiling was painted cream along with the walls, and the front of the room had a large white presentation screen ready for us. The seats were curved around to favor the small platform at the front of the room, so we could all get a good look at the lecturer.

"Nothing to be worried about," Oliver assured me, but I wondered if it was truly for my benefit or his own as his amber eyes flicked around the room nervously.

More students filed in, and I spied two lecturers standing

at the front of the room going over notes and setting up a presentation screen.

The white board came to life as the projector beamed down on it, the symbol of a phoenix on a shield at the center of it.

"You know, my life would've been so much easier if I could've made it here for the Orientation week," I mumbled.

"Don't worry, why do you think Lucas had to show us to our room? I skipped it. Was kinda… incapacitated. As a cat," Oliver muttered.

I watched as the second lecturer left, leaving the main one with us.

I'd missed Orientation week, meaning I was plunged headfirst into all this. The University had been quite understanding with me and handled getting my magic class sorted for me, which was one of things I would've done in the orientation week. Along with just familiarizing myself with the campus. At least I'd gone over my map.

"Good morning all!" The lecturer's voice rang out, hushing the chattering crowd and plunging the room into silence.

"I may have met some of you last week when you were getting yourselves acquainted with the campus and getting some of your classes sorted. For some of you, this will be my first time meeting you, and I'd like to formally welcome you to the Corviticus University." The lecturer beamed as she straightened her white button-up blouse. Her dark hair was done up in a professional bun, and she wore a pencil skirt with some small black heels.

"My name is Dr. Thawne, and I'll be one of your wonderful team of lecturers here to help you learn," she said as she pushed her wiry framed glasses up her crooked nose. She looked no older than forty.

"Today, we'll go over your syllabus, and we'll get your practical and laboratory days assigned. We run a few lectures on the same topics, so you can structure your schedule to suit you. Once we're done with that, we'll move on to the introduction to Animal Management for Veterinarians, which I will be your main lecturer for," Dr. Thawne's voice rung loud and clear in the rather small lecture hall.

It couldn't house more than two hundred students, and barely half of the seats were filled.

I rested my hands on my notebook, my eyes flicking to Oliver as he rummaged in his own laptop bag to pull out a notebook.

We waited patiently for the papers to reach us as they were passed along by the other students. Thankfully, we'd sat at the back behind some others, so we didn't have to get up as the stack made its way to us.

I eyed the syllabus that Oliver handed me, scanning over the topics we'd be covering this semester. Good. I had all of these textbooks already.

"Now, let's move on to choosing your practical days. You have two weeks to come to me if the days are no longer suitable, but you are required to complete six hours of prac per animal grouping. This is the timetable available, and I'll organize you all into groups by your preference," Mrs. Thawne explained as she clicked her laptop and the projector screen changed to a list of days.

It would be one full day of prac for some, or split days. It was possible to group your prac altogether to complete them in one day.

"What do you think?" Oliver asked me in a hushed tone as murmurs filled the room.

"I'm not sure, we could do Tuesday, that way it keeps it all in the one day and we stay in the mindset," I said as I flicked my gaze over the timetable. Tuesday would be good, I'd finish my day at three and could go to work afterwards for a few hours.

And then on the Tuesdays with no prac, I could work full days, considering how it appeared we'd get every second week off from prac if we didn't split the days.

"All right, we'll do that then." Oliver nodded firmly as he jotted it down.

We waited for Mrs. Thawne to ask the students who wanted to do the full day on Tuesday, and we put our hands up.

With the schedules out of the way, we moved onto our actual lecture, and I bowed forward as I jotted down as many notes as I could before I exchanged the notebook for the laptop. I owed Lucas big time.

"So, first lecture wasn't so bad." Oliver grinned as we sat under the shade of a large fig tree set away on the edge of the campus courtyard. Our next lecture didn't start until ten-thirty, in the building opposite where our first lecture was. There were many smaller buildings all around the campus, and it was set up in a large O shape, the large reception and office building with the library in the second story being the main entry point, although there was some parking for students if you followed a side street down to the back of the University. Then more buildings were down towards the back forming the O shape. The Athletics track was found at the end of it, just before the carpark at the back, and the center of the O consisted of smaller buildings, the main courtyard for lunch, assorted food kiosks, and even some small shops.

My map had informed me that the Veterinary clinic we'd

be doing our prac in was located behind the student car park down the back.

"How many students come here?" I asked as I enjoyed the break in the overhead clouds and soaked up the sun's warmth.

"About 3,000, I think. It can't accommodate much more, and many students choose to go down to the Brisbane Universities after school, better chance of getting a job afterwards in the city." Ollie shrugged as he pulled out a caramello koala from his bag.

I rolled my eyes at his snack, and he just winked as he bit its head off.

"Mostly students come from on the range here, maybe a bit further out. You get the odd bunch from the coast like you," Ollie mumbled through a mouthful of chocolate and caramel goodness.

"Well, I'm just glad that almost all the animal husbandry and handling can be done on the campus down at the clinic. It's cool that they offer almost free services to the public to train us." I grinned. It was an awesome concept, because we also did work on farm animals right here, all but the pigs, as they were a bio-security issue, and would be handled at a piggery off campus.

"Yeah, it'll be good. We don't have our first specialized day until week three. Horse in the morning, sheep in the afternoon." Oliver nodded as he checked his notes again. The teacher would make a list available on the student portal and a template schedule that we could use to build ours with.

"I've never worked with farm animals," I murmured. I'd handled dogs, cats, birds, etc, but nothing farm wise.

"Huh, my grandfather owns a property out from Maple Grove a bit, I spent a lot of time from my childhood there, we even rode the horses, and I helped with the cows sometimes. He said us shifters were the best for working with animals because we could sense when things weren't quite right. I still wish we could find out about your ability though, you said it's only really life-threatening stuff you sense, right?" Ollie cocked his head at me as he sat cross-legged in the shade beside me.

"Yeah, always bad stuff I sense. Cancer was a big one, and now poison, apparently. Not so much the minor things unless I really try to search for it, even then, it's luck of the draw," I mused as I pondered over it. My old dog from childhood, Maisy, had had a few issues with her over the years, and I'd picked up on a few, others I'd missed.

She had been limping once, and despite my best efforts, I couldn't figure out why until a few days later when I sensed a small infection in her paw. She had a splinter. She got a cough a few times, but I never could tell what that had been from, and when she got arthritis when she got older, I hadn't sensed that, just known it had come about with her age.

I had sensed her time was up a few days before it came, wailing and crying in my sleep as she lay on the end of my bed. I could never quite understand that, it was just like I knew there was nothing that could be done.

I'd copped it big time for that when my Aunt came in, being woken up from her sleep by my wailing and finding the dog inside.

Maisy had been an outside dog, but in her old age I didn't want her outside on winter nights, so I'd sneak her in when everyone else was asleep, and sneak her out before they woke. She never gave me away or went to the toilet inside.

I explained this to Oliver, whose face dropped at my sad tale about Maisy and my bitchy Aunt. I also told him how the pendant I'd worn only seemed to block my mischief magic, not my sense for things.

"It sounds like maybe you sensed the splinter because the

infection could've turned really bad, maybe," he offered his thoughts.

"Yeah, maybe." I nodded thoughtfully. I wish I knew more about this ability. Maybe my fae magical class could help.

"Hey." Ollie leaned forward to rest a hand on my knee with a soft smile. "I'm sorry about your Aunt, you deserved better than her anger. And despite her, you turned out kind and sweet," he said, his amber eyes filled with warmth.

"Thanks, Ollie," I murmured as I covered his hand with mine. How I wanted to confide in him the full truth. The darkness I'd grown up with while with my Aunt. She was only one of my problems.

The gesture made a tingle run through me as our hands touched, and he gave me his boyish grin as he looked down at his phone.

"We should get moving though, the next lecture starts in less than ten."

The Animal and Veterinary Biology lecture went smoothly, and we were doing our prac every second week as well, on Wednesday morning. This would give me more hours that I could work if needed, although I wasn't too sure how my afternoon would go yet, I still had one last course lecture to attend after lunch to get my schedule fully sorted out.

Well, that and then the magical classes.

My stomach fluttered at the thought of it, and I drew in a sharp breath as Oliver led me through the courtyard to one of the kiosks for lunch.

Students wandered around, some sat at the tables, others headed for the small cafe located up in the main building on the bottom floor.

"Sausage roll?" Ollie asked as he peered back at me while he stepped into line.

"Um, hang on," I murmured as I slipped my hand into my bag to find my wallet. I pulled out the little wallet with a cute fox face on in, although a number of strings were hanging from the edges and the fox's face was worn and faded.

I checked my notes and coins, biting my lip. I should've just bought lunch with me.

"On m.," Oliver waved me off.

"No, I can buy my own food," I scowled, but he shook his head playfully with a grin.

"Nope, I'll shout the pretty lady," he said with a wink. Warmth rushed to my cheeks at the mild compliment, and then he was moving up to the counter to order.

I'd barely even looked at the menu, although it seemed they were a small bakery kiosk.

"I'll take a sausage roll and a tropical juice, you?" Oliver turned back to me, his amber eyes glinting brightly in the sun that had finally revealed itself.

"Blueberry muffin and iced coffee?" I mumbled.

"What she said." Oliver nodded, and the man behind the counter just smiled as he got our order out of the cabinet and fridge.

"I can pay for myself, y'know," I said, not turning down the muffin that the kiosk attendant held out to me with an iced coffee from the fridge.

"I know, but I don't mind." Ollie shrugged as he reached for the bottle of sauce on offer beside the napkin stand. He squirted a line of thick tomato sauce on the sausage roll before grinning and setting it down.

"Want some sausage roll with that sauce?" I snickered, and he just snorted as he took a hefty bite from it.

"OLLLLIIIIEEEE!"

My headed whipped round at the singsong shout from across the courtyard.

"Shit," Oliver barely managed to say through his mouthful of food.

I watched wide-eyed as the rather short girl came sprinting up to us with a grin plastered across her face, her blonde piggy-tails bouncing on her shoulders in her tiny pink dress.

"Hey, Glenda." Oliver managed a weak wave as his amber eyes flicked to me for assistance.

I had no idea who this bubbly little pink powder puff was.

"I'd heard you were starting your studies here! I ran into your sister during orientation, she's still as bitchy as ever, can't believe she hasn't finished her course." The blonde rolled her eyes and did a dramatic sigh.

I turned to Oliver, who looked utterly stunned at this new development.

Who was this little girl who reached only my shoulder? Surely she wasn't studying here?

"So, who's your friend?" The girl's big blue eyes fell on me as her mouth curved into a sneer.

Great. Definitely not someone I wanted to know.

"This is… um… this is Ally," Oliver finally got out, still caught completely off guard with his sausage roll now forgotten as he held it at his side.

"Well, she's certainly not an upgrade." The girl gave me a sarcastic grin as she crossed her arms. "I'll have you know I've moved on now, I'm with Grayson, he's a true shifter." The girl cocked an eyebrow as she flicked those amused eyes between us. "Did he tell you that he's cursed and no longer a true shifter, aye, Ally?" she said, making sure to draw out my name in a tooth-grinding way.

"Wait, are you his ex?" I asked with a frown. Okay. So

Ollie had an ex. Damn, he needed to raise his expectations, big time. This little kitten was still stuck in high school by the looks of things, and judging by those pushed up little boobs, she was trying way too hard.

She scoffed as she rolled her eyes. "Why, has he told you all about me?" she purred, looking a little pleased with herself as she crossed her arms.

"He said he'd dated a little powder puff girl for a while, but she was too immature and obsessed with pink for his tastes." I shrugged, rolling with it.

Her pleased look turned to one of fury as Oliver choked beside me.

"At least I can still shift into anything I want!" she shot back, glaring daggers at Oliver.

"Look, kiddo, I think you should cool ya tits, run on back to high school and your friends," I said, disbelieving my sudden confidence with this little terror. I did not like how she was trying to make Ollie feel, and to be frank, I was worried it'd force something unwanted. I didn't want this little pink bitch to ruin his first day of uni.

She fumed, huffing as she stepped towards me.

"I'll have you know I'm studying right here, and my *friends* are just over there," she said as she pointed a pink fingernail at one of the distant tables.

"Let me guess, beauty?" I gave her a charming smile as she boiled.

"Glenda! Aren't you nice and bright today? Almost like a pig in a herd of sheep, maybe tone down the brightness."

My shoulders relaxed as Skip sauntered up, beaming at Glenda.

"Skip." She managed a half-smile, almost a flirtatious little smirk, before his words sunk in and she scowled at him.

"Come, Lucas and I are sitting over under the fig, you

should join us. I'm sure Glenda here would like to get back to her friends, right?" Skip turned his focus onto the little pink ball of rage.

She opened her mouth but Skip waved her off. "See ya, Glenda!"

Oliver seemed overly grateful as Skip steered him away, and I gave Glenda a quick nod with a smirk before following the pair.

"What on earth were you thinking, Ollie?" I turned on him as soon as we joined Lucas under the fig tree. He was sitting up against the trunk with a book of spells in his lap and a peach in hand. He certainly liked his fruits, and today he wore a navy suit again, this time with a green tie with little stars on it.

"Give me a break," Ollie groaned as he sat down and finally remembered his sausage roll in his hand. He sighed as he took a bite of it, his gaze moving to look across the court-yard to where his ex was still glaring at him.

"Damn, would not have thought that little psycho would come to uni," Skip remarked as he plopped down on the grass beside us.

"How did you date her? She's… I can't even come up with a word for *that*," I said distastefully as I raised my iced coffee to my lips.

"So much pink, still." Skip frowned as he stared at the distant pink beacon. A bright pink that did not belong on the campus at all. Not to mention it barely covered her.

"She always loved pink." Lucas chuckled.

"Why?" I mumbled as I bit into my muffin, baffled that Oliver could ever have been with such a prima-donna.

"She knew my family, her family are true shifters from Noosa. Why on Earth she came here to study is beyond me, and Grayson, ugh." Oliver rolled his eyes.

"Wait, she's with your cousin now?" Skip turned to Ollie with a look of complete shock.

"Apparently. Oh, and she thinks Ally's my girlfriend." He sighed, and then gave me a cheesy grin.

"I will fake it just to piss that little pig off," I said immediately, drawing a laugh from Skip.

"You guys were together, what, when you were fourteen? It lasted not even a year," Lucas sniggered, his eyes still on his book.

"She never got over it, though. Ollie was the one, apparently." Skip fluttered his eyes at me and I snorted.

"Yeah, well, that bitch fucked up my life," Ollie snapped.

Skip's face dropped as he chewed his cheek and looked away. Even Lucas shifted uncomfortably as Oliver took a swig from his juice bottle, a deep frown marring his normally sweet face.

"How?" I murmured. He'd said it with such hate and a dark look in his eye.

"Because," he grumbled as he stood.

"Where you going?" Skip asked.

"For a walk, I'll be back," Oliver muttered as he strode over to the closest bin and tossed the remaining bit of his sausage roll and stormed off.

I went to stand but Lucas held out an arm to stop me.

"Let him be. She's the reason he's cursed," Lucas murmured.

"What? How?" I gaped.

"When they were dating, he, his cousins, and his sister were harassing the witch neighbor, just usual kid stuff. Glenda was there too, and she threw a tennis ball at the witch. It hit her in the back of the head, and when the witch turned back, she assumed it was Oliver who was standing beside Glenda. She struck him with the curse, forcing him into cat form. He never dobbed Glenda in, and then the witch moved after informing his parents that his curse wouldn't lift until he was twenty. Glenda left him, she wanted to be with a true shifter, and Ollie was no longer that, and then his family... well, let's just say a few months later he moved in with me," Lucas explained.

"Jesus, that little bitch," I murmured in disbelief. "Did he tell the truth when they split?" I asked.

"Yes, but the damage was done. His parents contacted the witch but it couldn't be lifted, not even by the witch who cast it, she cursed him badly in a moment of anger, and she regretted it when she learned the truth." Lucas sighed, giving me a sad smile.

"Poor Ollie," I mumbled as I set my iced coffee down. He didn't deserve any of this.

And now this little wench was here. Here to screw with his head some more.

"I hate her," I stated bluntly.

"Join the club," Skip scoffed.

I stared off in the direction Oliver had headed, my heart squeezing for him.

And Lucas had mentioned his family too. What had happened there? Why would no one tell me?

13

I found my way to my next lecture after lunch with Skip and Lucas.

I was beyond relieved when I headed inside and saw Oliver slouched in a corner seat.

"Hey," I murmured as I sat down beside him.

"Hey," he mumbled.

"Got you something." I smiled as I pulled the caramello koala out of my bag. I'd bought it at one of the kiosks on the way through the courtyard.

He smiled and shook his head, but accepted the offering.

"Don't let that little pink barbie get you down." I squeezed his arm. "I could fight her for you? I have wolf in me, and she's tiny," I offered, drawing a chuckle from him.

"She's a true shifter, and your wolf side isn't your dominant side. It's obvious as hell." He grinned.

"Why?" I feigned shock at this information.

"Werewolves are more badass, you're definitely favoring your fae/pixie side." He shrugged. "Although, you were quick with your wittiness today." He gave me a sly smile.

"You saying I'm not a badass?" I gaped at him, and he grinned.

"I think you could be, no question about it. But you don't give off the vibe."

"I can't believe she's going to be studying here this year. And she's dating my cousin," he groaned as he slouched forward and began unwrapping his caramello koala.

"Who cares, she's not worth your worry, besides, you've got me to protect you." I winked as I gave his arm a soft punch.

"Y'know she could turn into an elephant and trample you, right?" He raised an eyebrow at me.

I instantly pictured an elephant wearing a bright pink tutu and snorted at the image.

"What?" Oliver chuckled as I shook my head.

"Just picturing an elephant in a pink tutu," I said, unable to stop myself from grinning.

Oliver rolled his eyes but chuckled as well.

We settled as the lecturer started the introduction, and I was grateful he'd relaxed and gotten somewhat back to his usual cheery self.

I wouldn't let that little pink demonic barbie drag him down. She didn't deserve the light of day for what she'd caused. And she obviously didn't give two fucks about it, which only pissed me off more.

Thursdays were our tutorial and prac days, we'd attend different tutorials on Thursday morning, and then in April our workshops would begin.

"We can't miss any of the tutorials, but lectures are made available online the day after for students who couldn't make them," Oliver said as we began the walk through the court-yard. Our magical classes were located in buildings down towards the back of the campus, so we'd walk partway together.

"I'd prefer to attend most of my lectures in person, you can't ask questions in a recording," I said as I shifted the weight of my laptop bag on my shoulder. The sun beat down on us with a fury, and the day had significantly warmed since the clouds had passed.

"Yeah, it's good though, if I have any issues, worst case is that I'd have to watch them from home," he said as he flicked a bug off his arm.

"Or, y'know, I could bring you in as a cat," I offered with a smirk.

"Haha." He rolled his eyes. "But the staff actually have been made aware that there could be shifting problems with me, thankfully," he said, and I could sense his shame in having to inform the teacher body of that.

"What will the magic class be like?" I asked, trying to shift his mind off of it. Not to mention I was actually curious.

"They'll give you a run-down of the abilities of your kind, they may even split you up, like with me, I'll go to a shifter class, but according to Skip, I'll be split from the group with the other true shifters to practice with them. Although, to be honest, I might not attend much, I can't do much of the stuff I should be able to do," he muttered as he kicked his jogger against the pathway in annoyance.

"And fae?" I asked.

"They may separate you by your sub-species. So true fae in one class, pixies, sprites, etc, in others. You'll also be tested for an elemental ability, and sometimes they'll pair you up if there's someone who knows a bit more if you need additional help." He smiled as he turned to me. "Don't worry, it'll be fine."

"I know barely anything about myself except for some reading I've just done," I groaned.

"You'll be fine, you've managed this far." Oliver grinned as he pulled us up just outside of the buildings we were headed for. "Meet back at the fig tree after? That way we can walk home together?" he suggested with those sweet amber eyes relaxed and at ease.

"Sounds like a plan." I nodded as I brushed my fingers against my laptop bag. I hadn't once taken my iPod out of the side pocket today. That was an unusual feat.

"Awesome, and good luck." He beamed as he moved forward and pulled me into a tight, warm hug. It sent sweet shivers coursing through me, and I clung to him for a few moments longer than was necessary. He was so warm and smelled of sweet caramel. Maybe that was just thanks to his love of caramello koalas.

"You too, don't go getting stuck in cat form." I chuckled as he pulled back and stuck his tongue out playfully.

We parted ways, and I headed to my class with an uneasy knot in my stomach. The lectures and working out my schedule were the easy part.

I sucked in a deep breath, wondering what would await me in the lecture hall I was headed for.

The amount of first-year fae that greeted me in the room was more than I'd expected.

At least fifty fae were spread out in the room, and I froze as I took in the lecture hall with wide eyes.

All these people were fae, and there was no doubt in my mind they knew everything there was to know about themselves.

I spied a vacant spot closer to the back, and I made a beeline for it, glancing around at the people I passed.

Many were true fae, even I could tell. They had that extra glow and beauty that only the true, full fae had, the other pixies, sprites, and whatever else, were still stunning in looks, but they didn't have the obvious fae glow.

And not to be crude, but there wasn't a single one in this room who looked a little overweight. A side effect of being a fae. They were actually incapable of becoming overweight, something many supes had in common thanks to their genetic makeup. It was even more strange for fae, since they adored sweet things.

I sat down in the dark, cushioned navy seat away from the cluster of students, satisfied I'd avoided being pulled into conversation with any of them.

"Hey, you mind if I sit here?"

I internally groaned as the silver haired girl walked down my aisle to stand beside me.

There were a heap of seats around, why this one next to me?

She seemed to understand my confusion as those gray eyes lit up and she smiled.

"You're a halfling, like me, I'd rather sit with you than the rest," she said.

She could tell I was only a halfling? Damn. Well, guess they all already knew how to sense each other. I hadn't even bothered to open up my power to see if there were other halflings.

I was drawing a few unwanted stares already. True fae were arseholes, stuck up creatures who thought of themselves as royalty. Like my Aunt and her family, even if they weren't rich. Their kind were just proud. Sometimes I was glad I was a halfling with more pixie in me than true fae.

"I'm Emma." She thrust out her hand, those strange gray eyes taking me in with a broad smile. Her silvery white hair was done up in a braid that fell down over her shoulder, and I wondered briefly if it was dyed. Some supes had unique hair colors, just a genetic thing, although rare.

"Allison," I accepted her handshake, and her smile widened as she sat down beside me in her jeans and dark gray singlet.

"So, you're a wolf halfling, and pixie?" She frowned, cocking her head as she analyzed me. Probably sensing what I was through that colored aura thing.

"Yeah, that's me." I shrugged, focusing on sensing what she was, not that I understood the colors.

She was a swirl of purple and pink, and I grinned as I recognized the colors thanks to the boys teaching me a little.

"And you're a pixie witch?" I checked, and she nodded.

"Yep, us halflings should stick together, the full-bloods look down on us most of the time, although some consider us special," Emma said.

"Guess they think we're like mutts, huh," I muttered.

"Yeah, most creatures try to stick to their own kind when it comes to relationships, except fae, some of them will get with vamps, but vamps can be with any creature since they can't reproduce," Emma said as she sat her bag down beside her on the vacant seat.

"Why do I get the feeling it's like how the world had problems with interracial couples?" I murmured.

"Cause it is. They prefer same species to stick together, although they don't mind cross-shifters, say a dingo and a border collie or something like that. Or fae and pixie, etc. Although fae can be odd about their own crossing with the subspecies. But when the lines cross right over, like us, then they don't like it much, but they can't stop it." Emma frowned. "You don't know much, do ya?"

I cringed as she recognized my instant uncertainty with all things supernatural.

"I grew up pretty sheltered, including from the supernatural world," I admitted.

"Well, that sucks." She clucked her tongue as she leaned back in her seat. "Better late than never, I s'pose."

"Yeah." I managed a weak chuckle.

"Well, don't worry, you'll learn a lot here in these classes about yourself, and I can help you." She grinned, even her eyes lighting up. She sure was a bubbly one.

"So what are you studying?" I asked as the room filled with soft conversation as we waited for the lecturer.

"Sorcery and magic, not taking a standard mundane course with it like business or something, maybe in a year or two I might branch into something else, but my mom runs a successful potion store and needs more hands, so I'm learning here while she teaches me at home as well." She grinned as she leaned forward, and I could sense she'd been opened up like a book.

"My family is a long line of strong witches, potion makers mostly, my dad is a pixie, he's the odd one out in my family, but we were a weird bunch anyway, so he fits right in, although he gets some bad looks when he's out with mom from other supes, mostly faes. Shifters and witches are the most common of supes, true shifters are heaps rarer, practically royalty, faes are relatively uncommon, but you'll find plenty here as they'd rather attend this uni than the ones down at the city or Caboolture as it's more dangerous for them with newer vamps springing up all the time in those areas. Those with fae bloodlines smell yummy to vamps, like us with sweet things, they love us, but new vamps, especially those turned from humans, can be dangerous, they get a bloodlust and if they get a whiff of fae when they're first turned, they can hunt us down and kill us. A few years back there was an outbreak of murders in Brissy, fae drained completely by newborns, that's newly made vampires. Anyway, ever since then, less and less fae go to the city, they tend to stick to less populated areas, unless they're in warded zones, where the warding helps null their scent to vamps. It's still there, but they don't get that crazed hunger, and newborns can't sniff you out, either. That's some epic magic used in warding." She whistled as she beamed at me.

I was just amazed at the chopping and changing and her ability to hurl all those words together. She was practically bouncing in her seat as she spoke, but I kinda liked it. She was bubbly and energetic, alert, and had no misgivings about me.

"I grew up in Maroochydore, a warded area, so I guess I was lucky there. My cousin dated a vampire witch, too, so I guess I never really learned much about the issues with vamps and fae." I frowned.

"Vamps turned from supes are even less of a problem, they have better control than human turned ones." Emma shrugged.

"Can shifters be turned?" I asked.

"Yeah, although some lose the ability to shift and become more like a true vamp. Some creatures who are turned keep some of their abilities from their previous state. Witch vampires are a common one, they keep some of their magic abilities most of the time when they get turned," Emma said. "But nothing too epic, only the more moderate abilities. Some can still make potions infused with magic, others can hurl it, and are capable of a few spells. Everything else is gone though."

I pondered over this as the lecturer came into the hall finally.

So Marcus had some magic abilities? What could he do? He was an interesting one for sure.

"Shouldn't you be in a witch magic class?" I asked.

"I've been taught witch magic all my life, but my dad is quite busy, so I need to learn more about my pixie side and abilities," she stated with a smile.

We fell into silence as the lecturer called for quiet, and she informed us of our schedule. Every Monday afternoon we'd attend a magical class, pixies would meet in one room, full fae in another, sprites in another, and the list went on. Brownies were a thing, as were goblins, dwarves, and elves.

When I'd enrolled, I'd had to state what I was, my blood-lines, so they could make sure they had classes available to suit.

"Do you know what brownies are?" Emma whispered as the lecturer focused on speaking to the larger true fae group about what their classes would consist of.

"No," I murmured.

"Brownies are nature fae, think of them as the hippies of our kind, very earthy, their magic consists of harnessing nature, so they can make things grow and flourish. Most of them will probably be studying some kind of agricultural course. You should know about pixies, their mischief magic and such. All fae have a sweet tooth, although you'll find brownies are more fruit eaters. Goblins, contrary to popular belief, no longer look as hideous as they once did, although they don't have the same beauty as other types of fae. They're greedy though, and can be nasty. There's only a couple in this class, and I know for a fact that Jeremiah is studying law. He'll become a feared lawyer one day, they hate to lose anything, so they're good in that department.

Their magic is odd, similar to a low witch, can be honed in certain areas. Goblins aren't as ugly as they used to be a few centuries back thanks to careful cross-breeding with other types of fae and honing their magic to help promote better looks. Yeah, it's a weird history there, don't get me started," Emma snorted, earning her a look from the lecturer, who was now addressing the sprites.

Emma ignored this and continued in a hushed tone, her gray eyes flicking around excitedly as she spoke. "Sprites are water creatures, so they can breathe underwater and are excellent swimmers. Their magic is more water based, so they can sometimes be mistaken for elementals, but the difference is that they can't wield it as powerfully as an elemental, and they can communicate a little with water-life, like mermaids." Her eyes narrowed as she gave me a questioning look.

"My housemates told me about mermaids," I murmured, and she nodded as she moved onto the next one.

"Dwarves aren't common, normally they're short, but the few we have here are the more modern day form, where they're normal size. They're strong though, normally bulkier than the rest of us, and are great warriors and forgers. Their magic is usually infused into weapons, making them more powerful depending on the user. And then there's elves, they're the true warrior fae kind. Think *'Lord of the Rings'*. Damn, wasn't Orlando Bloom gorgeous?" She sighed as she got side-tracked for a moment, her eyes practically glazing over for a moment as she swooned over the elf. I'd never actually watched the movies, but I'd heard of it and knew of the elf man with gorgeous long blond locks.

"Anyway, they're capable of wielding weapons unlike others. They have a natural ability to hit their target with any weapon, they're capable of carefully inflicting wounds, as in, if they want to incapacitate you but not kill you, they're the main ones who can do that with ease. If they want to not do permanent damage or vice versa, that's them, too. And if you want a bullet or arrow to curve in mid-air around something or whatever, they can even do that," Emma said, her cheeks reddening as she ran out of breath.

Damn, she knew a lot. And some of the fae sub-species were utterly epic.

"True fae?" I queried.

"All of the above, some they can specialize in, but they have all the abilities of the subspecies." Emma nodded happily at her own knowledge, proud of herself. "But they never seem to hone it to the same perfection that the subspecies do. Guess they prefer to be a jack of all trades rather than a master of one."

I went to ask more, but the lecturer moved onto pixies, and we focused on what our classes would consist of.

It was up to us if we wanted to buddy up with another of our kind, and Emma was keen to be my buddy as she grinned at me. Maybe she just liked being able to teach me.

We'd learn to mask our magic when outside of warded areas, although many already knew how to do that. Then it was honing and controlling our magic, learning all the little things we could do with it.

Once she'd gone over the course outlines with everyone, we were informed our syllabus would be found on the online portal, but if we needed a printed copy, see her afterwards. We were now going to be tested for an elemental ability.

"How do they test us?" I asked Emma softly.

"They've got a warlock who comes in to do the elemental tests on the first day," Emma said as the door to the room opened.

I watched as the older gentleman walked in, his graying

hair slicked back as he held his hands behind his back. He walked with poise and grace, his short beard neatly trimmed and shaped, with a salt and pepper look. He wore a grey suit, and my first thought was actually Lucas and his love of suits.

"That's Mr. Brady," Emma hissed, her eyes wide at the sight of the warlock.

That name sounded awfully familiar, and I frowned as I tried to rake my brain for where I'd heard it.

"I heard he's got two kids attending the University, a son and daughter. His son is a warlock as well, his daughter is just a witch, but a powerful one. I'd be no match," Emma murmured as she nibbled on the end of her pen.

"Everyone just relax, this won't hurt, but those of you with an elemental affinity will be revealed," our lecturer said. Mrs. Johnson I believe she'd said her name was. Our magical classes would be with a Miss. Watson.

"How does he test?" I asked softly.

My question was answered as Mr. Brady planted himself before us and swept his arm out to the side.

A ripple of golden magic-like smoke flooded the hall, washing over us all.

Two girls stood up, gasping as they glowed softly, along with a boy on the far side of the room.

"Well, we've got three," Mrs. Johnson clapped her hands gleefully. "Do you know what your elemental abilities are?"

"Fire," the first girl said confidently, smiling brightly as she looked around the room smugly.

"I… I don't know," the second girl stammered, a brunette.

"I had no idea," the boy said when all eyes fell on him, and he shifted uncomfortably.

"Well, you three will come with me now then, you will have additional classes to hone your elemental ability," Mr. Brady said as he clasped his hands together and nodded at the three students. They all shot each other looks before gathering up their things and heading down to the front of the room to follow after him.

Once they were all gone, Mrs. Johnson turned her attention back on us.

"Now, for the rest of this introductory lecture, we'll be practicing warding our magic. In order to do this, you must learn to ward yourself. Those around you, other supes, will struggle to sense you when reaching out, that'll be a sign that you're picking it up. You'll be practicing it more with your specific tutors, but we'll go over the basics today," Mrs. Johnson said as she stood readily before us.

I focused all my attention on this, and Emma helped guide me through it when Mrs. Johnson's explanation wasn't helping too well.

In order to ward myself, Emma's explanation made more sense. Mrs. Johnson said to imagine a glow seeping out from me, shielding me from view of humans and twisting their reality. My magic would do this a little on its own apparently, but by mastering warding and concealing, I could completely conceal it rather than it just being a little twisted.

Emma's explanation made more sense. Imagine the energy that I feel, the same one I summon forth to see the supes around me, cloaking me, protecting me from sight and all my magic with it.

The rest of the class was practice, and we were set up in pairs or groups, whichever we chose.

"How come some of the elementals don't know what they are?" I asked softly.

"It doesn't always awaken without some effort. You could go your whole life not knowing you're one," Emma said.

"Hey, you said Mr. Brady has kids here, what are their names?" I asked as I watched her practice. I was reaching out to sense her, but I was only seeing the faintest line of color around her, but it was almost invisible. She already had been taught to conceal her magic, so we'd focused on me for most of the session. I was struggling to perfect it, but she was coaching me on.

"Cathy and Lucas," she said as she scrunched up her eyes in thought for a moment.

"Wait, Lucas Brady?" I frowned as I finally realized. The emails I'd shared with Lucas, his last name had been Brady.

"Yeah, he's the reject of his family, they didn't like his… uniqueness, so he left. Inherited his grandfather's place just down the road, lives with a bunch of guys, most of them are rejects of the supe community too."

"Why are they rejects?" I asked, my mind completely moving away from the practice we were meant to be doing. Maybe I would finally learn more about my housemates. And what did she mean by Lucas' uniqueness? Sure, he loved suits, and he could be a little flamboyant at times.

"Is Lucas gay?" I suddenly asked. I'd been curious about it, but hadn't asked anyone. Emma seemed more than happy to share, which was a good thing right now.

"No, he's bisexual, and very interesting, rumor has it that he experiments a lot, in strange ways." Emma wriggled her eyebrows with a cheeky grin.

"Oh," I breathed. So what was up with Skip and him then? Was there something there? Or was I looking too much into it?

"As for the others, Oliver, the true shifter, ran away from his family, although, truth be told, he was kinda run out by them. A stain against their good, upper class name, with his curse and all. A laughing stock. Not to mention his arranged girlfriend then left him. True shifters are all about arranged stuff, they're pretty old kingdom with that shit, wanting to keep true shifters pure. Then there's Skip, he's not so much a reject really, I guess. He bailed on his family's farm to study, and from my understanding, he's running away from something. And then there's the renowned vampire Marcus." Emma sighed as she frowned sadly at her notebook. She stabbed at it momentarily with her pen before clicking her tongue.

"Poor thing lost his whole family when he was turned, that news was big here, who would've thought such a thing could happen in this town? His maker murdered his family apparently." Emma pursed her lips, and I could see the pain in her eyes for Marcus.

Now I finally understood him, and my housemates, so much more.

Poor Oliver and Lucas, and Marcus, my God, I felt completely horrified for him. No one should have to experience such a thing like that.

My parents had died when I was little, but it was still painful at times, wondering about the life I could've had, what they were like. I barely remembered them at all, I was so young. But I knew I'd been loved.

"Most people here know about them, Oliver and Lucas' families are, like, royalty, and Marcus' were pretty well-known. Skip's grandmother was loved by all in this town, a social butterfly that one, right up until she passed," Emma said as she peered down at our lecturer, who was checking in on one of the groups down the front. "Small towns. Everyone knows everyone."

"I never knew," I murmured.

"Well, you're not from around here, but you would've found out eventually, sooner or later," she said. "Why so curious though?"

"Well…" I chewed my lip as I wondered if I should tell her. No harm in it.

"They're my new housemates."

"Hold the phone, you moved into that house? With four guys?" Emma's jaw dropped as those twinkling gray eyes widened.

"Yeah, I was running out of time to find a place, it popped up, and they seemed nice, so I applied." I sunk back into my chair. They seemed like a lovely bunch of guys, for the most part.

"Damn, what I wouldn't do to be stuck in that house." Emma swooned as she fanned herself with her notebook.

"What?" I snorted at her.

"Really? You haven't noticed how fine they are? They are sexy as hell," she moaned as she rolled her eyes.

"Well, I guess," I mumbled, my cheeks heating up. I wouldn't deny that they were all good-looking. But they were also my housemates.

Which meant they were out of bounds. Not to say I couldn't look though.

"I'm soooo jealous, you lucky bugger." Emma chuckled. "So, what's it like, living with them? How's that dark little vampire?"

"I haven't seen him much, I only moved in on Friday night," I admitted.

"Damn! You moved in late, didn't you?" Emma grinned, showing off her pearly whites.

"Well, I had a job and a rental, so I needed to help my housemate there find a replacement since I was breaking my lease. Left most of my stuff there, too, wasn't much anyway, a second-hand bed, a chest of drawers, figured it could help with finding a new housemate if it was a little furnished. Sadly my old housemate got ultra pissed about my breaking lease and tossed some things while I was packing. Clothes and such. A few dresses I loved."

"Did it help to find someone? And what a cow, guess you're not friends, huh?" she asked.

"Yeah, we found someone." I nodded. "And no, definitely not."

"We can go shopping sometime? Get you some pretty dresses?" she suggested with a bright smile.

"Maybe, I'd like to save a bit for some things first. Dresses can wait," I said, and she just nodded understandingly

"So, you didn't say, what's it like living with those guys?" Emma cocked her head at me with a mischievous glint in her eye.

"Interesting, I guess, they're nice, friendly, showed me around, watched TV shows with me and stuff." I shrugged, not sure what she was exactly hoping for.

"Seen any of them naked?" Emma asked slyly as she arched an eyebrow.

The image of Ollie poised on the end of my bed with that erect little member was the first thing to sear into my mind, and Emma's grin widened.

My cheeks must've reddened, because she clicked her tongue.

"Well, you're a lucky girl. As far as I'm aware, they're all single right now." Emma winked as she lounged back in her seat.

"Really? Huh," I murmured. I'd known Ollie was, and Lucas, kinda. Being bi gave me a little hope, though.

Skip was a player, so I wasn't sure how I felt about him, he was some delicious eye candy for sure. And then there was Marcus.

Marcus, whom I'd just discovered the reason to why he was such a jerk.

The lecturer ended our conversation as she called out that the class was finished, and to collect our schedules online or see her for our continuing classes with specific tutors.

"So, how you getting home?" Emma asked as she gathered up her things and stuffed them into her bag.

"I'll be walking with Ollie," I said.

Emma's mouth curved up at this, and I rolled my eyes. She sure liked my housemates.

"Okay, well, I'll see you next week in class, if not before. Or, you know, I could give you my number or you could add me on Facebook, then we could chat if you ever have any questions?" she offered as she slung her bag onto her back and stood.

"I'm between phones right now, but I'll probably make a new Facebook account tonight, so I can add you on that?" I said.

"Ouch, between phones, that must suck." She cringed at the thought as she held her phone in her hand. "But sure, I'll be under Emma Hall, you'll recognize the profile pic," she said with a smile. "But it was nice meeting you, Ally."

"You too." I nodded at her as I gathered up my things and packed my laptop bag before standing. We both headed down to the door where we parted ways, Emma bouncing on her toes as she looked forward to seeing me in my next class. We agreed we might try to catch up before then, but she knew I was still settling in at my new place with the boys.

I found Ollie at the fig tree like we agreed, and he was looking rather dejected as I joined him and sat down beside him.

"What's up?" I asked as I touched his arm softly.

"She's in my class," Ollie muttered.

"Glenda?" I raised an eyebrow at him.

"Yeah, all the true shifters are in one, the first years," he groaned.

"Do they offer more than one class?" I asked, but I had a feeling I knew the answer.

"There's only five true shifters this year, including her and I." he sighed as he played with a blade of grass.

"Do you have to attend them?"

"Well, no, not really. I wouldn't have minded, though," he said as he finally dragged those sad amber eyes up to meet mine.

"Well, maybe we can just practice outside of class. Skip and Lucas probably know a bit about what you'd learn, we can all help you outside of class?" I suggested.

"Yeah, I guess so. It's not like I can practice turning into different things anyway." He gave a sharp laugh. "I can't wait until this curse lifts, before it, I could turn into anything I wanted. I could fly over all of Maple Grove as an eagle, to feel the wind like that again, to fly so high over everything, I miss it," he breathed as he leaned back on his hands, staring up at the blue sky overhead.

"Wow, that would've been amazing." I awed as I followed his gaze.

"Yeah, it really is. Being a true shifter was something I loved so much, becoming anything you wanted, there was so much you could do. A lot of mischief, too." He chuckled. "But I'm past that now, I paid the price for playing around."

"Well, it wasn't really you, though, was it?" I remarked softly.

He turned his head to me, those amber eyes softening as he gave me a small smile.

"Nah, but that doesn't change anything," he said quietly. "Anyway, Lucas texted offering to hang around and drive us home, you probably missed his car this morning, he's got this fancy silver Mercedes 4x4." Ollie grinned. "I told him we'd just walk, it's a nice day today."

"Yeah, we can walk," I agreed. "So, apart from that, how was your first shifter class? Do you guys have magic, too?"

"It was good, and not really, our shifter classes teach us how to fight in different forms, how to shift into many things. Our magic is the ability to shift.

'We learn about everything we can do, even how to only shift parts of our bodies. Want some claws but nothing else? They'll teach us that, amongst other things," he said as he climbed to his feet and offered me his hand.

I allowed him to pull me up, feeling sorry for him. Emma had said he'd run away, but his family had also pretty much run him out. He didn't deserve that. He was such a sweet, cheerful guy.

"So, I met a girl today, think we might be becoming friends, she's very knowledgeable, taught me a fair bit more than my lecturer today actually," I said as we began walking.

I wanted to ask him about what she said. About everyone. About Lucas being bi and being the reject of his family, about Marcus' family, and what Skip was running from. And I wanted to know why his family had abandoned him. Was it seriously because of his curse? His so called 'taint' against their name?

"Oh yeah, what's her name?" Ollie asked as he kept in step with me.

"Emma, Emma Hall," I said.

Oliver clenched his jaw as he stopped, staring hard at me.

"White-haired chick?" he asked, frowning uneasily.

"Yeah, why?" I asked, uncertainty washing through me now.

"You should be careful with her," he said.

"Why? She seems really nice. A halfling like me, witch/pixie." I shook my head. She'd been overly kind to me, and helpful.

"She's also a psychic witch, and a pixie with psychic powers makes for a bad combo," Ollie murmured.

"Why?" I asked.

"They can sometimes read minds."

14

"You're bullshitting me, right?" I stared dumbly at Oliver.

"Nope, she can read minds on occasion," he said seriously.

"Damn," I murmured. So Emma could see into my head. Whenever she chose too? Oh God. Oliver. Naked.

"Whenever she wants?" I asked softly, not wanting to know the answer.

"I think she can choose when to, but when she was growing up, she could hear in randomly, whenever her mischief magic flared up. She's learned how to better control it now, I think." Oliver shrugged.

"That must be a weird power to have while growing up," I mused as we reached the edge of the campus and headed out onto the street. Other students were making their way off the campus or onto it, and I wondered how many students didn't bother attending their lectures and just watched them on the online portal instead.

"Yeah, psychics are interesting ones, they can normally just commune with the dead, the whole tarot cards and whatnot, they're the real deal version of them," Oliver informed me.

"I don't see why reading minds should stop me from being her friend." I frowned.

"It doesn't have to, but if you've got some crap in there you don't want her knowing, then be careful," Ollie said as he tapped his head to emphasize his point.

"I'm sure I can just ask her not to look into my mind," I said, but I wondered if it were true. Could she choose to not listen in? Or would it randomly happen? Was she always listening?

"Maybe, I don't quite know how it works, just that she struggled through primary school and ended up being home-schooled because she was bullied a lot. She'd accidentally share something she'd heard. I remember hearing how she told one of her classes that her teacher was out of sorts because her husband was having an affair on her. She landed in detention for that. It was true, though, she'd overheard the teacher's thoughts," Oliver shared.

It sounded like that cheery, bubbly girl I'd met today had had it hard growing up.

Fine, if everyone else wanted to act weird about her, I'd make it my job to be her friend. She'd been only nice to me, I had no reason to want to not be friends with her. Especially not just because she was a little different.

"How do you know all this?" I asked.

"Maple Grove is a small town, we tend to know all the residents well, gossip and news spreads easily," he said with a shrug.

"Right," I breathed as I fiddled with my bracelet.

"We went to the same school, too. Everyone who lives here sends their kids to the Maple Grove primary school. Just makes sense," he added.

I pursed my lips at this. How different would life have been if I'd grown up here?

"Hey, can you help me set up a proper Facebook later today?" I asked as I reveled in the warm sunlight. It wasn't too hot of a day, which I was grateful for.

"Sure! You should really invest in a phone soon, an iPhone would be good, we've all got them at home, so you'd never go without a charger." Oliver grinned.

"I might have to wait a while, I need to buy this MacBook off Lucas, I don't want to just use it for ages." I sighed.

"Don't stress about it, I'm sure he doesn't mind. Actually, there might even be an old iPhone lying around at home somewhere. I'll see if I can find it for you," Oliver said thoughtfully.

"No, I can't keep borrowing things, I need to buy them myself," I groaned. As much as I loved how sweet he was being, I hated relying on others for stuff. Especially expensive stuff.

"You can buy it off me if you really want to. And I doubt Lucas wants you to pay for the MacBook immediately, money isn't exactly a priority for him." Ollie gave me a knowing smile.

"Okay, how much would you want for the phone?" I asked carefully.

"I'll tell you what, since you've organized your schedule to match up with mine, and if you promise to help me out with any shifting troubles should they arise at uni, then you can just have it. Consider it a gift," he said warmly.

"No, no way, I can't accept it as a gift, they cost hundreds of dollars," I scowled.

"So? I've upgraded, I have no use for it. I would've just sold it eventually, but we'll be helping each other out this way." He gave me his boyish, bright grin that reached his eyes.

"Let me give you something for it, please?" I practically begged. I couldn't just accept it.

Although the thought of finally having a new phone did thrill me.

"How about you shout my pizzas for the next four times we get them?" he suggested with a sly smile.

"That'll be the equivalent of maybe $100, if you get a large pizza," I groaned. And that was if he got them from the wood-fired place.

"And?" He shrugged.

"How is $100 enough for an iPhone?" I said in bewilderment.

"It's fine, it's old anyway, jeez, just take the offer, Ally." He rolled his eyes playfully.

"Ugh, fine." I accepted begrudgingly, even if it did thrill me.

He pulled up and jutted out his hand, and I laughed as I shook it.

"Now, let's get home and see if I can find it for you and get it charged. You still have a sim for your old phone?" he asked.

"Yeah, it's in my bag. My plan included my phone, but since I dropped it, I couldn't afford to replace it," I said.

"So you've been paying for a plan you're not even using?" He frowned as we continued walking home.

"Well, only for about a month, I was saving up to buy a second-hand one, but then put my money towards bond here instead."

"Well, we'll get you with a phone." He nodded confidently. "And then Facebook. So was it an iPhone you had before?"

"Yeah, I was paying off one, dropped it after only being a year into my contract," I muttered.

"That sucks. What'd you have before that?"

"A flip phone, cost me $50 back when I was fourteen, had it ever since. Did the job, but finally decided to upgrade."

"And you never got Facebook despite having an iPhone?" He just gave me the most astonished look. "What are you? Some kind of freak?"

"Hey! I didn't have time for it," I said as I hit his arm playfully and he snorted. "Besides, I didn't really have friends, I just texted and called everyone. And technically I had a Facebook, just a crappy, fake one with my old email address so I could get Tinder. Deleted it when I had too much work going on, along with Tinder."

"You're nineteen and never had a proper Facebook, you are probably only one of a few in the entire world," he exaggerated. "Why didn't you just use it if you went to the effort of making one for Tinder? And why'd you have Tinder?"

"Yeah, well, we'll get it tonight, properly." I smiled. "And because I didn't really have friends or any reason for it. As for Tinder, probably the same reason most people have it," I said as I rolled my eyes at the obvious answered. He was watching me with an intrigued look, as if he hadn't expected such a thing of me. And there was something else lying there, a darker look. An interested one.

"Well, we'll be the first people you'll add to your real Facebook then," he said proudly, his deep amber eyes still taking me in. Like he was seeing me in a new light. Strange. Was it all because I'd mentioned Tinder?

We walked the rest of the way in minor conversation about the weather and plans for the weekend. Mine was working, whereas Ollie wanted to read and maybe go visit his grandfather. I didn't ask about the fact that he had no contact with his family anymore.

Maybe things were different with his grandfather.

He offered for me to join him, as sometimes the other boys would, but I couldn't say yes yet. I needed to find out what half shift my bosses wanted me to work.

Once home, Ollie was off searching for the iPhone almost immediately, and I tromped up the stairs to put away my laptop bag. I set it on the desk and eyed the stack of books I still wanted to read about supernatural creatures. Not to mention I had actual studying to do.

I decided to pull out the MacBook and sit down at my desk, opening up the student portal and finding my login details in my emails. I sifted through and deleted all my junk emails, and then logged into the portal to check it all out. My student account had all my courses linked up. I found the template for schedules, and got to work setting it up after checking my pixie magical class details. It took only a short while before I had it all set up in a neat timetable, two pages, first week and the second week, as some of my classes rotated, mostly the practicals.

"Hey! I found the phone, I've reset it already, and it's got a decent amount of charge." Oliver popped his head through my open doorway.

"Awesome!" I turned to him, excitement coursing through me as he strode over to sit on the end of my bed near me.

"You have a backup of your old one?" he asked as he peered down at the iPhone in his hand.

"Nah, lost it all since my old laptop died. I'll be starting from scratch," I said unhappily. So many photos just gone. Thankfully, those that were important to me, I'd emailed to myself as a safety precaution.

"Well, let's get started then, here," he said as he handed it to me. "It's got a glass screen protector on it already."

"Great, thank you," I murmured as I turned the phone over in my hands. It looked brand new to be honest. "This is awesome. You're awesome."

"Aw, thanks," he said bashfully, his cheeks reddening. God, he was cute as heck.

I pushed the home button, revealing the hello screen. We then went through the steps setting it up, signing in with my apple ID after connecting to the wi-fi. I was still trying to understand their password for it. 'LucyisQueen123'. Ollie had said it had something to do with Lucas. It just made me smile stupidly.

I linked up my emails first before moving onto the app store to download the Facebook app.

"We can set it up on your laptop first if you'd like? While we wait for the app to download?" Ollie suggested.

"Right," I nodded as I set the phone down on the desk and swiveled back to face my MacBook.

Ollie stayed on the bed, guiding me through the step-by-step process of creating an account. I could've done it alone, but he seemed eager to help me along, so I didn't stop him. Although, I couldn't remember setting up my old one. It was more out of necessity than need, since I'd needed Tinder. Yes, totally needed it.

"You should take a profile picture too!" he said excitedly now that we'd got the basics for it set up after some time.

"Um, okay." I shrugged. I'd done the odd selfie here and there, but it was more for personal use really, generally a photo with an ex or something for Tinder.

"Here, I'll take it." Oliver beamed as he plucked my phone off the desk. "The app will finish downloading in ten minutes, we can finish setting your profile up then."

I just nodded as Ollie stood before me carefully with my

phone at the ready.

"Smile," he said, and I did as told. He took a few photos from different angles before handing it back to me to check through them.

"Surprisingly, you take decent photos, most guys take shit photos of their girlfriends." I chuckled with a wink.

He looked completely stunned for a moment, and I wondered if I'd overstepped my boundaries with the joke. But then he grinned and rolled his eyes.

"You seriously going to pretend to be my girlfriend whenever Glenda is around?" he mused.

"Yeah, I don't like her," I stated as I went through the photos and decided on the third one. It was a good angle looking down on me, showing off my decent boobs and making my chocolate eyes pop.

"Join the club," he muttered.

"She said she ran into your sister, she's studying beauty, right?" I asked.

"Yeah, Bec, she's been studying it for two years already. It's not a long course, Corviticus offers some courses that you'd usually find at Tafe. But you get more hours to complete it or something. She better get her arse into gear or she'll fail it, they only give her three years to complete it, full-time you should be able to complete it in eighteen months," Oliver scoffed.

"Not very close, huh?" I raised an eyebrow as I checked the app store on my phone. It was down to seven minutes until the download was complete.

"Nope. She's twenty, two years older than me. Haven't really seen her since I left home to be honest, but I hear about her occasionally. She hasn't changed much, still a party girl. Social life comes first. Mom and Dad wanted her to studying business or something better than beauty, but she had her mind set. I'm surprised they allowed her to be honest." He shook his head.

"You never talk about your parents," I murmured.

"Yeah, well, nothing to talk about." He shifted uneasily, and I saw the barriers slam up behind those amber eyes. They'd cast him out. He hadn't just run away. And it still pained him.

I could see it so clearly, the hurt and grief in his eyes.

"Well, tomorrow we have our first Animal Management Practical day. You looking forward to it?" I asked, shifting the topic.

"Yeah, I guess so. We're starting with cats and dogs, so it should be good. I can focus more on my ability. I can recognize pain in many animals if I actively search for it, but my magic can also allow me to ease their pain too. I'd like to use it more. I used to help my grandfather out on his farm, I spent a lot of time there as a kid, so did Lucas, Skip, and Marcus. We could be real kids there, no overbearing families trying to make you act a certain way," he said with a sigh. "Every now and then he'd have a horse go lame, and I could help ease the pain and try to understand where it was originating from. My grandfather taught me a fair bit about finding the source of pain using my magic, but it's been a while since I've seen him."

"You guys are on good terms?" I asked.

"Oh yeah, Pop was the only one who didn't go weird on me after the curse thing. I think Lucas confided in him about the truth early on, but made him swear not to tell. I've seen him a fair bit over the years since I left home, but last time I saw him was a few months ago now." He frowned.

"If I'm not working the afternoon shift Sunday, I'd love to come meet him," I said honestly. I was also eager to visit a farm. I'd never actually been to one growing up.

"Of course, you know what, we'll work it around your shift. If you work in the morning, we'll go in the arvo, if you work the arvo, we'll go in the morning." He grinned. "Pop will love you, he's a true shifter too, my entire lineage is."

"What's his farm like?"

"He mostly rescues dogger horses from the sales and retrains them. Sometimes gets some thoroughbreds right off the track for retraining. He also has a few rescue cows, he's vegetarian, so he doesn't eat meat."

"How old is he?" I frowned. Retraining horses? I was picturing an old man in his seventies or eighties.

"Seventy-two, but he seems a lot younger. Don't worry, he's got a few workers who help him retrain the horses too now, he doesn't do it all himself." Oliver laughed, under-standing my bewilderment.

"I was going to say, jeez," I breathed.

"How's the download coming along?" he asked as his amber eyes flicked to my phone.

"Two minutes," I said as I checked it.

"Well, once you've got it, upload your photo, and I'll help you get your privacy settings and everything set up. Oh, and we'll add messenger too, you'll want that," he added.

We spent the next half an hour setting up my Facebook once it had downloaded to my phone, adding the boys to my friends list, and Emma from uni.

Oliver also added me to a few supernatural Facebook groups. They were hidden groups that you needed links for, which he sent me, and then your identity would be verified as supe. You needed to answer a series of questions before they'd accept you, like your date of birth, family name if not the one listed on Facebook, and a few other things. I'd be accepted into the groups within forty-eight hours once they did a background search on me.

"So, what are these supe groups for anyway?" I asked. The idea that there were Facebook specific groups for supes was boggling, but apparently there was more to Mr. Zuckerberg than we thought. He was one of us, a supernatural creature, although it was kept pretty quiet as to what he was. I couldn't help but be curious as to what the Facebook genius could be.

"They're for finding out about events in the area for just our kind, keeping updated on news on us. I've added you into the University group, the Events group for the Coast, and the buy, sell, swap page too for South East Queensland. Oh, and just a social group." He beamed.

"There's a buy, sell, swap group for supes?" I muttered in disbelief.

"Um, yeah. Where else would you buy all the potions and enchanted objects from? Many witches will also offer their services to humans, but they are less potent for humans. Just the way it is for some reason, you need magic inside you to activate potions to their full extent."

"Great." So was that where my aunt had gotten the pendant for me? From a Facebook group?

"Hey, I'm going to go do some reading for my Animal Management stuff in the library, want to join? It's only just after four-thirty now, and Skip said he's making dinner."

"I might just hang around here for a bit, lie down and do some standard reading on supernatural creatures. But I might pop down soon."

"Okay, well, enjoy the phone," he said with that gorgeous, boyish grin.

"I will, and thanks again, I owe you." I smiled back.

"Just shout some pizzas and we're even!" he shot over his shoulder as he headed out of the room.

I flinched as my phone sounded off, and I flicked it onto

vibrate.

Emma had accepted my friend request and had sent me a message.

'Hey Ally! Good to see you got Facebook finally. I was thinking we should catch up sometime outside of uni. I have a feeling we'll be paired up, and if you have any questions, just let me know :)'

I smiled at the message. Emma was sweet, and I liked her already. Besides, it couldn't hurt to make some friends. Finally some friends like me.

What I wouldn't do for some real friends for a change. I'd lost contact with most of my school friends, and I didn't feel like rekindling the relationships. They could never truly know me, and it just made things harder.

'Sounds great! I do have one question, I have the ability to sense when animals have serious illness, things that are life-threatening, but I've been told fae don't have that ability.'

I shot the message back, moving to my bed to lie down.

Skip had accepted my friend request, and I decided to check out his profile.

Yep. Definitely Skip. His profile picture was him posing in front of his beast of a landcruiser. I trawled through his photos, finding some from a few years back of his family.

He had a little sister, only a few years younger than him by the looks of her.

Emma messaged back, and I moved my focus to the message.

'Yeah, that is a weird one. Shifters have it, maybe it's your wolf side.'

'Lucas said that my shifter gene isn't the dominant one, which is why it's really weird,' I sent back.

I waited as she typed back quickly.

'That is weird. I'll do some digging. You got class

tomorrow?'

'Yep, prac. Got lunch at 11.'

'Damn, I'll be in class. Maybe we could hang after classes? Pop into Dingo Diner maybe for a coffee or something.'

I snorted at the suggestion.

'I start work there Saturday, but sounds good.'

'Oh awesome, guess I'll see you in there, I grab my coffees from there, they're so much better than the uni ones.'

I contemplated telling her I would be joining the barista team. I did make a decent coffee.

'Cool, I finish at 3 tomorrow. Wanna meet out the front afterwards?'

'Sounds like a plan, see you then.'

Huh. Maybe making friends wasn't so hard.

Although, I'd have to talk to her in person about this reading minds thing. I didn't think it was appropriate over message.

I smiled as Lucas accepted my friend request, and sent me a winky face to greet me.

I shot a laughing emoji back, which he liked.

"All right, no more Facebook, you need to learn about your new world," I muttered as I set the phone down on my bedside table.

Not to mention I'd start my study for my Animal Management.

I reached down to the pile of books beside my bed and picked up the encyclopedia. I was intrigued by all the different supes out there, although I'd covered the common ones a fair bit. I had so much learning to do in order to fit in. I was the black sheep here, the supernatural with barely any knowledge.

I'd change that.

· · ·

I padded down the stairs in my socks and pajamas after having had my shower. It was just after seven-thirty, and Skip had messaged me to inform me dinner was ready.

Spaghetti bog. Something I hadn't had in a while.

"I'm just saying, if it were up to me, your sister shouldn't even be at uni anymore. C'mon, one year left, and she's done how much of her course?" Skip scoffed as he sat down at the dining table with Lucas and Ollie.

"Apparently, next to nothing from what I hear," Ollie muttered as his eyes moved to trail over me in my pajamas.

I was suddenly very aware that I had no bra on, and the cooler night air had made its mark.

This didn't go unnoticed as Ollie's eyes dropped to check out my perky nipples before flicking away.

Skip was less inconspicuous.

"Bit cold, huh?" He gave me his charming smile as I folded my arms over my chest.

"Skip," Lucas scolded him before waving for me to join them.

I kept my arms covering my breasts as I sat down in the free seat beside him, with the other two straight across from me.

The pot of spaghetti bog was perched on a wooden chopping board between us all, and it was apparently self serve.

"Want a drink?" Lucas asked as he served me up a sizable amount.

"Um, sure," I said as I tried to avoid meeting Skip's gaze.

"So, Ally, meet any good-looking fellas today?" Skip asked as Lucas waved his hand and some orange juice floated out of the fridge. It glided over and poured into my cup just under full before flitting back into the open fridge.

I smiled every time Lucas did that, and he appeared to enjoy my amazement as he watched me with a soft smile.

"Um, no," I said as I caught Skip's expectant gaze.

"Really? No one?" His mouth curved into a smirk as he jammed his fork into his spaghetti.

"Didn't really have time," I muttered as I had a mouthful of the hot spaghetti bog. Damn, it was good, saucy with seasoned mince.

"That's just sad. Especially if it's been a while since your ex," he snickered. "Might be getting lonely."

"I never said it's been a while in that department," I retorted, causing him to chuckle.

"Well, seems our little pixie is quite the minx." He winked, causing the heat to flood my cheeks.

I didn't have a good response to that, so I just settled for reaching for my juice and taking a large gulp.

"I've never been with a pixie, would love to see how that mischief magic works," Skip said casually as he shoved another mouthful of spaghetti bog into his mouth.

I just stared at him in shock, trying to decipher what he was saying.

"Skip, she's going to take that the wrong way." Oliver sighed.

"Oh, nah, she can take it however she likes." Skip gave me a crooked grin with a wink as he wiggled his eyebrows.

I felt like my face was on fire right now. The thought of Skip naked and in my bed was definitely a hot one, and it was warming me up. I was quick to squash it down before it heated me up too much.

"Jesus, Skip, you'll be the death of her." Lucas chuckled.

"I'm just saying, I'm down for anything." Skip shrugged.

I focused on my plate, staring dumbly at my spaghetti as my body quivered at the suggestion.

Was he insinuating he'd sleep with me?

I mean, I wouldn't pretend I wasn't an okay-looking girl, and I'd snagged quite a few one-night stands on Tinder. But he was my housemate for crying out loud.

"Ally, relax, he's just playing with you," Lucas assured me.

"He just wants you to believe that." Skip laughed. "He just wants you to himself."

"On the contrary, if I did want Ally, you know perfectly well that *I'm* always up for sharing." Lucas' mouth curved into a playful grin.

"Oh yes, Lucy does love to have fun," Skip snorted.

"Ollie likes to get involved too sometimes, don't ya?" Skip turned on Ollie and elbowed him, whose face lit up like a red fairy light.

"What is going on?" I squeaked, and Lucas laughed as Skip just shook his head.

As if he'd timed it, Marcus walked in right then, glancing around at all of us at the table.

"Marcus, save me," I mumbled as I groaned and reached for my half empty glass of juice.

"Let me guess, they couldn't keep up their cover that this isn't a sex house?" Marcus mused, and I just gaped at him.

"What?" I nearly choked as my eyes flicked around to my housemates.

"What exactly do you think happens on their party nights, VB? You're in a house of man-whores," Marcus said with a straight face as he opened up the fridge.

He pulled out his cool bag and removed a small blood bag for himself before stuffing it back into the fridge. He leaned against the closed door as those frosty eyes settled on me with an amused glint.

"Guilty as charged," Skip admitted with one hand raised

to the flag.

"I'm not a man-whore." Ollie pouted.

"Oh, but you do sneak into the action when you can, don't deny it." Skip laughed as Oliver's ashamed eyes fell on me.

What the hell was going on right now?

Had the charade been given away? Were they all just playing the part of being sweet housemates when in truth I was their next plaything?

And despite the way it unnerved me and even freaked me out, it excited me.

I had to inwardly scold myself at the thought.

"Ally, relax, don't get stressed. Everyone likes to get laid every once in a while, and we're all single, so sometimes, we have some… friends, come over. I'm sure you know the drill." Lucas turned to me, those calm forest green eyes sparkling with amusement.

"Yeah, I guess." I shrugged, but my face was burning and my body was ready to jump to life. Right. I couldn't be annoyed at them for it, I'd had quite a few one-night stands myself.

And they were young men.

"So, wait, you bring them back here?" I asked.

"Yeah, although we generally give a heads up via messenger. I'll add you to the group chat." Skip grinned as he reached for his phone on the table.

I just looked around at my four housemates, stunned. I had not expected to find that out tonight.

I mean, I knew they'd be doing stuff, but I didn't realize they'd be so open about it.

"If you wanna bring a guy back, just give us a heads up, but we don't like to share with outsiders." Skip gave me his charming grin, and I took a moment to try to gauge if he was joking or not.

"Just know that sometimes we may talk about it, and Skip most certainly will talk about it. He wasn't meant to until you'd settled in so we didn't scare you off," Lucas said pointedly at Skip, who just rolled his eyes as he polished off his plate.

"I'm not that easy to scare off," I said instantly, which drew a deep chuckle from Marcus.

"Oh, but you've only brushed the surface, VB, trust me," he said, drawing my attention. He was sipping from the small blood bag, using the tube to suck it out. It looked like it was right out of a hospital. Wouldn't surprise me.

My mind flicked momentarily to the stories my cousin had told me of sex while being bitten by a vamp. Apparently the best she'd ever had.

I shoved the thought aside as I dragged my eyes away from him.

"Even you, Ollie?" I turned to my best mate with a playful pout.

"No!" he barked, his eyes widening.

"Aw, isn't that cute. You don't want her to know, I think someone's got a crush." Marcus chuckled, and I found myself happily warming at the sound.

"No, that's not it!" Ollie sunk into his seat as he averted his eyes.

It wasn't like he'd tried to hide his interest in me, I just wasn't sure how interested. Just a little crush, or a jump my bones if given the chance? Probably the second, he was a guy after all.

"Hey, leave him alone." Lucas chuckled.

"Hey, he's been the first one naked with her." Skip grinned, and I rolled my eyes as the image of Ollie naked on my bed that first morning flared into my mind.

"It wasn't like that!" Ollie snapped as his eyes flashed

brightly.

"Oh shit." Lucas sighed, and I just stared dumbly as Oliver disappeared from sight.

"What?" I muttered as I glanced around the room.

"Oh, crap, I'm sorry." Skip cringed as he looked down at the seat beside him.

Oh, dear God.

"Look what you did! He's got his first prac day tomorrow!" I said, horrified as I stood, the orange and white cat sitting unhappily on the seat in a puddle of clothing, his shirt hanging from his shoulder. He had such a grumpy cat face that I couldn't keep from smiling despite feeling mortified for him.

"Oh boy, hopefully it'll just be a short one," Skip murmured as he stood and began gathering plates, obviously wanting to pretend like it wasn't his fault.

'I hate you.'

I flinched at the words that rung out in my mind as clear as day. Oliver's voice.

The cat was glaring at Skip's back, his tail twitching manically.

"Right, Ally, you'll hear his voice now, thanks to your bracelet," Lucas reminded me.

Crap. I'd forgotten that.

Ollie leaped down off the chair, stalking over to Skip who was rinsing the plates and stacking the dishwasher.

'I had prac tomorrow!' Ollie snapped, and his small form yowled as he leaped at Skip.

I watched in shock as Ollie attacked Skip's leg, clawing and biting him like a savage little beast.

"I'm sorry! Ow…. Ow! Fuck off!" Skip cursed as he flailed his leg in an attempt to shake him off.

Ollie hissed as he shot back, his back arching up.

"Boys, seriously? In front of Ally?" Lucas sighed. "C'mon Ollie, let's try that relaxation spell, see if we can't try to get you to turn back before tomorrow," he said.

"A spell?" I murmured softly.

"Sometimes a relaxation spell can help reverse it sooner. It's a gamble, sometimes it works, sometimes it doesn't. It focuses on relaxing him, and if the shift was caused by an emotional outburst rather than just a random shift, then sometimes it can fix it," Lucas explained.

"Well, that'd be good, but he needs to do his prac," I said as I looked down at the cat stalking past me. He stopped as he looked up at me, and then crouched down before pouncing up on the table beside where I was sitting.

'I forgot to tell you, I met a dingo shifter today. Said his name was Derek, that was the guy you told me about, right? He could smell you on me, asked how I knew you,' Oliver said, his amber eyes narrowed into slits as he looked at me with curiosity.

"Derek was in your shifter class?" I mumbled, my stomach twisting at the thought. God, no, why was he here?

"Who's Derek?" Skip asked as he checked his scratched up leg.

'Ally's ex,' Oliver stated as his tail twitched unhappily. *'He was in my shifter class until we got split.'*

I sunk deeper into my seat as I thought about him. He wasn't a fan of my mischief magic when it flared up once. That had been the big turning point in our relationship.

He'd also been a narcissistic arsehole. And more.

"Why are we only just hearing about this?" Skip smirked.

"Because she doesn't want to talk about it," Marcus spoke up from his stance against the fridge.

I caught those frosty blue eyes, and for a moment, I knew that he understood me. He knew how I felt right now, and why Derek was not a talking point for me. Those icy blue eyes were soft and saddened.

I guess the real Marcus was showing through.

"Why not? Did he hurt you?" Lucas asked softly as he touched my arm.

I flinched and pulled away, standing up in a huff.

"I think I'll head to bed, thank you for dinner, Skip." I nodded at the confused man by the dishwasher.

'Ally...' Oliver murmured, but I shook my head.

"I don't want to talk about it," I mumbled.

"If he hurt you, we can fuck him up," Skip growled.

"We won't let him touch you, Ally," Lucas said, but I was already shaking my head as I wrapped my arms around me, the uneasiness churning inside me as fear and anger boiled beneath the surface.

Why was he at this University? Why now?

"Ally," Lucas said firmly as I squeezed my eyes shut.

"Fucking spaghetti!" Skip shrieked.

My eyes popped open, and I just watched numbly as the spaghetti bog clambered out of the pot like a writhing mass of worms.

It split into sections, and each one launched at the closest person.

I watched as a large blob of spaghetti bog splattered against Lucas' chest, snarling and writhing as a strange little mouth tried to bite him. Thankfully, spaghetti had no teeth.

'Help!' Ollie shrieked as he hissed and scrambled to leap off the table. He wasn't fast enough as a chunk of spaghetti bog latched onto his tail before he jumped.

He yowled and ran crazily around the kitchen with it hanging from his tail, all the while Skip was battling his attacker as it splattered onto the floor and snarled at him. He was wielding a chopping board and spatula to defend himself.

Marcus was too far away at the fridge, and there hadn't been enough spaghetti left to target him, so he was just watching in mild amusement.

"Ally, calm down, you need to breathe. You need to reclaim your magic," Lucas said as he waved his hand and the attacking mass on his chest floated back to the pot, writhing and howling softly.

I just stared at the orange stain on his white undershirt, his suit a mess now.

Well, at least my overwhelming fear and uncertainty had eased a bit.

"How?" I asked softly, knowing I had to handle this. I couldn't just have my powers running havoc, even if I just wanted to hide and wish the day away.

"Close your eyes, imagine that same tingling washing over you, imagine your energy and power being sucked out of the spaghetti and returning to you," Lucas murmured.

I did as he said, drawing in some calming breaths as my stomach still churned from the news.

I ignored the frantic cursing from Skip and the mad dashing of Ollie.

I envisioned the energy in my mind, my power, slowly returning to me, washing over me in that unique, tingling, electric sensation.

I felt the soft spark surge through my body returning to me and settling deep inside. Skip sighed, and I heard him set the chopping board down.

'Thank God,' Ollie muttered. *'I thought it was going to eat my head.'*

I managed a chuckle at his words, and I opened my eyes to look around apologetically.

"I'm sorry," I said sheepishly as Skip began gathering up the now dead spaghetti bog off the floor with paper towels.

"Don't be, I shouldn't have pushed," Skip apologized in return. "I lack a filter, according to everyone else, I speak before I think," he mumbled, obviously annoyed with himself.

"I know you were only worried," I murmured, and he gave me a sad smile as he carried the spaghetti to the bin.

"Well, looks like there won't be any leftovers after all." Skip sighed as he tossed the spaghetti into the bin.

"Just be grateful Ollie didn't get eaten." Marcus smirked, and Ollie hissed in response.

I looked at Marcus, at the understanding I saw in his eyes. I was grateful he was trying to make light of the situation, if not a little surprised.

"Well, we'll clean up here, you head on to bed if you want to, you should get some rest after your first day." Lucas stood and looked down at his dirtied shirt.

"Sorry," I apologized again.

"Stop saying that, you can't help that no one taught you to control your magic. Besides, it's just a shirt, nothing magic and a wash can't fix," he said with a wink.

I nodded, looking down at Ollie on the floor as he groomed his tail.

"Don't worry about him, we'll give the spell a go, and if we're lucky, he'll be back to himself for prac tomorrow," Lucas said as he flicked his hands and the spaghetti bog pile behind Ollie floated into the air.

"Okay, cool. And thanks, for helping me fix it," I said as I rubbed my arm awkwardly.

"Don't mention it." Lucas gave me a warm smile.

I turned to say goodnight to Skip, and my eyes fell on Marcus, who was giving me an odd, curious look.

I left it alone as I headed upstairs, wanting to fall into a deep sleep with dreams that took away all my worries.

15

"How was work?" Derek asked as he walked me to my door. I was grateful my housemate was still working, so I'd get some alone time with him. He'd turned up at my place after my shift to hang out.

"It was fine." I shrugged.

"Really? Something tells me there's more to it than that." He chuckled, his dark eyes glittering with interest as he wrapped an arm around my shoulders. He was a fair bit taller than me at roughly 6'2, with me at just 5'4, according to my driver's license.

"Ugh, I had this douchebag come in. Wasn't happy with the cake he ordered with his coffee, despite having eaten the whole thing," I spat as I unlocked my door and headed in. I dumped my handbag on the white laminate counter and started taking off my name-tag and pendant. I always wore it out, but once home and alone, I liked to take it off sometimes. It was just something I did, to feel more like myself.

Little did I know it would be the first time I'd taken it off in front of Derek.

"What was wrong with the cake?" he asked as he

slouched against the counter and ran his hand down the side of my face, making me sigh.

"Apparently it was too dry or some shit, but he made a huge scene out of it when I said there wasn't much I could do since he'd eaten the whole thing. I offered him a replacement, but that wasn't enough," I rolled my eyes as the scene replayed in my head. That large, lumbering idiot had caused the whole shop to fall silent as they all watched the furious man bellowing about his cake. Seriously, who gets that pissed about cake?

"Whoa, what the fuck?" Derek stumbled back against the sink, and I frowned at him, before following his gaze to the fruit bowl beside me.

The apple was convulsing, a small mouth forming as it hissed and shrieked in anger.

Small legs protruded, and it marched out of the bowl, soft snarls coming from it.

Great. Just what I wanted to eat right now. A goddamn apple.

"Sorry," I muttered as I snatched it up and took a bite out of it, causing the small red apple to shriek and squirm in my grip.

"Ally, what the fuck is wrong with that apple?" Derek's wide eyes were focused on the monstrosity I was munching into.

"Mischief magic, apparently. I'm a pixie." I sighed as I continued biting into the apple.

"A pixie?" Derek frowned and winced as I bit into the apple again. Its cries were dying down now, and soon it faded back to a normal apple as I ate right through to the core in record time.

"I thought you were fae," he murmured as I tossed the core into the bin.

"No, you assumed that. I never corrected you, but my mother had pixie lines mostly," I said.

"Mischief magic." He scowled, and I was taken aback by how his shoulders had risen.

"What's wrong?" I asked as I moved closer to him, but he stepped away from me with his eyes dark and stormy.

"You keep lying to me, not telling me things. You said I was your first boyfriend, but you obviously weren't a virgin," he scoffed as he shook his head. "And now you're telling me you're a pixie?"

"You know why I wasn't a virgin," I murmured, shifting uneasily at his sudden change in demeanor. It wasn't the first time either.

"Because you were abused? You really expect me to believe that?" he spat. "And a pixie? C'mon. Everyone knows they're always causing trouble. You're probably lying about what happened to you," he barked.

Wow. Full fucking change right there.

Hold up.

"What the fuck?" I muttered, shocked at his words. How had the man I'd been falling for snap so suddenly like this? There had to be something else causing this outburst.

"Derek, what's gotten into you?" I murmured as I moved backwards, my chest tightening as he balled his hands into fists.

"Nothing. I'm just sick of this, of your lies. You did this. You never come clean, you hid your past for over a month, even after we first had sex, you wouldn't tell me the truth as to why you weren't a virgin if I was your first boyfriend. Then you tell me some sob story to make me stay around. You refuse to come out to parties with me, and now you're telling me you're a pixie?" He threw his arms up in disbelief.

"Seriously? I work, a lot," I growled as I snatched up my

pendant from the counter. Better hang onto it in case my magic flared up. Didn't need him going psycho even more. He'd switched like this before, always brought up my past after we had sex. He knew I hated it, hated being reminded, but he just couldn't understand it.

"I didn't tell you about my past because of exactly this, thinking you might freak out on me," I said, hating how the tears threatened to spill and my voice hitched.

"I stayed with you, even when you didn't want to have sex at first. I waited until you were ready, you kept going on that I was your first boyfriend, you wanted it to be right. But I wasn't your first, you're just a damn slut trying to throw others under the bus for your own mistakes. And you have days off, you could come out with me then," he spat.

I just stared at him, trembling at the nasty look in his eye. Why was he so split like this? One day he was my charming boyfriend, treating me like the girl he loved, then the next he was hurling harsh words at me.

This wasn't the man I'd fallen for. This wasn't the man who'd spent a few nights teaching me how to shift, loping through the national park with me, as a dingo and wolf. This wasn't the man I'd opened up to, had sex with. This was that nasty side that showed itself afterwards, that mean, cruel side that never failed to rear its ugly head.

"I don't understand how such a small thing has turned into this," I stammered, wrapping my arms around myself as he advanced on me.

Please, not again.

The slap knocked me against the counter, and I slid to the floor as I held my stinging cheek, the tears streaking down.

"Because you lie! I'm your partner. There shouldn't be any lies between us," he growled as he stood over me.

I awoke with my heart pounding and sweat beading on

my forehead. So much for dreams that would take away my worries.

I sat up, drawing in a deep breath as I calmed myself, balling my shaking hands up as I pulled my knees to my chest.

Derek. My ex. My first ever boyfriend.

He'd always turned angry and violent when he got confused, upset, or scared. It was like he couldn't accept those emotions, so he'd just lose it instead. That had been the last fight we'd had. I'd ended things after that and found a new rental. My boss was very understanding and banned him from the shop when I told her he'd hit me.

I didn't tell her it wasn't the first time.

I'd stayed with him despite his major mood swings, because he was my first boyfriend. And the abuse, the mental and physical? I'd grown up with that already. I'd thought it was normal, but a part of me always knew it was wrong.

"Of course you're here," I muttered.

I thought I'd left him behind, moved on and away from him.

Guess my luck had run out. We'd only been together a few months, would he even remember me? It'd be nearly three years now.

I turned to pluck my phone off the bedside table, groaning at the four-thirty time on it.

I pulled myself out of bed, not willing to try to return to sleep for another hour or so. I didn't want another bad dream. A wretched memory.

Instead, I changed and fixed up my hair before sitting down on the end of my bed.

I reached for the encyclopedia, but then decided against it as I picked up a history book.

Time to learn some supernatural history.

I spent the next few hours learning that supes dated back to the vikings, probably further, but the history was scattered beyond that. I learned Leonardo Da Vinci had been a witch who specialized in dream-walking, a rare witch ability that allowed him to explore alternate realities, and to delve into the dreams of others. He used this to inspire some of his creations. I tried not to think too much of these alternate realities, the more I did, the more it weirded me out.

Many great people from normal history had a supernatural twist, which I was finding utterly fascinating.

There was the era of witch-burning, a harsh time for supes, where they tried even harder to blend in. Their magic evolved with them, thankfully, and witch-burning was left behind when witches could hide themselves easier. Many innocents, humans as well, died in that time.

The Supernatural Council came into effect in the late 1400s, although before that there had been country based organizations that handled all supernatural affairs in that region. The Supernatural Council was the one ruling Council, the High Council managing the most major of issues concerning supes. This included Hitler, who had been brought back to life as a child thanks to a warlock. This resulted in a sick, twisted man who struggled with the two sides of himself. Those who were brought back had a darkness inside them, a remnant from the afterlife that tainted them.

He was carefully destroyed and covered up, but not after significant damage had been done. The crackdown on warlocks only worsened after that, and all warlocks were put under watch, tracked down by the Council's very own warlock, who had mastered the magic of prolonged life.

I pursed my lips as my phone vibrated, informing me I'd been accepted into the Facebook groups for supes.

I set my book down, now curious about the groups. What would they contain?

The buy, swap, sell group was just like Oliver had said. Mostly charmed objects, potions, spell books, study books, jobs for supes. I only scrolled through a few listings before checking out another page.

The University one had information on events coming up, and it offered the link and code to the supernatural web. The code changed every few days, so it was best to make an account.

"Supernatural web?" I frowned. A quick read over their post informed me it was google—for supes. So real sites with real info, all carefully protected and warded so only those on the supernatural web could access it.

Intrigued, I clicked through to the website, where it asked for the code and then an identity check. It would create an account for me once I was verified as supe. Of course.

I entered my details, keen to know what lay in this supernatural web. It could take a few days to verify, though, which bummed me out.

My requests for the supe social and events group were still pending, so I set my phone down.

The time was now six-thirty, and I figured I might as well go get breakfast, I needed to be at the Veterinary clinic on campus before eight for my prac day.

Hopefully Ollie was himself again.

I walked out into the hall, pulling my old gray jacket tight around my shoulders. It was still pretty cool in the morning.

I found Lucas up bright and peachy in an extravagant purple suit in the kitchen.

"Morning." He turned and grinned at me.

"Morning," I said as I stifled a yawn.

"Bad sleep?" he asked with a frown.

"That easy to tell?" I scoffed as I set about making some toast. Some peanut butter and jam sounded good, and I'd made sure to buy them.

"Was it because of what Ollie told you?" he asked gently as he put the kettle on.

"Yeah." I sighed. No point in lying, last night had made it clear that there were issues involving Derek.

"Anything I can do to help?" he asked.

"Nope, you can't undo the past." I gave him a forced smile as I popped two pieces of bread in the toaster.

"Did he hurt you?" Lucas asked, and I could hear the underlying venom in his voice.

"It's nothing to worry about. It was years ago," I said, wishing he'd just drop it.

He must've got the hint, because he didn't say another word as he set about making a tea.

"You want one?" he asked.

"Sure," I murmured as I waited patiently for my toast to pop. I'd gathered up the peanut butter and strawberry jam and set it on the counter with a plate.

"Mornin."

I smiled as I turned to spy Ollie walking in, rubbing his eyes sleepily.

"Glad you're back to normal," I said as he managed a tired smile.

"Yeah, well, it happened sometime during the night. Guess the spell worked, thank God," he said gratefully.

"Tea?" Lucas offered.

"Hot milo?" Oliver asked eagerly, and Lucas just rolled his eyes but nodded.

"Excited for today?" I asked as my toast finally popped and I carefully plucked the pieces out and tossed them onto the plate before I burnt my fingers.

"I guess so, it'll be interesting," he said as he sat down at the table.

"Hey, got a question, the supernatural web, what's on it?" I asked.

"Supernatural google. Want real facts, history, memes, whatnot. Anything supernatural will be on there, and it's all hidden from humans, only accessible by us," Lucas said.

"Want to know what actors are supes, you go there, want to learn more about spells, abilities, places, etc, that's where you go. It's the main doorway to the supernatural world," Oliver added.

"Could I learn about my ability on there?" I asked.

"Don't think so. I tried searching it there, along with my grandfather's books, but nothing came up about a pixie with that ability. It's weird, you'd think there'd be something, somewhere," Lucas remarked as the kettle boiled and he got to work on the hot drinks.

"Oh, okay," I murmured dejectedly. I'd been hoping I might find some answers there.

"Hey, did you look for any family on Facebook?" Ollie asked.

"Um, no, not really. I wouldn't even know where to start. I don't want anything to do with my aunt and cousin," and her boyfriend, but I didn't say that, "but I never really knew any other family apart from them. They weren't exactly family people, they never saw anyone, barely spoke of any of them. I doubt I'd even know if they were related to me if I came across any family relatives," I said.

"That sucks." Ollie pouted, but it turned to a smile as the hot milo floated over to sit before him. Lucas carried his and mine over as he joined us at the dining table.

I bit into my toasted peanut butter and jam sandwich,

sighing at the sweetness. Speaking of, I still had Freddos in the fridge. I'd take one with me today.

"I know some people, I could find out some relatives of yours if you'd like?" Lucas suggested.

"I don't know, would that be weird? I wouldn't even know them," I mumbled through a mouthful of my breakfast as I used my hand to cover my mouth.

"No, not at all. I'm sure they'd understand why you weren't in contact if your parents passed away and your aunt was a bitch," Lucas said.

"Maybe a relative would know more about my ability," I said thoughtfully.

"Possibly," Lucas said as he sipped his tea.

"Okay, well, if you know someone who can find relatives, then I guess I might as well," I said before biting into my toasted sandwich again.

The morning was uneventful, and Lucas offered to drive us. Skip didn't start until later, and I was getting used to only seeing Marcus in the evening hours.

I finally got to see Lucas' fancy 4x4 Mercedes, with its luxurious interior and wood paneling on the dash and doors. It was beautiful.

The drive was short, but the day was already heating up at just before eight in the morning. He parked down in the back carpark, and we parted ways with a wave and agreed to meet at the fig tree for lunch.

Ollie hooked his arm through mine with an excited grin, and we were off to our first practical day.

We assisted the older students and professors, learning as we went and being taught what all the tools were and what we would be assisting in for the first few weeks.

By the time lunch rolled around, I was giddy with excitement. I was really doing this, pursuing a proper career that could give me a real life.

Because living in a room in a house of guys was not a real life. Ha! It sure was an interesting one.

But this was what people did. They studied and got good jobs. That was how it worked.

Skip joined us for lunch, and I annihilated my freddo in seconds despite telling myself to make it last after eating the cheese and ham sandwich I'd prepared this morning. I'd even bought a water bottle when I'd done groceries, one of those metal bottles that stayed really cold.

"So, it's going well?" Lucas asked as he ate a sandwich for a change, although he had an apple with him, too.

Ollie was stuffing his face with a wrap he'd bought at a kiosk, and Skip had a homemade sandwich as well.

"Yeah, we love it." Ollie gave him a thumbs up as he bit into his wrap.

"Good, that's good." Lucas nodded.

"How's yours going?" I asked.

"The business is pretty boring but necessary, the sorcery and magic, that's the fun one." He grinned, those earthy green eyes flashing enthusiastically.

"Well, I got to study the cells of plants today, amongst other things, so that's a bonus." Skip shrugged. "I won't see you guys this arvo, I've got work."

"Right, you're working as a chippy?" I checked.

"Yeah, working with a mate's dad from primary school. Don't talk to his son much anymore, but he gives me work some arvos, and I work there for a full day every Thursday, it covers my bills," he said.

"You like it?" I asked as I sipped my water, the sun

burning my legs. I pulled them back into the shade of the fig, glancing around the courtyard vacantly.

"Yeah, I like working with my hands, making things, fixing things," he said.

"Oh, you so do love working with your hands," Lucas purred, and I breathed in my mouthful of water which resulted in a choking fit.

Skip just laughed as Lucas chuckled, while Ollie was the only one to come to my aid and pat my back.

I regained myself as I flicked my eyes between the pair.

"Okay, you can't keep making jokes like that, not inside ones, I want to know," I gasped as I regained myself, nodding at Ollie in thanks.

"Trust me, you probably don't." Skip smirked as he bit into his sandwich. He'd almost finished it in just four bites. That had to be a record.

"Oh, I think I do," I retorted.

"Skip's good with the ladies when it comes to his hands," Lucas stated, and Ollie groaned.

"Is sex really all you can think about?" I let out an exasperated sigh, but my interest was piqued. Just how good was he with his hands?

"Uh, most of the time." Skip gave me a stupefied look.

"It's natural at this age." Lucas shrugged, but his lip was pulled back into a sly smirk.

"I don't," I shot back.

"Really? You don't think about it? About that moment when your bodies are all wrapped up, naked and hot, desperate for satisfaction? When all you want is something more, that final finish, that bliss and pure ecstasy coursing through you as you connect with another person?" Skip purred as he leaned forward, the words rolling off his tongue like velvet.

Holy hell, that caused a reaction.

He sensed it too, I realized, as his eyes dilated.

"Word of caution, shifters can smell arousal," Lucas murmured.

Oh fuck.

"Seems our little pixie does think of sex more than she cares to admit." Skip chuckled, but those blue eyes were fixated on me. I could see his interest deep in them, the hunger, the... desire.

"All right, enough of this." I put my hand up, afraid I'd jump the kangaroo shifter if he kept that up. I seriously needed to buy myself a new toy, and soon.

"I'm just playing with you." Skip grinned as he pulled back.

Yeah, sure. That was all it was.

I turned to ask Ollie to back me up, but my mouth formed no words at the way those amber eyes were trailing over me.

Ugh. Shifters.

"Here, let's sort this." Lucas sighed as he waved his hand.

"You're no fun." Skip pouted, and Ollie relaxed a little as he averted his gaze, his brow creasing.

"What'd you do?" I asked as I turned to eye Lucas, who was watching me with an amused crooked smile.

"Got rid of the scent," he stated obviously.

"This is embarrassing," I muttered.

"Get used to it. You live with shifters, and a vampire. I'm probably the only one who won't smell it." Lucas chuckled. "And relax, we're used to these things. We grew up like this, sex is pretty normal."

"I'm not having sex with anyone," I said, then realized what I'd said. Why had I said that, God, foot in mouth much?

"Aw, and here I was thinking you were falling for me." Skip feigned heartache as he held his hands to his chest.

If only you knew, I thought to myself.

Lucas just chuckled, and I could've sworn Ollie pouted before covering it by biting his wrap.

"Well, my lunch break is over, you two behave, I don't want you scaring our new housemate off," Lucas said firmly to the two boys as he stood.

"We'd never do that." Skip gave him a bright, cheeky grin.

No, not at all.

Great. I was seriously wishing I could toss aside my need to keep my relationship with my boys strictly business. They were so damn tempting at times, not to mention they obviously had some interest. Or maybe it was just a shifter reaction? *No, stop that, Ally. They are a no go, no matter how any of you feel.*

I sighed, hating my logical side right now.

Maybe I'd get tinder on my new phone with my real Facebook, that would help. And once I had some money, I'd get myself a new toy.

"How was your day?" Emma asked vibrantly as I met her out the front of the campus. I'd informed Ollie I would find my way home later, so he got a lift with Lucas. Emma skipped over to walk beside me, her white hair up in a high ponytail today.

"Good, yours?" I asked as she began leading the way. Dingo Diner was only a ten-minute walk, and we'd agreed to go there. To be honest, a milkshake sounded damn good right now as the sun beat down on me with a vengeance.

"Eh, all right. Practiced magic stuff," she said.

"You're a psychic, right?" I checked, and her shoulders slumped.

"Yeah," she mumbled, her face downcast, all her bubbliness gone in an instant.

"Hey, I don't care, I was just wondering," I tried to reassure her.

"Yeah, sure, I bet your housemates told you all about me," she murmured, refusing to look at me.

"Yeah, so? I don't give a rat's arse about it. Although, can you choose when to read minds?" I asked carefully.

"Not always. I've learned to wall myself off, but sometimes things slip through. Some people broadcast loudly, but other times I'm not focusing enough on keeping my guard up and it lets some through. Other times I'll let it down," she said uneasily, gauging my reaction.

"Like when you asked about seeing one of the boys naked?" I smirked as I raised an eyebrow.

She pursed her lips, but I could see the smile threatening to break.

"Sorry," she said, but I could tell she really wasn't. "Could you blame me? Those boys are hot as fuck!"

I laughed and shook my head as she lightened and smiled.

"Sounds like it's a lot of work keeping people's thoughts out," I said.

"Yeah, it is." Emma frowned, as if she hadn't expected me to care or understand.

"So what do you do? I've read psychics can have an array of abilities depending on their bloodlines."

"Well, obviously there's the mind-reading, although I try not to advertise that," she scoffed, "then there's the communing with dead, readings, and occasional visions. And since I'm still a witch, I specialize in potions like the rest of my family. I'm still learning to control my visions, as sometimes they happen randomly. Can be past, current or future things."

"That's pretty epic." Being able to glimpse the future? Now that was wicked, and communing with the dead? I instantly thought of my parents, but pushed it away. They'd died long ago now, no need to dig it back up.

"I guess, I'm fairly used to it, I'm not the only one in the family with it, but I'm the only one with the mind-reading thing, thanks to my dad being a pixie," she said nonchalantly.

"Must be hard, being able to hear thoughts like that," I murmured. "You must hear some nasty stuff."

"Yeah, you learn things you'd rather not know. Ever read the *Sookie Stackhouse* series by Charlaine Harris? She hits the nail on the head in that. If you haven't, maybe the show, *True Blood*?" Emma looked at me, those gray eyes bright and cheery again.

"No, sorry, I do read, but not as much as I did before I started working full time. Moving here should free up a fair chunk of time though, maybe I'll see if the Maleny library has them," I mused.

"I can lend them to you? I own them," Emma said eagerly.

"Awesome, I'd like that."

"So any luck with figuring out why you've got the ability to sense animal illnesses?" Emma asked as we slid into one of the booths at Dingo Diner.

Gina was wearing the actual uniform today, as the one she'd previously worn wasn't the same as mine. It consisted of a black shirt with the Dingo Diner logo sprawled on it, and black shorts. The text was a sandy, desert orange with a cut-out of Ayers rock behind it. She greeted us warmly and expressed her excitement for my starting day on Saturday. She seemed almost more excited than I was. Henry was too busy frying up orders for the other waiting patrons, but he gave me a quick wave before focusing back on the task at hand.

We ordered some milkshakes and a small hot chips to share, and Gina said she'd bring it out.

"No, Lucas said he checked the supernatural web but got no answers," I said. "Nothing in the info about pixies either that states anything."

"Huh, weird. I've never heard of it either, maybe it is your werewolf side somehow. Maybe you're the first ever genetic anomaly." She grinned as those eyebrows rose nearly into her hairline.

"Doubt it." I chuckled.

"Hey, ever done a reading? Maybe it'll give you some answers?" she suggested as she tapped those bright red fingernails on the table.

"No, what do you do?" I asked.

"I use special supe tarot cards that my mom got for me. I use your aura and energy to select out cards that line up with you. It's a bit hard to explain, but it's the real deal with us psychics, not that fake crap most of the humans do," she said with a roll of her eyes.

"Only most of the humans?"

"Yeah, some have trace lines of psychic in them, not enough to be supe, but enough to access a little of the magic. It's a different kind of magic to most, an otherworldly kind." She waved it off as she delved into her bag.

She pulled out a deck of cards and set it on the table.

"You keen?" she asked with a wide smile.

"Sure, why not." I shrugged. What harm could be done? Besides, I was curious how it worked.

Just at that moment, Gina strode over to deliver our milkshakes and hot chips in record time.

"Enjoy." Gina nodded, giving me a bright smile before heading back behind the counter. It seemed the afternoon was a rather busy period. Good to know.

"All right, so, to start, what is it you want to get some insight on today?" Emma asked as her expression turned serious and she withdrew the deck of gold-backed cards from their wooden case.

"My ability," I said as I sipped my vanilla malt milkshake.

"Anything else?" she asked as she shuffled the deck, and I could swear there was a faint green glow to her eyes.

"My future?" I shrugged, and Emma's mouth curved into a smirk.

"Doesn't everyone?" she murmured as she divided the deck into four piles.

"When were you born?" she asked.

I gave her my birth date.

"Parents' names?"

"Gerard and Christine Smoak," I murmured, hating that I had to bring them up. It was always a little difficult for me. I'd never had a chance to really know them. They'd died when I was six.

"They're deceased?" Emma clarified. I didn't remember ever telling her that, but she was a psychic.

I just nodded.

"How?" she asked, and normally the question would've made my chest squeeze, but this time I knew it was just part of the process.

"Car accident."

"Hmm." She pursed her lips.

"What?" I frowned.

"Nothing," she said as she removed two of the four piles and set them back into the case.

"All right, close your eyes, I'm going to focus on your energy for this one, channel it to choose a pile," she said as she held a hand over the piles and offered me her other one.

I did as told and took her warm hand, shivering as I felt a strange, foreign tingling sensation coursing through me.

Nothing like my own electric one, this one felt strange and soft, rippling through my own energy.

"Okay, it'll be this one," she said after a moment, and released my hand. "You can open your eyes."

I did, glancing down at the last remaining pile.

"This next part will be completely my doing. I'll use your aura to choose the cards, and I'll decipher their meaning," she said as she plucked a chip from the box and tossed it back.

I grabbed a few for myself as she swirled her hand over the pile slowly.

It glowed with a faint green, eerie color as the pile floated up and the cards began shuffling themselves.

I watched in amazement, glancing around at the other patrons hesitantly.

Gina was watching with mild interest, but most other patrons didn't care about our little card reading session. Right. Supes. It was normal to them.

Five cards floated out of the pile, setting face down on the table before us. The glowing pile drifted to the side, and Emma caught it and set it back into the box as the glowing subsided.

"All right," she breathed as she began flipping the cards over.

I read the cards, impressed at the hand-painted images on each. The first one read 'The Father', and had a stoic man posed on it. The second was 'The Eye', the iris an array of vibrant colors. The third was 'The Lone Wolf', a beautifully painted white wolf standing alone in a forest. The fourth was

'Family', picturing faceless figures embracing. And the final one was 'The Banshee', it had a strange, shadowy figure floating on it in a hood and white flowing dress.

Emma's eyes glowed a soft green as she flicked them over the five cards, studying them.

I munched on some more chips, my eyes constantly drifting back to the Banshee one. I'd read about them, a rare creature that brought death with it. Was it the supe version of the death card?

God, I hoped not.

I slurped my milkshake uneasily, but then Emma frowned and sat back.

"It's not the clearest interpretation, the spirits aren't very forthcoming today," she said, her eyes perplexed.

"The spirits?" I arched an eyebrow.

"I use a combination of my magic and communing with the dead to get the best result. Some of these are vague, but some aren't. The first one, 'The Father', symbolizes that all the answers you seek come from him. So I'm understanding this as meaning your ability is coming from his side of the family. So maybe an anomaly with the werewolf gene," she said. "Hard to tell, but definitely your father."

"He was just a werewolf." I frowned. All the answers? I'd only really had one question.

"Did you though?" Emma asked, and I saw her mentally slap herself when she realized I hadn't said it aloud. "Sorry, my walls go down a bit when I do this," she apologized before clearing her throat and moving on. "'The Eye' symbolizes you're being watched over or sought out, but this is a little obscure. I don't get a positive vibe from this, so best be careful. 'The Lone Wolf' is clear. It says you've lost your main family and are estranged from all others. Your own choosing, for the best ,too. I get a feeling that there's some dark history with your aunt, more-so her partner, well, more than one partner." Emma frowned, pursing her lips at me in hopes I'd elaborate on this meaning.

"Yeah, I'd rather not talk about it," I said as I stiffened. I hadn't expected the reading to reveal that. It was something I preferred to pretend never happened.

"Okay," she breathed, accepting my unwillingness to share. I was glad she didn't push it. "The 'Family' card symbolizes your new family, relationships that will flourish in the time to come. Romance seems to be entwined in this one, too." sShe winked, moving completely away from the previous issue, which relaxed me. "And strangely, the whispers say it's not monogamous." She chuckled.

"What does that mean?" I asked, baffled by this revelation.

"More than one partner?" She gave me a stupefied look.

"I know what monogamous means." I chuckled.

"It's vague. I have a feeling it's your housemates." She winked.

"Is that your intuitive side or your wishful side?" I shot back, and she just grinned mischievously.

Her expressed sobered as she looked back down at the last card.

"This last one is a worry. The reading is extremely weird for this one. It's hard for me to decipher. Something about your past, present, and future, all in one. You've lost some people, although their death is not what it seems. Death will be a part of your life, but as to how, it's vague. Maybe your illness sensing in animals, it's mostly fatal stuff, right?"

I nodded, a chill running through me at her words. Their death was not what it seemed? Was that my parents? They died in a car accident. At least, that was what the reports said, and what I'd been told.

"Could just be that. I'm sorry, this one's really hard to gauge. Normally it's a symbol of an upcoming death. The Banshee is said to wail before someone dies, the bringer of death." She frowned.

"Not creepy or concerning at all," I muttered.

"Don't take it to heart, it's not a very accurate reading, which is weird. Most of the time I can do readings quite well. You're unique." She grinned as she took a big gulp of her strawberry milkshake.

"So don't be worried about 'The Banshee'?"

"No, whatever it means, you can't change it anyway. I could get my mom to do a reading on you if you'd like, she's been doing it far longer, may get a better idea," she suggested.

"Maybe, it couldn't hurt," I murmured, perplexed at this reading. What did it all mean? A death not what it seemed, the romance aspect, and then the banshee? It was definitely confusing.

And quite worrying.

16

I stared around the darkened house, fear niggling inside me as the moon shone eerily through the window.

"Marrrrcccccuuuusss," a singsong voice called out from upstairs.

I knew I wasn't Marcus, I was me, and yet, at the same time, I was him.

And I knew who the voice belonged to, because it terrified me.

"Anna," I murmured, my voice a mix of my own feminine voice and Marcus' low voice.

I shot up the stairs, moving with the speed of a newly turned vampire.

Memories of Annabelle turning me despite my protests, of her draining me dry and declaring our eternal life together was imminent.

I'd awoken, well, Marcus had, to find myself in a shallow grave on an old farm on the outskirts of Maple Grove. I'd clawed my way through the dirt, surprisingly not choking on it as I struggled to rise. I didn't gasp for air when I surfaced, for my *lungs required no oxygen. A hunger filled me, driving me to head into town, but I fought the urge to enter any of the homes where I could hear those steady thumpings beckoning me. Heartbeats.*

Instead, I flitted home at a speed I'd never had before, knocking over the green garbage bin outside my home as I struggled to stop. Outside Marcus' home.

We knew something was wrong.

And now we were on the second floor, gingerly making our way to the upstairs library room.

I already had an idea of what awaited me there, but I fought it. I didn't want to believe it, even though the air was thick with the stench of fresh blood.

I choked as I stepped into the room, my eyes flicking between the bloody faces of my family.

My parents, their terrified eyes clouded over and their mouths open in silent screams. Their arms stretched out as they reached for one another, their fingers barely touching.

Then I froze, unable to take my eyes off of little Ariel, my baby sister. Only thirteen years old, her body hanging limp in the arms of her killer.

Those dark locks were matted with her own blood, and her usually bright blue eyes lifeless, staring blankly at me.

I just stared, struggling to comprehend what was going on.

Dead.

They were all dead.

I crumpled to the floor, their faces dancing in my mind as I stared at my family, bloody and not breathing.

"I told you, you're mine now. You'll get over them."

I don't know how I managed it, but I dragged my eyes to meet those cruel, uncaring jade eyes. Those eyes of the girl who'd decided to claim me as her own.

The girl I'd recognized as what she truly was when we'd first kissed.

A monster of the night, darker than any of the others I'd met before. There was something twisted inside her.

"Marcus, don't look so sad, everything will be all right."
Anna pouted at me before grinning and giggling as she stroked Ariel's hair. "Such a pretty little thing, I should've kept her. She'd have been a good pet."

Rage tore through me as she held my little sister in her arms, acting as if she was nothing more than a doll.

I screamed, the shriek tearing through the house as power surged forth from me.

Annabelle's startled eyes widened as she shot to her feet, but then a dark smile spread across her face.

"You're not a powerful witch, you never were, and you're less of one now." She giggled as she licked the blood from those crimson lips, a dark stain against her ghostly white skin.

But I knew my power surge was enough, for the next instance, Mr. Brady appeared in the room.

He was the town's main warlock, and he was the Area Enforcer. I knew he'd feel my wave of complete power.

My call for help.

"What the hell?" he mumbled as he looked around the room, having been summoned here with my last act of magic.

"You called for help?!" Annabelle screeched as her fangs elongated. "You're mine, you always will be!" she snarled, launching at Mr. Brady who was still getting his bearings.

He threw his hands up defensively as the vampire came for him, and a strange sensation washed over me as she went up in flames, shrieking and screaming as she flailed.

I knew Mr. Brady had already gathered what had

happened in those few seconds beforehand. He'd put two and two together.

Vampires that kill freely are to be punished. And attacking an Area Enforcer only adds to that.

I slumped forward, crawling forward to where Ariel had been tossed aside, her body twisted like a rag-doll.

"Ariel," I whimpered as I pulled her into my arms.

"God dammit," Mr. Brady mumbled, but I barely heard him. I was too consumed by what had happened.

Ariel was dead.

No more random art sessions outside, no more watching as she practiced her witch magic, no more teaching her about her powers.

She was gone.

I shot awake screaming, drenched in sweat with tears running down my face. My cries died down as my chest heaved, and I heard the commotion as my housemates burst to life.

Oliver was the first one tearing through my door, with Skip hot on his heels.

But I barely registered their frantic questions as the light flicked on and Oliver leaped onto the bed to check me over.

I just stared, horrified, as Marcus stood at the door, slumped against the frame with watery eyes.

So much for my first week going smoothly. It was Friday night with my first shift tomorrow, and now I had no clue what was happening.

"How'd you do that?" Marcus murmured, his voice piercing through the worried words of the other three boys. Lucas had arrived as well, and had swooped into my room in his matching set of pants and long-sleeved pajama top. It was purple with small golden stars all over. I would have found it comical if I didn't currently feel like I'd just lost my family and had my heart ripped out.

"What are you saying?" Lucas frowned as he stood beside Skip at the foot of my bed and turned to peer at Marcus.

"She got in my head," Marcus murmured, his horrified eyes focused solely on me. "And I saw hers."

My heart faltered at those whispered words, and I instantly knew.

He knew everything about me. In that moment, everything had changed. I knew everything there was to know about him, too.

But how?

How did I know he'd loved the smell of lavender in the house when he was growing up, or that his favorite color was an ocean blue, and his favorite food had been Indian before he was turned?

Not to mention the woman who killed his family. Annabelle Drew. A fae turned vampire, which was the reason he'd been so strange around me. Turned faes lost their humanity the most when turned, and they became dark tricksters and users of others.

She'd decided she'd wanted him.

And he'd paid a hefty price for catching her attention.

"Brett," Marcus murmured, and I flinched at the name. He knew. God, he knew everything.

"What's going on?" Lucas demanded answers as Ollie sat cross-legged before me, gently caressing my covered legs to sooth me. "You saw inside his head?" Lucas turned to me for clarification.

"I saw everything, somehow," I mumbled as I rested my chin on my knees. My chest hurt, and my face was wet from crying. And I had no fucking idea what was going on.

"I was catching a momentary nap, and I saw her in my dreams. We…" Marcus hesitated as his brow furrowed.

Kissed. I knew what he'd been going to say.

That was how it had started before I got sucked into that scene.

We were in a moonlight clearing in a forest, hungry and desperate for the other's touch. Why? I had no idea.

But that was the feeling I'd had, and then we'd drifted closer, him teasing me as he'd run those icy hands over me, and I moaned as I moved in to kiss him.

"We were in a dream together, when we touched, everything changed," Marcus murmured, those frosty eyes filled with pain, sorrow, hatred, and despair.

"Who's Brett?" Skip asked.

"No one!" I snapped, and Oliver's gentle caressing faltered on my leg.

"He hurt her," Marcus whispered, the silence filling the room after. It was suffocating, and I wanted them to leave, for me to get some answers away from them. I didn't want to explain anything to them.

I didn't want them to know what I was running from.

What'd I'd lived through.

"Like some kind of dream-walking, maybe? Although, pulling someone else into your head is not something I've heard of," Lucas pondered, although his eyes were perplexed as he glanced between us.

"I'm so sorry," I choked, the tears threatening to spill once more as I caught Marcus' eyes. I'd endured it all, felt everything. Even though I was back to myself now, it still lingered, like it was a part of me.

"So am I," he murmured, those icy eyes hardening as he clenched his jaw.

"You can trust us, Bee Sting," Skip murmured as he sat

on the end of the bed behind Ollie, who shuffled to the side so I could see him easier.

"It's not that I don't," I muttered.

"It's that it hurts," Marcus said, taking the words right from my mouth.

I gazed over at him, completely shocked. He looked just as unnerved as I felt.

"This is freaky," Ollie murmured, his hand still on my leg comfortingly.

"I'm guessing it has something to do with your witch powers flaring up, maybe," Lucas suggested as he looked to Marcus.

"Didn't feel like that," Marcus said as he crossed his arms. He wore a black long-sleeved shirt and long pants tonight, apparently his favorite choice since he wore the same colors every night. Black or navy.

And yet, I knew immediately it was because he was trying to hide himself. He didn't want to stand out or draw attention with bright colors. He didn't want to catch the attention of someone like Annabelle again.

He'd not known what she was at first, considering it was daytime the first time they'd met, in full sunlight at a local market. Turned fae weren't affected by the sun, making them more deadly.

"What else could have done it then?" Lucas asked, but no answer revealed itself.

"How you feeling?" Ollie asked with a soft smile as he shuffled forward.

"Like I just got tossed into a blender with Marcus," I said honestly. I felt connected to him, like we were in some strange sync.

"Charming," Skip muttered, but I could sense his unease at this strange affair.

"Well, I'll do some digging, see if I can find some answers. But whatever happened, it seems to have died down. You should try to sleep again, you've got your first shift in the morning, although if you're not up for it, I'm sure Gina will understand," Lucas said.

Right, my job.

I couldn't just skip out on my first day, even if I was in shock. At least the terror and heartache was fading away.

"Are you sure we should do that? Maybe we should call your dad?" Skip murmured, and Lucas stiffened.

"No. I don't need him getting involved," Lucas growled. "I don't need anything from him."

"He's the Area Enforcer, right?" I murmured, remembering him from the scene with Marcus' dead family. He'd been there.

"Yeah." Skip nodded. Ollie looked like he wanted to be anywhere but on the bed now, but he stayed with me, his hand moving to cover mine.

"Still, I doubt he'll know. If I can't dig anything up by Sunday night, then we'll ask for help. I think whatever happened is over. I did feel a strange magic spike in the house, but it's gone now," Lucas said as he crossed his arms and moved to stand closer to my desk.

I now had the chance to see the fluffy pink bunny slippers he was wearing. I just raised an eyebrow at them. Yep, definitely a unique Lucas thing for sure.

"I can stay with you, if you'd like?" Ollie offered.

"It's okay, you go back to bed, you must be tired." I smiled reassuringly.

He shook his head, but admitted defeat with a stifled yawn. This started a domino effect, all except Marcus, who was still watching me quietly from his position against the doorframe.

"Well, you know where my room is if you need me, or Ollie," Skip murmured as he stood. "Just come grab us, or shout, we'll be right in."

"Thanks," I said, honestly grateful for his kind words. The past week had been an interesting one, I was getting into my classes, and Emma had spent a few afternoons with me in the library teaching me more about the supernatural world. My initial fear about my reading had simmered down, and I'd told her not to worry about getting her mother to do a reading on me. She seemed fairly busy, with her home business of potion making and charming objects. I wouldn't disrupt that just because I was worried about some cards. But times like now, it did seep back into my mind.

And the boys had made my time here fun, watching movies, inviting me to play board games with them, helping me continue learning how to mask my energy. They were beyond helpful really.

"Hey, Lucas?" I called out just as the guys were preparing to leave.

Ollie had patted my arm before clambering off my bed, and Skip gave me a soft nod of goodnight.

"Yeah?" He stopped in the doorway beside Marcus, the two other guys continuing to their rooms.

"Any luck with any relatives?" I asked.

"I should have some news back tomorrow," he said with a soft smile as he flicked my bedroom light off. "Get some sleep, Cupcake."

Marcus remained at my door, the hall light illuminating his figure.

"Seems we both have demons we're fighting," he murmured.

"Yeah."

"Wanna come sit on the verandah? I don't know about

you, but I'm not game to sleep anytime soon." He gave a soft, sharp laugh.

"I thought you slept during the day?"

"Mostly. Sometimes I get bored and nap." He shrugged, and I could just see those frosty eyes in the soft lighting.

"Okay," I murmured as I reached for my jacket on the end of the bed. I slipped into it and followed him out onto the verandah, the night air a rather pleasant temperature. I could almost forgo the jacket.

We sat down at the outdoor table on the cushioned, wooden seats as we looked out over the backyard.

"So, Brett hurt you, but so did Wayne. Both your aunt's partners," Marcus murmured as we sat side by side in the seats.

"Yeah," I breathed. No point in hiding it, he knew it all.

"I'm sorry," he said softly as he turned to me, that devilishly handsome face saddened. Those icy eyes stared into mine, and for some strange reason, I felt completely comfortable right here with him. At ease despite everything.

"So am I. Your family." I frowned, my throat tightening at the memory.

His face hardened, and he looked back out across the backyard. The stars glittered overhead, and the moon stood watch over us.

"I'm glad she's dead, Annabelle," I said.

"So am I," he said, his voice cold and pained.

We fell silent for a few moments, the only sound was a soft wind rustling through the backyard trees.

"So, your favorite color is ocean blue," I said, wanting to lighten the mood a little.

"And yours is sky blue," he said, a smile tugging at the corner of his mouth. "You own practically nothing, mostly old clothes from op shops, and you have a thing for all the guys here," he said, a deep rumble sounding from inside his chest.

Laughter.

"Oh dear God," I groaned. But as he'd said it, I knew too.

"You've been drawn to me since day one." I smirked.

"You're a pixie, it's normal," he shot back. "You have fantasized at one point or another about the boys. Even me," he said, a sly smile spreading across his face.

This was Marcus. The real Marcus. The one hidden beneath the layers of pain and heartache.

And somehow, I'd broken through that. We'd shared our pain, created some strange bond.

"Well, I also know you've had an interesting dream about me," I shot back.

"I'm a guy, even if I'm undead." He chuckled.

"Your blood doesn't really run, therefore you shouldn't technically be able to have sex," I said playfully.

"We're supernatural creatures, magic runs in us," he said, his deep, smooth voice making me quiver.

"This is so strange. I feel like I know everything about you, everything you've felt, even your thoughts," I said, shaking my head in complete bewilderment.

"It's weird. I've not heard of magic like that before. I mean, there's actual bonding spells and such, but they're complete rituals, not just random magical occurrences," he said.

I just stared at him, relaxed at the air about him. He seemed... less on edge. Like the tension had melted away.

There was nothing to hide between us, no need for masks or fake smiles. We knew exactly what the other had been through.

And suddenly, I wanted to kiss him. Like in that dream leading up to the nightmare. The dream where we were desperate to feel each other. And when those icy eyes dilated, I knew he felt it, too.

This strange connection, this bond.

Marcus' hand cupped the side of my face, and then those cool, soft lips were brushing mine questioningly.

I leaned into it, a surge of power coursing through me.

Marcus moved quickly with his vampire speed, pulling me from my seat and moving me to perch on his lap so he could wrap his arms around me as he kissed me.

I could feel his desire mingled with my own, beckoning me.

Tempting me.

I slid my hands up under his shirt, moaning at those perfect abs that I trailed my fingers over. He shivered beneath me as his lips moved against mine. His tongue rolled over my bottom lip, begging for entrance.

I welcomed him, the hungry, passionate kiss sending fire shooting through me, and my lady parts ached and throbbed.

It had been quite some time. And right now, I wanted this to progress further.

God, I wanted it so bad, to feel him inside me, to feel his lust and hunger becoming one with my own.

I trembled, gasping against his mouth as his hands slid up under my shirt, his smooth thumb running over my pebbled nipple and sending delicious jolts through me.

I moved against his arousal as it pushed into me through those baggy trackies. It wouldn't take much for me to have that inside me, to get what I truly desired right now.

"Is that really what you want?" Marcus broke the kiss to nuzzle my neck, his hands cupping and caressing my breasts under my shirt.

It was getting way too hot out here now despite how cool his body and touch was.

'I could fuck you right here, make you mine,' he growled, but I knew instantly that he hadn't said it aloud.

But I didn't care either. I needed him. It was madness, this desire, the primal urging.

Marcus lifted me up like I was nothing, and I wrapped my legs around his waist.

The next thing I knew, we were in his room, and he was laying me down on the bed.

My heart hammered in anticipation, and he pulled free from me to tug off his clothing. He moved so quickly that I barely even saw the movements, just the final image.

And hot damn.

He stood in nothing but some black briefs, and he was definitely made of marble and designed as a stunning piece of art.

Those chiseled abs—he was certainly giving Skip a run for his money in that department.

"Really, you're thinking of Skip right now?" he groaned as he slid onto the bed to hover over me.

"You gotta admit, your housemates are all good looking," I breathed.

"If you let them, they'd probably all have you in a heartbeat." He chuckled as he swooped down to claim my mouth again.

My mind strayed to the other three men in the house, and the image of them all coveting me made heat scorch through me.

Marcus smiled against my mouth but didn't break our kiss. Was he seeing my dirty thoughts? Probably.

And then I could see what he was planning to do, how he was going to have his fun with me, take it slow, enjoy it.

And…

"You're going to bite me?" I broke the kiss, my mouth curving upward.

"Unless you don't want me to," he purred, but I could see the disappointment in his eyes.

"No, I've just never... been bitten," I murmured as my fingers danced across his chest. So cool to touch, and yet the fire between us was like nothing else.

"I won't hurt you, VB," he said softly as he dove down to capture my mouth once more.

He didn't break our kiss as he worked my jacket off.

Our bodies entwined, and my hands explored his almost naked body as his hands strayed under my shirt once more. He teased my nipples, drawing soft moans from me before pulling my top clean off.

In a movement I barely captured, he'd ducked down and yanked my pants and underwear off, leaving me completely naked beneath him.

"Not fair, you still have them on." I pouted as my fingers slid down to tug on the waistband of his briefs.

He growled as he caught my mouth, pushing his body down against mine, sending chilly shivers through me.

I loved it.

When he broke the kiss this time to allow me to breathe, he sat right back, those icy eyes trailing over me with a delicious, sly smile. My eyes fell to the erection pushing against his briefs, and I fought the urge to reach out and touch it. To trail my fingers over it and pump it, making him moan in anticipation.

"How do you look so damn good if all you do is play games on the laptop?" I mused as he leaned over me again.

"Wow, you really want to ask that right now?" he scoffed as he cocked his head. Fuck, he looked divine right now.

"I got turned looking like this. I retain this figure no

matter what. And being a supe before, I didn't have to try hard to look this good," he snickered as his head dipped to nibble on my earlobe.

I sighed as I ran my fingers down his cool back, wishing he'd take those wretched briefs off so I could feel all of him.

"Do they bother you?" he murmured as he leaned back, his fingers trailing along my collarbone and settling on the two small scars on it.

"Sometimes, if people see them. I guess I was lucky he only went for areas not easily visible."

Marcus frowned, sitting back as those soft fingertips danced down across my breast and to my abdomen, where another small, ugly scattering of them was.

"He never did pay, did he?" Marcus growled.

I was in his head again, seeing the images he'd seen in my own replaying. My aunt's first boyfriend, Brett, was pinning me down, holding his cigarette over my collarbone. He'd disapproved of the low-cut dress I was wearing at the time, and he wanted me to pay for it.

"Tell me, little one, how does it feel, how does it feel for your flesh to burn?"

"Your back, too," Marcus murmured as he moved to hover over me again, his eyes pained and sad.

Way to kill the mood.

Brett had moved to marking only my back when someone at school had caught sight of some of them. I'd had to make some crappy lie up.

"You really think they believed that it was a pencil that did that?" Marcus sighed.

"I was nine, it was the best lie I had," I muttered.

"Lucas could probably do a spell or potion to get rid of them, if you wanted," he murmured as he dipped down to leave a gentle kiss against the scars on my collarbone.

"Do they bother you?" I asked softly, my stomach tightening at the thought.

He thought for a moment before answering. "No, they're a part of who you were, how you became who you are now. But sometimes, you need to completely let go of the past to move on, to have a better life. And sometimes, we need help with that."

"Have you moved on?"

"No, not really," he admitted with a small smirk. "I never said it was easy."

"You know, we were going to have sex, and then you killed it." I sighed.

"Oh, did I?" he gave me a sly smile. "I'm sure I can fix that."

He moved in to kiss me again, this time some of the hunger was gone, and instead it was a sweet, deep kiss, one of understanding and need.

One I'd never felt before.

His left hand strayed to my left breast, caressing it and rubbing the nipple, sending hot shivers throughout my body.

His other hand danced its way down to rest on my hip, and he ground down into me, rubbing himself against me.

I moaned as I closed my eyes, my hands moving to run down his chest and settle on his waistband.

He pulled back to move to kiss my neck once more.

"You are so tempting, VB," he purred.

"And you're a tease," I groaned as I hooked my fingers into his waistband, intent to pull them down and free that arousal. I wanted to finally see it, to feel it.

"Uh-uh, not so fast." Marcus chuckled as he caught my hands. "I'm going to enjoy this."

He pinned my hands out to the sides, cocking his head before a dark look filled his eye.

I saw what he planned to do, and quivered at the idea.

He flitted off the bed and returned in seconds with a belt.

"Trust me?" he murmured, and I managed a small nod.

If you asked me yesterday, you might have gotten a different answer. But I knew him inside and out now, somehow, and I knew he'd never hurt me.

He strapped my hands to the metal rails at the top of the bed. It was elegantly welded into swirls, giving it a gothic, whimsical look. It suited him perfectly.

With my hands now bound, he got to work, exploring my body with his mouth and hands.

"A little birdie told me your orgasms taste like honey," Marcus purred as he nipped my nipple and drew a squeak from me.

"Of course you heard that," I muttered, but the heat was turning into a desperate throb between my legs now.

God, I wanted him inside, so fucking badly.

"Being a vampire means I don't eat, if I do, I can't taste anything, I'm wondering If I'll be able to taste that," he mused, his cool breath washing over my nipple and making me shiver.

Damn, the thought of that devilish face between my legs, that tongue flicking out, tasting me. I moaned as I arched up. God, he was going to kill me with this teasing.

He nipped my nipple again, this time a little harder than the first time, and I gasped, following it with a moan as he engulfed my nipple with his mouth. He sucked and swirled his tongue over it, using his other hand to knead and stroke my other breast, all the while occasionally grinding against me. I was dripping with desire, I knew it. I could feel it.

He pushed his clothed dick against my wetness, and he moaned against me blissfully as I soaked the front of his briefs with my own arousal.

"I didn't think you were such a minx," he moaned. "But I know better now."

Right, he'd seen everything. All my tinder flings, my one-night stands. Keith, my second boyfriend, all the fun stuff we'd gotten up to.

My mind was pulled back into the here and now as he switched sides, favoring my right breast now. His hand had other plans, though.

I arched into him as his fingers swooped down to brush across my thigh and then came to rest on my inner thigh in an utterly annoying way. He was so close.

"You're going to finish for me, VB," he purred as he nuzzled my breast.

Hell, I didn't doubt he was wrong there. I'd never felt anything like this crazy desire before, not with any of my previous partners. I needed him, and I knew that once he was inside me, there would be nothing but bliss.

Those fingers danced over my inner thigh as he continued suckling, and I quivered and moved beneath him, desperate for more.

After a few excruciating moments, those fingers finally found their way to my arousal, getting slick with desire as he moved them around my entrance, lubing his fingers. Not that he needed to.

I shuddered and gasped as he slipped his forefinger in, and he moaned against me.

"You're so warm," he rasped.

I'd adjusted to his cool body, actually grateful for it considering how hot I'd gotten now.

He began stroking my walls inside with soft, deliberate motions as I let out soft mews.

He moved his face up to kiss me again, and I deepened it

as I moved against him, moaning in ecstasy as he inserted another finger.

He knew what he was doing as his thumb began swirling over my clit, my moans growing louder as he worked on me.

I pulled against my restraints, wanting to touch him and hold him, but he just chuckled against me.

He broke the kiss to shimmy down my body, and I just watched through hooded eyes as he stopped down between my legs, his fingers still working on me. The moonlight glinted off his raven hair through the opening in the curtains, the little sliver giving us enough light to see.

"Look how excited you are," he breathed, that cool breath brushing my inner thigh and sending sweet tingles through me.

I closed my eyes as that wet tongue flicked out to slide over my thigh before he followed it with a gentle kiss.

"You love to fucking tease," I growled.

"Now, listen to that, our little pixie swears." He chuckled, his fingers slowing in the motions which made me squirm against him.

I twinged as his cool breath washed over my wetness instead, and then he was tasting me, that cool, wet tongue flicking over my folds as he continued to caress my g-spot expertly.

He nuzzled and kissed around my entrance, and then those perfect lips settled against my clit, and I moaned as his tongue flicked over it. He teased and tempted me, the ecstasy coiling deep inside me, building up as he began suckling my clit.

I gasped and moaned as he used his free hand to hold me in place when I began to rock and writhe against him.

So goddamn good, so close.

I wanted that orgasmic bliss, I could feel it coming, that utter perfection and euphoria.

I almost screamed in agony when he pulled away, removing his mouth and hands from my wetness when I was on the brink of release.

And then it came like a tidal wave as those fangs pierced my inner thigh.

I arched and quaked with the rippling orgasm, stars dancing before my eyes as energy and satisfaction tore through me.

And it didn't stop. Wave after wave rolled through me as he drank from me, and I lolled my head back as I trembled and shook with each one.

It died down after a few moments, and I felt Marcus release my thigh, running his thumb over the puncture marks. I knew what he was doing. He'd bitten his thumb and was healing my tiny punctures with his own blood. Another way to link us.

"Goddamn, it's sparkly," he snickered as his tongue lapped at my orgasmic juices, and he moaned blissfully.

"And it's fucking honey," he said against my folds as he savored my sweet juices.

I couldn't move as I lay sweaty and sated, my chest heaving in the aftermath of that incredible orgasm.

I'd never experienced anything like it.

Now I understood the fascination fae had with vamps, why they got with them even if it was a little risky. And I knew I tasted like sweet goodness to Marcus.

"Damn." He sighed as he cleaned me completely, licking up every last drop.

I knew instantly that he was a little disappointed he couldn't have more fun with me, considering he'd accidentally finished while feeding off me. He'd never fed from a fae before.

And it gave him the same rush and orgasmic effect that his bite did for me, if he was in that headspace.

He slithered up to lie beside me, undoing the belt to release my hands.

"How was it?" he purred in my ear. I knew I didn't have to say it out loud. It had been utterly amazing.

He just nuzzled me and urged me to roll over so he could spoon me.

If you'd have asked me a week ago if I'd be falling asleep in his arms, I would've laughed in your face.

But that's exactly what happened.

17

MARCUS

Wayne crept into the room, padding over to Allison's bed. She was only fourteen at the time, but he'd had a few drinks, and her aunt had already gone to bed.

Allison was pretending to be asleep, the blanket rising and falling with her steady, forced breathing.

He didn't care as he wiped his mouth, a smirk forming. Allison was peering at him through her eyelashes, hoping he'd miraculously leave.

He'd never left before.

Why would he start this night?

My eyes shot open as I drew in a sharp breath, and I turned to look at Allison, looking so content and perfect as she slept, doused in a soft glow from the moonlight.

How could she be so sweet and caring despite what her aunt's second boyfriend had done to her? Hell, what they'd both done to her?

Why was she so willing to move past it? I knew it still hurt her, and yet, the nightmares that scared her the most were the ones where she got burned by her aunt's first boyfriend, Brett. Maybe it was because Wayne had died an ugly death.

He'd paid for his crimes against her.

But Brett, he was still kicking.

I reached out to stroke her arm, causing her to shiver at the cool touch. I sighed as I quietly slipped out of bed and tucked her in with the blanket. I didn't need to sleep anyway, but falling asleep with her in my arms, that had been perfect. And yet, so strange.

I'd been drawn to her from the moment I saw her, but last night, things went crazy after that dream. I had to have her in some way, and as much as I wanted to connect our bodies, I fought it.

I couldn't shake the knowledge that she'd been abused, and I wanted her to feel completely safe with me before I did that with her. So, instead, I tasted her, and she was just as incredible as I'd thought a fae would be. Not to mention her juices. It was the first time I'd tasted anything but the coppery, metallic taste of blood. Her blood had been sweeter, but her juices, they'd been sweet nectar. Honey.

And it was addictive. I'd lapped every last drop up.

I couldn't have had her anyway, I'd orgasmed just from tasting her blood. So sweet and intoxicating, so over-whelming on the senses. I could feel her own orgasms pulsing through her, wave after blissful wave, and I'd joined her in her finish. I would've needed a few minutes to recharge at least.

There was much to her that I suddenly knew, too. Like how she had always felt like the odd one out, the one cut off from the supernatural world, despite her aunt and cousin being a part of it.

I knew of her previous partners and one-night stands, and

I knew she longed for a new toy thanks to joining our house. We were all too tempting.

A pang of jealousy tore through me, but I shoved it aside as I dressed and sat down at my desk.

Just because we had this special connection didn't mean we were a thing now. Did I want to screw her and make her mine? Yes.

But a part of me was still uncertain, still wary about letting her in, even though I knew everything there was to know about her.

How could she ever love a creature like me? One of the night? Who lived only for blood?

No. I'd keep this from becoming more. Did I still want to have her? Hell yes. But only when she wanted me to. I'd make it on her terms. I knew she felt for the others, especially Oliver. But the other two had grown on her over the last week as well. Days spent having lunch together, spending the daylight hours in the afternoon studying or watching Kit and Red play PlayStation. And she was curious about Lucas, she had figured out he was bisexual. I wondered if she'd seen the full truth from my mind? I'd seen everything about her, but not really the friendships, not in depth, just a basic overview. Maybe she'd seen the same. Knew the same.

I sighed as I ran a hand through my hair.

What the hell was this anyway? Why had this happened? The magic I'd felt during that dream, and then in the strange linking of our minds, it was unique. Something I'd never felt or seen before. And I was certain it had come from her.

She was more than a pixie/werewolf mix. I knew that for certain. I'd talk to Lucas, see what he could find.

Because she deserved to know. She knew there was something different about her, and not just as a pixie, she'd sensed it for a long time but pretended not to, not wanting to believe it. She needed answers. We all did.

Because right now, it felt like she was a part of me. A part I wanted to protect and cherish, to make as happy as possible. Was this what love felt like?

I scoffed. Love. As if.

No, this was some magic binding. Something I couldn't fight. Maybe it could be undone. I didn't care if it wasn't, though. It wasn't so bad, having someone to talk to. Someone who knew absolutely everything. No pretending to understand. She truly did. And it made us closer than I'd ever felt with my three good friends in this house.

I pulled out the bottom drawer of the desk, staring hard at the sketchbook in there with the pencil case on top.

It'd been so long since I'd drawn. But she looked so beautiful tonight. So peaceful and perfect. I wanted to capture it, highlight every little detail I could see as she slept.

And for the first time in years, I pulled out my sketchbook and pencil.

And I drew.

18

LUCAS

"So, this chick I've been getting with, she keeps bringing up a threesome." Skip sighed as he sat on the lounge beside me. Oliver was perched on the other lounge, stuck in his little cat form unhappily. He was sitting in the one spot where the sunlight was filtering through the window, lighting him up like a little angelic cat.

"And?" I mused as I sat back and put my legs up on the coffee table.

"With another guy," Skip said in disbelief, like the thought was absurd.

"And?" I cocked my head at him, a smile playing on my lips.

"Dude, that's gay," Skip scoffed.

"Two guys banging the one chick is gay?" I laughed.

"Well...." Skip grumbled, seeing the slight fault in his logic.

"Sex is sex. There shouldn't be any labels around it. If you like someone, you can screw 'em. If you want to share, then you share, if she wants to be shared, why not try it? You might find you like it." I smirked.

"*Have you ever had a threesome?*" Skip queried, his face sober. This was something he was really curious about.

"*Of course. Unlike you, I'm willing to adventure around a bit,*" I said playfully as I danced my fingers up his arm.

He quivered at my touch, but didn't pull away.

It was a strange thing we had going. He was always adamant he wasn't gay, but he'd never turned down my slight flirtation. Go figure.

"*What's it like?*" he asked, and I left my hand on his shoulder as I furrowed my brow in thought.

"*Fun, exciting, exotic. Sometimes it'll be a girl and guy, sometimes I'll mix it up. I've perfected a very interesting spell.*" I winked.

"*What spell?*" he asked.

"*I can turn myself into a woman if I so please.*" I shrugged like it was nothing.

In fact, it was a rare spell to master, only warlocks were capable of it.

It was used for many things, such as infiltration, spying, sabotage, and more.

I'd mastered it simply for the chance to feel a woman's orgasm. I wanted to see how everything felt for them. And you know what? It was bloody fun.

Skip's eyes widened and even Oliver sat up in shock as they both stared silently at me.

"*What? You've never wondered what it would be like? What an orgasm would feel like?*" I wiggled my eyebrows, and I could've sworn Skip was on the verge of worshipping me. I'd achieved the greatest thing ever in his eyes.

And there was something else in those bright blue eyes, a curious look.

A look that sent hot shivers through me.

. . .

I smiled as I remembered the moment Skip learned my dirty little secret. How it had opened up our interesting relationship. I was eighteen at the time and Skip was seventeen. He was visiting to celebrate me moving into my grandfather's house. Oliver had moved in after being cursed and being practically run out by his family for being the laughing stock of their name.

Dickheads. I wouldn't forgive them for that. He was just a boy.

I stared at the laptop before me, raising an eyebrow as it pinged with a new email.

Ah, James had gotten back to me, my friend in the force. He was one of my occasional flings, well, until he'd moved to Brisbane. Although, I did still have fun with him when he came back to visit.

I'd asked him to help me find some family of Allison's, so I opened the email hopefully.

The usual sweet words and update on his life. Mostly work, and a new dog.

Good for him.

But what piqued my interest was the info he'd dug up.

The odd death of her parents, and some relatives on her dad's side.

Strangely, all other relatives were deceased or living internationally. Except for her aunt and cousin, who still resided down at Maroochydore.

There was an aunt and uncle on her father's side, Natalie Smoak and Dixon Smoak. Natalie was her father's sister, his only sibling. And she was living at Maryborough.

Good.

I opened up Facebook and searched for her, having to sift through a number of profiles before finding hers, to my surprise. I'd expected it to be private or non-existent for some reason.

"Hey."

I growled at the intrusion as I turned in my chair to spy Marcus entering the library.

"Relax, didn't mean to intrude on your study." He rolled his eyes.

I cocked my head, sensing a shift in his aura. My mouth tugged upwards, although I wasn't overly pleased inwardly.

"You slept with her?" I asked, although I already knew.

"Yeah, unexpected, but whatever that dream thing was about, it made us crazy. Drawn together," he said as he folded his arms. He was trying to act like it meant nothing, but I knew there was more to this than the occasional hook-up he had at our little parties.

"I know, I sensed that. I was hoping by finding some family, I could figure out what's going on," I said as I turned back to my laptop.

"And?" Marcus sighed as he strode over to peer over my shoulder.

"Just an aunt. All other relatives are either dead, living overseas, or that horrible wench from Maroochydore," I murmured.

"Right," he breathed. "Is her aunt's ex-boyfriend Brett still alive?"

"Yes, they split years ago, though," I said, although I could sense his annoyance. I'd dug up info about her aunt when Oliver had told me about her scars. I wanted to know. Her aunt's two partners whilst Ally was living with her were known to law enforcement for assault and misdemeanors. One of them was responsible.

"And Wayne died," Marcus clarified.

"Yeah, messy death." I frowned. "Actually, I noticed some similarities between his death and her parents."

"Like what?" Marcus leaned closer, reading over the email, his interest caught. Too bad the info wasn't there. It was from database searches I could use myself, although tracking Ally's family had been difficult, so I'd asked James for help, knowing he had more resources at hand than I did. Supernatural law enforcement files.

He'd attached some files to this email for me to check over, birth and death certificates, family trees, etc.

"They were all eaten. The supernatural council covered up her parents' death as a car accident, although from the sealed reports they have, the car was attacked and the parents eaten. The bodies were mauled and mangled, difficult to identify."

"Allison doesn't know that," Marcus murmured, and the pain that lined his face made me purse my lips. He really was connected to her somehow.

"And probably better she doesn't. It's not a pretty way to die, no need to tell her," I said firmly.

"No guarantees she won't find out. We can see into each other's heads apparently," he muttered. "Know what the other is feeling."

"I can help shield you. A small spell, should lessen this bond, although I don't want to press it too much as I don't know what it is," I said. I knew a few spells to help with telepathic stuff, or bondings by magic. I'd even been asked to use the tele-pathic blocking stuff on those afraid of Emma Hall finding out their secrets. Who, of course, was now a good friend of Ally's.

Not that I cared much about her, my mind was blocked from her ability, and those inside this house were warded while within its walls. It was just part of the strong warding I had on it for safekeeping. My grandfather had a lot of old, valuable stuff, so the warding protected it from those who were not given permission to enter.

"That'd be good," he murmured, although I could tell his mind was elsewhere. Probably wondering what had mauled her parents and aunt's boyfriend.

"Could've been a werewolf attack, or any other shifter. Hard to say, although they were never able to pin it on anyone, and the bite marks were unique, too, not distinctive to any known shifter species," I said, although it did bother me a bit.

I liked Ally, she was sweet and beautiful, and had a natural way with all of us. She fit in perfectly here, and I knew that I wasn't the only one with a soft spot for her. Even Marcus had one for her, which was glaringly obvious now.

"She can't just be pixie, there has to be something else in her," Marcus said firmly as he straightened and stretched, following it with a yawn.

Dawn would be upon us soon, and he'd retreat to his bedroom like usual.

"Well, I can do some digging into her family tree that James found. He's given me some links to databases to add to my collection to search through if needed."

"James, he's the police officer you get with sometimes?"

"Yeah." I nodded.

"Well, let me know if you find anything," he murmured as he glanced out the window. The sky was slowly graying as the sun contemplated rising.

"She has work today, maybe wake her up before the other two," I suggested.

"Right." Marcus smirked, knowing full well how our two other housemates would react to the knowledge she'd been with Marcus.

Ollie, little Ollie who was the most innocent of us at times, but definitely more experimental in the bedroom than the other two despite what they might think, would be a little crushed by it. He'd been coveting after her since she'd come here. But he had been respectful, understanding that she may not want to ruin the housemate vibe by starting anything.

Then there was Skip. He'd had the hots for her since he met her, and finding out what it could be like to be with a pixie had only made her more a prize in his eyes. I'd done my best to sate his desire to stop him from trying to have her, but he didn't exactly hide his interest in her. He wanted to see if it was true about her orgasms, something I'd heard about animatedly from him. I knew it was true, as I'd been with a pixie myself, but he wanted to find out himself, not taking my word for it.

Typical.

As for me? Maybe there were no housemate off-limit rules anymore. Marcus had crushed that rule. And I had a feeling she wasn't just going to settle down with him because of one night of fun. Maybe I'd try my luck.

19

I awoke shivering as someone shook my arm gently.

"Mmmm?" I groaned as I opened my eyes and struggled to see. I rubbed them in an attempt to clear my vision before tugging the blanket around me.

"You need to get up, you've got work today. Not to mention I don't think you'll want the others to know you were in here." Marcus chuckled as he stroked my face.

I blinked as I adjusted to his voice, and then everything flooded back.

Well, technically we hadn't had proper sex.

"Work," I muttered, hating that I had to get up. But to be honest, it was probably warmer elsewhere once I was dressed. Marcus was freezing me right now with his morning cuddle.

"Sorry, I can't help it. I am kinda dead." He smirked as he nuzzled my back.

"I thought you spent your nights doing stuff? Have you been in bed this whole time?" I asked, touched at the thought.

"No, I left after a while to do stuff, I try to only sleep during the day mostly, but I came back a while ago. Wanted to enjoy it a bit before I woke you up," he breathed as he kissed my still naked back.

"Are any of the others up?" I asked softly. Guilt chewed at me at what Oliver would think. I knew he had a thing for me, he couldn't hide it well.

"No, well, just Lucas." He sighed, a hint of annoyance in his voice. "You really worried what Kit will think?"

"I know he likes me," I murmured.

"Well, that's obvious," he said bluntly.

"And I don't exactly know what this means. Last night, it was…" I pursed my lips as I pulled myself into a sitting position, staring down into those icy, gorgeous eyes as they stared up at me. His dark hair was tussled as he lay back against the pillow.

"Great, but you also don't understand the pull," he murmured.

"Do you?" I frowned.

"Not really. Since we shared that dream, I've been drawn to you so much more than before. I don't understand it," he said as his jaw hardened.

"Why did we share it? What magic did that?"

"Yours, I think. Lucas thinks it could've been me, but I know it was you," he said honestly.

"My mischief magic?" I snorted.

"No, something else," he mused as he reached up to stroke my cheek tenderly.

The sight of his naked torso was enough to make my cheeks flush once more. At least he had the rest of himself covered, or I might struggle to get to work on time.

He smirked as he read my mind.

"I can't wait to have you," he purred.

"Yeah, but I've got work, and they'll be up," I said as I flicked my head at his bedroom door.

"Why does that bother you?" he asked softly.

"What?"

"The other guys knowing."

My cheeks flushed as I mulled this over, but the unsettled grunt he gave told me he'd found the answer.

"You like them all, and you're not sure you want to settle down," he said. I couldn't detect the tone in his voice, and nothing came to me from his thoughts or feelings.

"Can you tell what I'm thinking all the time?" I asked, wanting to change the subject.

He knew this, but humored me anyway.

"Almost always, ever since yesterday's dream thing, I can sort of... I don't know, I guess reach out, feel your feelings and thoughts. Some just get broadcast pretty loudly, mostly the sexual ones," he said.

"Weird, it's not the same back, I can see a fair bit, but not everything, can't feel everything. Not today," I murmured, and his frosty eyes flashed momentarily before he smiled softly.

"I am curious what it means, what your power is. I mean, if someone had asked me if I'd be pissed to be linked with you before yesterday, I probably would've said yes. But since it happened, I dunno." He frowned, that godly beautiful face lit up by his bedside lamp in a soft golden glow.

"Same here." I smirked. "But for some reason, we're connected now. We know each other inside and out."

"Still strange, but it's like I know there's no point trying to..." He pondered it for a moment, and I reached out with my mind. It was strange, like I just knew how to do it all of a sudden.

"Hiding, putting up your walls," I finished for him. It wasn't so easy, seeing into his head, almost like it was masked a little.

"See? Wouldn't have thought I'd be a fan, but I don't hate it," he said. "It's like... I don't know. Like you're a part of me. I can be myself, and I know that you know exactly what I went through, as I know everything you did."

"Yeah." I cringed. I hated that he knew everything about me. All my secrets, my ugly past.

"Hey, I won't tell," he said as he sat up with me, his voice low and soothing.

"Thank you," I murmured as I looked around the room. My eyes fell on the open sketchbook on his desk, and I slid out from the covers to investigate. The boys had said he'd stopped his art when he'd been turned. Maybe he'd just been hiding it.

Marcus flitted up to join me, trailing his cool fingertips down my bare back and making me shiver.

"I guess I finally got inspired. Had something to draw," he murmured as I looked at the realistic sketch of me sleeping. I just stared, my lips slightly parted at the breathtakingly real image. He'd even begun coloring it in.

"It's beautiful," I breathed, wanting to touch it but fighting the urge. I didn't want to ruin the perfect sketch. I was sprawled out in the bed with sheets covering most of me. The moon was seeping in through the open window, dousing me in a soft glow and casting shadows.

It was a peaceful, beautiful picture, and it was hard to believe that it was, indeed, me.

"I had a beautiful model," he said smoothly as he kissed my shoulder.

I quivered at the touch but groaned.

"I need to shower and get ready, what's the time?" I asked, wishing I could see if the sun had risen outside. But the tinting had moved into place, guess that answered the question.

"Probably around six-thirty or nearly seven now," he said softly.

"Oh." I guess I had more time than I thought.

Movement from out in the hall made my stomach knot up, and I turned back to Marcus. He just shrugged, his eyes trailing over my naked form hungrily.

"I should shower and get ready," I said softly, although the look in his eye made it hard to leave.

He just nodded, but leaned forward to leave a sweet kiss on my lips. It was almost enough to make me stay and climb into bed with him. God, I wanted to.

But today was my first day at work. And I needed this job.

I gathered up my clothes as Marcus sighed and crawled back into bed, and I murmured a soft goodbye as I dressed and hurried out into the hall.

"Have fun, Cupcake?"

I nearly screamed as I practically ran into Lucas standing in the hallway.

My cheeks burned as I stammered in an attempt to form words, but he just gave me his lopsided grin, his hair a disheveled mess. He wore the same pajama set from last night, the purple one with stars, and the pink bunny slippers.

"Relax, it's your sex life." He chuckled. "We've all got one."

I gave him a half-hearted smile as I tried to release the tension in my shoulders.

"Guess the housemate boundary rules are in the wind?" he mused as he cocked his head at me.

"Um…" I didn't know how to answer that. Were there actual rules? They'd just been my own personal rules, but I'd broken them.

"Skip will take this as you being fair game now." He

winked as he turned towards said shifter's bedroom door. "As will the rest of us."

I just gaped after him as he gave me a little wave before slipping into Skip's room. There were so many things to question about this moment. Including him going into Skip's room. I guess that confirmed my suspicions.

Or he could be waking him up if he's got an early class? I thought to myself.

An instant dirty thought shot into my mind at that. There was one way he could wake him up.

I mentally slapped myself for the thought. Even if it had put my arousal into overdrive. Maybe I should head back into Marcus' room.

No. I still needed to figure all that out. Something weird was going on between us, although last night had been deliciously fun.

I continued into my bedroom, keeping an ear out to see if Lucas came back out of Skip's room. I didn't hear the door reopen by the time I was heading into the bathroom for a shower. Although I could've sworn I'd heard soft moans.

Definitely shower time, especially now that my head was coming up with a million scenarios playing out behind that door. All of them arousing.

Skip must be bisexual then, and I already knew Lucas was thanks to Emma.

Do they do threesomes?

I groaned as the thought sent heat rushing through me as I stripped down.

Goddamn. It was like last night had kick-started my sex drive again. It'd been lying beneath the surface, but I'd been focusing on uni and getting myself settled, doing my best to push it down. Now it was making itself known with a vengeance.

I started the shower, testing the water as my mind wandered to Skip and his two pronged penis. What exactly did that look like? Where did the second prong come out from?

Guess I'll google a kangaroo's penis.

Yeah, cause anyone seeing that search history wasn't going to question things.

I stepped under the warm water, sighing as it relaxed my tense muscles.

Last night had been wonderful. Ever since my last toy had broke, I hadn't orgasmed. It was quite a build-up, knowing you wanted it, but unable to finish yourself off with just your hands. On my own, I needed more, and vibrators worked best. They got me off quickly.

But with a partner, the game changed. I was aroused easier and pushed to my release, with the right partners, of course. Derek, my first boyfriend, had helped me orgasm once or twice, but then it was always about him after that, despite gentle urging. Keith had been better, but after the first few months, our sex life died down when I picked up more work hours and so did he. We were too tired to do the deed, and then we fell apart.

My tinder dates after that were hit or miss. Sometimes I got lucky with a guy who wanted to please, other times it was a guy who just wanted a quick fuck. I'd never contacted those ones again. Hell, I'd only contacted a few of those in the first lot a second time, but never a third. I didn't want to grow any attachments.

But now? This was a whole new thing for me. I was going to be living here until I completed my degree, which years away. I had meant to keep things strictly friends and business, but that had bitten me on the arse.

My body flushed under the warm water as my mind

moved to Marcus, of how things went so incredibly perfect last night. I did want to know what it would be like to have him, fully have him. To feel him inside me, moving against me, our bodies entwined.

My lady parts throbbed as I imagined it, a sensual, cool night under the covers, exploring each other's bodies. I hadn't even been able to see him fully, he'd kept those briefs on, only changing into clean ones afterwards. I'd wanted so badly to touch it, to feel it, but he'd had other plans.

I'd get my chance. I knew that.

I tried to push all the sexy thoughts from my mind as I washed myself, but it only made it worse as my mind moved to Oliver. Sweet Ollie, who'd been a godsend, helping me to my classes and being a good friend. I was meant to be looking out for him in case of a sporadic shift, but he'd helped me settle into uni easily, sticking by my side through our classes and bringing me many laughs.

And I'd noticed his eyes lingering on me at times, the way they'd sweep over me as he checked me out.

It wasn't one sided, either. I'd seen him fully naked, and I'd liked what I'd seen.

"For God's sake," I muttered as I pressed my back against the cool tiles of the shower wall. The sudden coolness snapped my mind out of its hazy arousal. Good. I had work, and I needed to hurry up.

I focused on what today might bring, of what this new workplace might be like. I'd popped in a few times this week after uni, and was happy to see they were getting regular business.

I climbed out of the shower, glad that I'd battled off my onset of arousal. I wrapped my towel around me and glanced at my dirty clothes. Well, they weren't really dirty. I'd re-wear the pajamas, but the undies needed washing.

I'd pick them up when I came in to brush my teeth, and I made sure to kick my shirt over my undies in case anyone came in while I was dressing or having breakfast.

I headed out into the hall, humming some soft tune I vaguely knew. Probably a nursery rhyme from childhood.

"Morning."

I stopped before my door as Skip walked out of his room, looking mighty pleased with himself.

His cheeks were rosy and his hair a mess. Lucas was nowhere in sight, but I couldn't help the warmth that flooded my cheeks.

Naturally, he was wearing only some batman boxers.

"Don't think I didn't know." He chuckled as he stepped closer and leaned on the wall before me, those bright blue eyes trailing over me in my towel. One eyebrow raised as he found his way back to my eyes.

"Know what?" I shrugged, but my heart skipped a beat.

"You got the dirty on." He grinned.

"I…" I just held my towel against my chest, unable to lie straight to his face.

His grin only widened.

"You know what that means, right?" he murmured as he edged closer, that strikingly handsome face only centimeters from my face. He'd not shaved for a few days, and the stubble suited him.

"What?" I gulped, too stubborn to step away. Besides, I could feel the heat radiating off his golden tanned chest, and I so wanted to reach out and press my hand against it, to feel him.

"Game on," he breathed as he moved his lips up to my ear.

"Game on?" I questioned, but squeaked as he grabbed my arms gently and pushed me up against my bedroom door.

"No more rules. Lucas said we were to let you be, but Marcus broke them, so now, you're free game," he purred against my ear, his hot breath washing over it. Tingles shot through me as his hands slid down my arms slowly.

I just stared at him, shocked and lost for words.

He just gave me that charming smile as his forehead pressed against mine.

"We all want you, Bee Sting. It's just a matter of who wins."

"I'm not some game," I managed to say, my eyes locked onto those delicious blue orbs. Up close like this, they reminded me of a summer day with a clear blue sky.

"No, but you are the prize."

You can find book 2 available at my website.

www.jecluney.com

About the Author

J.E.Cluney is a full-time author who lives on the Sunshine Coast in Australia. She spends her days writing, binging on TV shows, and reading. With a slight addiction to chocolate to fuel her midnight ravings.

Acknowledgments

Cover created by the wonderful Loraine Van Tonder.
https://www.rynkatryn.com/
Huge thank you to my wonderful beta team for all their hard work. And to all my readers who keep the passion alive to create stories for you to devour. I couldn't do this without you.

GLOSSARY

Arvo - afternoon

Bogan - is Australian and New Zealand slang for a person whose speech, clothing, attitude and behaviour are considered unrefined or unsophisticated.

Bottle-o - Liquor store

Chippy - Carpenter

IGA - Grocery store

Fortnight - two weeks

Gumtree - either a tree or the Australian Craigslist

Kiwi - New Zealand origin person

Op Shop - Second-hand store that donates money raised to causes

Singlets - tank tops

Skippy - Australian Kangaroo show (popular and known)

Stubbies - bottles of beer

Thongs - flip-flops

Trackies - Tracksuit pants

Verandah - Porch

Woolies/Woolworths - Grocery store

Printed in Great Britain
by Amazon